Environmental devastation has left Earth a wasteland, but an even more nightmarish fate looms if the woman known as H124 can't stop an extinction-level asteroid from destroying the planet.

The Skyfire Saga

On the run from a dangerous media empire, H124 places her hope in learning more about the Rovers, the last bastion of humans to embrace science as a solution to Earth's ongoing environmental catastrophe. But with the planet under imminent threat from plummeting asteroid fragments, H124 must take on a perilous new mission: find and assemble the pieces of an ancient spacecraft capable of pushing the deadly projectiles off course.

Her journey will lead her to the hurricane-ravaged remains of the east coast, and onto the brutal streets of Murder City, where she learns a startling secret about her own past. Death Riders and night stalkers prowl the Badlands, but an even greater danger lurks above as H124 fights to build the craft that is humanity's only hope for survival.

Visit us at www.kensingtonbooks.com

The Skyfire Saga by Alice Henderson

Shattered Roads
Shattered Lands

SHATTERED LANDS

The Skyfire Saga

Alice Henderson

REBEL BASE BOOKS
Kensington Publishing Corp.
www.kensingtonbooks.com

For all of the activists like Jason, who passionately work to help wildlife

For all of the non-profits who set aside wildlands to be protected

And for my parents, who shared my love of the natural world

Chapter 1

Even with the heat suit on, H124 felt like her insides were cooking. She trudged along beside the others, the heat waves shimmering on the ground before her, distorting the landscape. The oxygen coolant fan rattled inside her suit. The tech was old, which wasn't reassuring. Even with it wheezing away, the air she breathed nearly seared her lungs. She checked the outside temperature gauge on her wrist: 152° F.

In front of her, Raven turned around, his face obscured by the rising heat. The sun flashed off the red metal of his suit. "One more mile," he told them. She almost hadn't come. He hadn't wanted her to risk it, even though the medpod had done its work restoring her shattered body. She still ached in more bones than she'd ever known she had.

But she'd come this far, and she was not about to let a formerly broken body get in her way. Back in her previous life, when she'd been a laborer in a megacity, she'd discovered an ancient university in ruins, upon which the city had been built. Deep in the university's interior, she'd found a machine warning of an imminent asteroid collision with the Earth. Her only hope had been to find the Rovers, a legendary group of people who continued to embrace science. And she had found them. Now she had to see this through.

They'd been unable to fly into the location because it was too hot; the air was too light to land a plane or helicopter. So they'd driven close in a climate-controlled all-terrain vehicle. But it was too heavy to venture into this precarious place, the site of an ancient city now overtaken by desert sands. There were too many places where the vehicle could get bogged down.

So for now, they walked.

"Will you look at that!" Rivet said. A slender red-haired engineer in her mid-thirties, she was always animated. Her pale, freckled face lit up as she pointed to an elaborate spire sticking up out of the sand, the tilted remains of a destroyed building, once proud and gleaming, now a sand-scoured mass of twisted steel and shattered glass. "Can you image what this place must have looked like?" She powered on across the sand, easily the most exuberant of their little party.

"I can imagine a lot of things. Like how right now I'm being cooked to a crisp inside this damn suit," Cal grumbled. In his late fifties, with grey rumpled hair and a face permanently reddened and creased in a frown, he was as dour and grumpy as Rivet was cheerful. But as he was an expert in radar, they needed him for this mission. Today they'd find out how close the asteroid fragments were to hitting.

H124 looked up at the sky expectantly. She could almost feel those incoming rocks out there, making her cringe.

"You holding up okay?" Raven asked, moving next to her.

She nodded, even though she felt like her face was on fire. The heat felt kind of good on her mending bones though.

Raven operated a maglev sled carrying a UV charging station. Four small rotors hovered above the ground, each fitted with a powerful magnet that levitated a flat surface. He'd programmed it to follow them. Hopefully the charger would be powerful enough for their mission. Orion trudged along behind it. He was a slim man in his early forties, with deep umber skin and short black hair that was starting to recede. His long fascination with astronomy made him their best candidate to figure out how to deflect the asteroid. On his back he carried a sandblower.

"I hope we find this place before we melt," Cal said. He carried a mapping unit that kept track of how far they'd walked while highlighting the location of their target. "It's still another mile to the north-northeast."

They'd come out here to find an ancient radar facility. In the last week, while she'd been recovering with the Rovers, she'd seen them use radar to determine if any Public Programming Control airships were on the move in their area. But this radar was something different. The Rovers believed that at one time, humans had used radar to image objects in space, to get an accurate idea of their size and trajectory. If they had any chance of deflecting the oncoming asteroid and its fragments, they had to get updated information on how big they were and when they were due to hit. The data she'd brought from the buried university in New Atlantic was still being studied and retrieved. The data storage technology was old, some of it older than anything the Rovers had on hand. They'd had to reverse engineer ways to read it. Rowan, the Badlander who had helped her escape New Atlantic, had been instrumental in figuring that out. He was truly a tech whiz.

She hoped Rowan was okay. He'd stayed behind with the all-terrain vehicle to protect it from theft. It was the only vehicle of its kind that the Badlanders possessed.

H124 trudged along, taking breaths as tiny as possible.

"It's hard to believe people actually lived here," Cal said, gasping inside his suit.

"It wasn't always like this," Raven told him. "It's hard to believe now, but this was once one of the most populated cities on the planet. It was a mecca of entertainment. People came from all over the world to work here."

H124 looked over at him. "What happened?"

"A combination of things. When the first Apollo Project came crashing down, incredibly high temperatures killed a lot of people." Raven had talked with her before about the geoengineering project designed to block some of the sun's incoming radiation in an effort to slow human-caused climate change. The project failed miserably. They'd made a second attempt, and it was still up there, its particles suspended in the stratosphere. They were designed to come down gradually, but instead had stayed up there permanently, causing unpredictable storms and chaos on a massive scale.

Raven went on. "Sea levels rose, inundating the popular coastal section. The place had already been dry, mainly surviving off irrigation. But megadrought depleted their water sources, and people couldn't live here anymore. The desert advanced, eventually taking over this valley."

Cal trudged ahead of them. "Well, this hell hole is an oven I can't wait to get out of."

"Are you serious?" Rivet said. "Think of the opportunity. Normally we'd never venture down here. Look at all these old buildings! And the sky, have you ever seen a more intense shade of blue?"

"Glad you're enjoying yourself," Cal retorted. "I feel like an overheated MRE." He slowed down, lifting one boot. "Damn. My boots are melting." As he lifted his leg, a long, stringy mass of melted material clung to the sand.

"Let's pick up the pace," Raven said. "We don't want these suits breaking down on us before we get there."

She thought of Rowan waiting in the huge armored car, and the giant wheels that had lifted them above the heavy heat of this place.

They all started walking faster, Cal taking the lead. Then he stopped. "Damn! This sand burns!" He limped a little farther, and let out a piercing scream. He wheeled around, facing H124 and Raven. "What is that?" he shouted. He flung aside the mapping unit and started ripping at his body. H124 saw something surge up inside his suit, swarming over his face. He thrashed around, grasping at his helmet. "Get them off!"

She rushed forward, hitting the face shield release, and the glass slid down with a click, revealing thousands of tiny grey bugs scuttling over his face and neck. He screamed again, throwing his arms up, scraping at his face with his heat gloves. They came away bloody, strips of flesh hanging off his fingers. He started to run, stumbling in the deep sand, then tripped and crashed down.

They all hurried over. Raven turned him over. "Get some water!" he shouted.

H124 ripped off her pack and pulled out her water bottle, kneeling beside Cal. Raven grabbed it, dumping the liquid on Cal's face.

It did nothing. The grey swarm shifted over him, blanketing every feature, even going up his nose. Cal gripped her hand, so tightly she thought he would break her newly mended fingers. She peered down the neck hole into his suit to see they'd swarmed over his entire body; his suit was alive with the wriggling mass.

Then he let go, and his hand fell limp.

The mass shifted abruptly, streaming down. As the bugs moved away, revealing Cal's head, H124 blinked at the horror. They'd stripped him of every last bit of flesh, leaving only gleaming white bone. Where there were once eye sockets, there were now windows to an empty skull.

Then she heard an eruption of insectoid clicking; the bugs were streaming from the hole in Cal's boot.

Raven stood up and grabbed her hand.

"Run!"

Chapter 2

H124's pack slammed against her back as she ran in the shimmering heat. Orion moved to the lead, grabbing the mapping unit and holding it out in front of him. "We're close!" he called back.

The sled whirred along behind them, matching their pace, the charging equipment sliding around erratically. H124 couldn't breathe. The air was too hot. She couldn't get enough oxygen, and the cooling fan was humming violently now, threatening to shut down. But she thought of Cal, his lifeless body lying back there in the sand, and ran on. She glanced back, not seeing anything moving on the ground.

"It's possible . . . they can't get into our suits," Raven said, his words coming in gasps. "It was the hole in his boot . . . that let them in. We've got to be careful . . . and limit exposure to the hot ground."

"This is it!" Orion cried. "Everybody stop." He set down the mapping unit, then hefted the sand blower off his back and blasted away at drifts by his feet.

The sun beat down on her back as she started sweating profusely in the confines of the suit. Her heart hammered at the thought of those things bursting up from underground. The sand blower revealed a rooftop vent. Orion turned off the blower and knelt, tugging at the grate covering the air vent.

Raven bent and helped him, and with a groan of rusted metal, the grate came free.

Orion stuck his head inside the dark opening. "There's a ladder," he told them. He picked up the mapping unit and entered the aperture. A moment later his head stuck back up. "It's safe."

Raven insisted H124 and Rivet go next, before he descended himself. The sled hovered, lowering down after him. He closed the vent above them, and in the darkness H124 could hear his boots on the metal rungs of the ladder growing louder as he went lower. "Is everyone okay?" he asked as he touched the bottom.

A murmur of assent answered back.

H124 turned on her headlamp. The four clustered at the bottom of the ladder, just a short distance from a cement stairwell leading down. They descended a flight, stopping at the next landing. It was much cooler here. She read 74° F off her temperature gauge, and opened her faceplate.

Orion slumped to the floor. "I can't believe he's gone. What the hell were those things?"

Rivet opened her faceplate, her eyes wide with shock. "They . . . ate him." H124 felt numb inside, staring out in disbelief.

Raven shook his head. "I can't believe it. "

Orion shot him a panicked look. "We're not going to make it out of here, are we?"

"Of course we are." Raven pointed up. "Those things got in because Cal's suit got compromised. We're on a ticking clock here. We can make it out. We need to get the radar information as quickly as possible, then get back up there. We'll wait until the coldest part of the night, just before dawn, then walk out to meet Rowan."

Rivet looked up at him, mouth agape. "Night? We're on foot! We'd be a walking buffet out there, lumbering around in these suits. What about night stalkers?"

Everyone went quiet. H124 had had more than one encounter with those things. They hunted in the dark, but that didn't slow them down.

Raven lifted his hand. "I know. But those things that killed Cal—if they sensed his skin through the tear in his boot, maybe the night stalkers are just as vulnerable. They might just stay away from the area."

Orion gave a low whistle. "That's a pretty big guess to bet our lives on."

Raven gestured down at his suit. "These things are old. At least a hundred years. Probably a lot more. We have no idea when they're going to fail. We know for certain if another of our suits breaks down, that person doesn't stand a chance. Going at night is our best bet."

Orion gave a ragged breath. "Okay. Okay."

Rivet glanced at Raven and H124. "I don't like this." She extended a hand to help Orion up. "Let's just keep moving. Do what we came to do and get out."

"But what do you think they were?" Orion asked again. "Insects of some kind?"

H124 had been voraciously flipping through books since she'd come to stay with the Rovers. She couldn't read them too well yet, though Raven had been helping her learn. But she'd read that some kinds of beetles stripped flesh off of bones.

"No," Raven said, panting. "Something else. Maybe something human-made." They all looked at each other in the dim light. "Let's find this radar equipment and start it up. We need to get out of here."

She thought of Rowan back there and worried. He probably wasn't walking around barefoot though. More likely he was sitting inside the climate-controlled vehicle, tinkering with his latest invention, whatever it might be. She switched on her PRD, bringing up a communication window in the floating display. She called him. Once his smiling face appeared she felt a little comfort.

"Wasn't expecting to hear from you so soon, H."

She was relieved to see him inside the vehicle, but dreaded the news she had to give him. "We had a . . . mishap. Cal is dead."

He immediately leaned forward. "What?"

"There's something out there, in the sand. Don't go outside."

"I'm coming to get you guys." He moved to the front of the vehicle to start it up.

"No, it's too dangerous. We're safe for now. I just wanted to let you know."

He withdrew his hands from the controls, albeit reluctantly. "I don't like this."

"Neither do we." She scanned the spooked faces around her. "We'll contact you when we're heading out. It'll be at night."

"Night . . . are you crazy?"

"Raven has a theory that the night stalkers are vulnerable to these things, too. They may steer clear of here."

He lifted his eyebrows. "A *theory?*" He glanced around, seeing the others through her PRD. "H," he said quietly.

She stepped away from the others. "Yes?"

"We don't really know this guy. He could be dead wrong about this."

She bit her lip. "We have to take the chance."

Rowan sighed in frustration. "If you're sure."

She looked back to see everyone nodding. They were still listening, apparently. "We're sure."

"You be careful."

"We will." She shut down the communication window.

Orion had switched the mapping unit to the plans of the building. "It's down here."

With heavy hearts they turned and descended the stairs.

Once they reached the subbasement, the old place creaked around them. A deep silence settled over them as they moved through a structure entombed and lifeless. Orion led the way, consulting an old schematic on the mapping unit. At last they reached a metal door with a sign: *Radar Astronomy Research.*

The rusted door came open with a piercing screech, admitting them to a vast room with several computer workstations, shelves of books, tables, and chairs. Some were still strewn with papers, the chairs pulled out slightly as if the researchers were due back any minute. Two coffee cups sat near one another on a table. H124 approached them. Grey dust coated their empty insides.

Cobwebs hung thick in some places. Orion chose a workstation and brushed the chair off, a plume of dust billowing up. He waved it away and stifled a sneeze. He couldn't hold back a second one, which thundered along the walls. He checked over the computer. "Looks okay."

Raven steered the sled over to the station, where they hooked up the UV charger. Rivet had drifted over to the books, browsing titles.

"Here goes," Orion said, pressing the power button on the computer. For a discouraging moment nothing happened. Then they heard the whir of a fan and a ticking noise. He switched on the monitor, which soon glowed. "Outstanding!" he cheered, clapping his hands together.

Once it booted up, he tinkered with the programs installed on the computer, clicking through icons and opening folders. H124 looked over his shoulder in fascination. It was the same kind of ancient tech she'd found under New Atlantic. So huge and bulky, so *physical*. Ingenious how the screen was made out of glass.

She wondered why it had all been left here, the cups on the tables, the loose papers, all of this equipment that must have been worth something back then. Maybe they'd meant to come back or had to leave suddenly. Maybe frequent megastorms had driven them out, or the crushing drought.

"I think I found it," Orion said. He looked up sheepishly. "But I'm a bit out of my depth here. I didn't go over this stuff with Cal. This isn't the kind of astronomy I do."

H124 gazed around the space at all the books, the equipment designed to study the stars, and a sudden sadness welled within her. How had all of this been lost? How could this all have been dropped in favor of mindless entertainment and ignorance?

Even the Rovers, who had held on to some of it, had lost so much. She'd asked Raven about that, and he'd told her that the Rovers hadn't existed continually since the great departure from science. They had formed later, from a group of people who realized that something vital had been lost— ways to study the earth, its systems. People who saw that whole ecosystems had been lost, whole biomes, and wanted to see if they could get some of that back, see if they could somehow restore balance to the Earth.

From the data disks and the small metal pieces, which she now knew to call *drives*, an ancient way of storing data, they'd learned about this facility and the capabilities of radar astronomy. They needed a more accurate picture. But so far the disks had not yielded up the information they needed most—how to stop the asteroid from hitting the Earth.

She looked back to see Orion sitting with his head in his hands, his shoulders trembling. "I don't think I can take Cal's place. We need him."

Raven steadied his shoulder with a palm. "You can do this."

Orion took a deep breath and faced the screen again. He set his jaw. "Okay. Here we go. The moment of truth." He clicked on something, and a window opened up. "I'm trying to establish communication with the radio telescope."

She didn't remember seeing anything like that on their walk in. "Where is it?"

"Miles away, in another valley." He looked over his shoulder at her. "The data you brought from New Atlantic said it was converted over to solar power in antiquity. Let's just hope it's still standing . . . and is operational." Orion looked back at the screen. "It'll be a miracle if it is." The window flashed, and they all crowded in. Orion clapped once more. "Communication has been established!" He ran a diagnostic check on the telescope. "There are a few minor problems, updates that need to be made, but it looks like I can still calibrate it. This'll take a bit."

He did so while H124 explored the room, joining Rivet over by the shelves. She saw now that the engineer hadn't been perusing the titles. She'd been crying behind the books. She noticed H124, and quickly wiped her eyes and nose. "Sorry," Rivet breathed.

"Don't be," H124 told her. "That was horrible out there."

Rivet took a ragged breath, and managed to crack a smile. "The old curmudgeon drove me crazy most of the time. Even someone with my cheerful disposition struggled with that jerk." She wiped away another tear. "But he was our jerk, you know?"

H124 smiled back. "Yes." She hadn't known Cal for long, but could see he had been an integral part of the Rover camp.

Rivet stared upward, toward the surface. "And now he's gone. That fast. I can't believe it."

She wanted to comfort the engineer, but wasn't sure how. H124 had grown up alone, only recently being in the company of other people. She didn't know if she should hug her or just squeeze her shoulder. She opted for the latter.

"Thanks," Rivet said. "I'll be all right."

H124 decided to give her some privacy and return to Orion.

Raven stood intently at the man's side as Orion kept nodding at the screen. "Okay. I've calibrated it. I'll aim it at the first fragment." He looked up at them and crossed his fingers. "I hope."

Bringing up the display of his PRD, he scanned through some notes and calculations. She knew he'd had a terrible time finding this first fragment. They'd managed to pull data off the disks she'd taken from the university to determine the orbits of the two other fragments and the main asteroid. Then Orion had searched the sky with his visual telescope, using a method described on the disks. In the general area where the pieces were supposed to be, he photographed the sky night after night, then had his PRD compare the images to see if any of the points of light were moving against the background of fixed stars. When one was, then he'd found the asteroid pieces.

But all weren't quite where they should have been, and one remained elusive. He'd wondered if the Yanofsky Effect might be responsible for some of the shifts in orbit. He'd read about it on one of the recovered disks and described it to them. It happened when sunlight struck the light or dark surface of an asteroid. Coupled with how the asteroid was shaped, that heat difference could end up affecting the object's orbit. But he still couldn't find the elusive fragment. He wondered if it had already hit some decades ago, but the problem was that it was too big to have hit unnoticed. It was still out there, he'd been sure. Then finally he'd found it, off course from where the disks had predicted.

That was the one he focused on now. "Okay. I'm targeting it with the radar. The waves will hit it and bounce back several times, and we'll get an idea of the size and shape of this thing, along with a much more accurate orbit than what a visual study can tell us."

While they waited, H124 looked through the titles of the books. One was filled with glorious color images that astounded her, taken by something called "*The Hubble Telescope*." They seemed to be pictures of things in outer space, though when she'd peered through Orion's telescope back at the Rover camp, she hadn't seen anything like these. They showed towering, green, ethereal clouds; distant galaxies brimming with golden stars; dense clusters of blue and white-hot stars being born in ruby mists. She thumbed through the entire book, taking a seat by one of the old coffee cups.

When she finished, she returned to the shelves, skimming the other books. She stopped at a section devoted to near-earth objects. Among the volumes was a binder labeled *Deflection Techniques*. She pulled it down. It was heavy, full of schematics and tabbed dividers. She thumbed through it, growing more excited with every turn of the page. "Hey, look at this," she said, walking back to the table and setting it down. "They were building a ship that could rendezvous with the asteroid and push it off course by detonating an explosive near it. It's called the 'blast deflection technique.'" She flipped through the pages. "Looks like they were doing it in a hurry, delegating the work to a number of different companies to speed up the process." One piece was located on the east coast, another in what was now Delta City, and the third in the west.

Raven approached and looked over her shoulder. She could feel the warmth from his body in this chilly place. She still wasn't used to being around other people, their constant proximity. For the first few days in the Rover camp, her throat had grown sore from saying more than two sentences in a row to people.

"Looks like they got pretty far with this," he said, flipping through the pages. He moved to a tab marked *Current Status*. "The ship was all but done. They just had to bring the pieces together, assemble, and launch." He frowned as he read on. "But the project lost funding. Their budget was cut by ninety percent. It says here this was the twentieth year they'd applied for the funding to finish the project, and were denied again. They were planning to reapply, but this final year, even more massive cuts meant everyone was laid off."

H124 stared around at the cavernous room. These people had been trying to save the planet. What was more important than that? "But without this project, no one would survive."

Raven exhaled slowly. "Maybe the problem wasn't immediate enough. Something so many years in the future might not have seemed as important. Back then, a huge amount was spent on military funding. It's probably where the money went."

Once more flipping through the pages of the binder, H124 found the section that detailed where all the disparate pieces had been built. "This is what we've been looking for," she said. "And there's finally some good news. Looks like a series of megastorms devastated two of the facilities early on, so they started assembling these pieces in the deep subbasements

of buildings. It was a required part of their protocol to protect the craft."
She looked up. "This means these pieces might still be there, buried like
that university I found." She met Raven's eyes. "We have to find them and
assemble this ship."

Raven smiled with a look of relief.

Orion spoke up. "And now we've got another bit of good news."

They all crowded around the monitor. He flipped through radar returns.
"Looks like the composition of these fragments is rocky, and not metallic."

"That's good?" Raven asked.

"Yes. It means the impacts won't be quite as devastating." He leaned
closer. "But oh, no. This isn't good."

"What is it?" H124 asked.

"That first fragment? It was impacted by another body in space, I think."
He pointed to the fragment's shape on the screen. It was a black and white
image of a jagged object. A second shape followed closely, with a stream of
smaller debris trailing behind. Orion pointed to the two main shapes. "See
these two pieces? I think they were originally just one, the first fragment.
Now there are two. This is why the thing was off course by so much."

He leaned in to a window that read *Ephemerides*.

"Oh, no. No, no, no."

H124 gripped the back of his chair. "What is it?" she and Raven asked
at the same time.

"Its orbit has really changed. From these calculations, it's going to hit
a lot sooner than we thought. Originally it was supposed to hit on its way
back from the sun. Now it's going to hit on its way toward it."

She leaned closer to study the orbital diagram, then the simulation of
where the first half of the initial fragment would hit—just off the coast
of New Atlantic. The second half would follow shortly afterward, hitting
land. A burst of crimson bloomed out from the impact site, sweeping over
a large area in all directions.

Then he turned the radar equipment to the other fragments of the main
asteroid, and they waited while he imaged them. The next main fragment
was going to strike some large islands north of continental Europe. The
third would hit the Pacific Ocean, followed by the main asteroid itself. She
held her breath. It was going to come straight down on top of Delta City.

"This is bad," Orion said, pointing to the impact site in Delta City.
"From what I've learned from those disks that H found, a large terrestrial
hit is far worse than an ocean impact. An ocean impact can cause tsunamis
and earthquakes, but a terrestrial hit sends so much material up into the
atmosphere that the effects are far more devastating. Global fires. The

shutdown of photosynthesis. This initial hit off the Atlantic is going to be bad enough. The tsunami there will wipe out New Atlantic. It would be even worse if there wasn't a continental shelf there. That'll help dissipate the wave a bit. But anything that survives that wave will be destroyed minutes later by the second half as it hits land."

As H124 studied the impact sites, an alarm went off inside her. "Wait a minute." She hurried back to the binder and flipped to the section that listed where all the spacecraft pieces were being built. "One of these pieces is just to the south of New Atlantic," she told them. "It's going to be destroyed."

Raven clenched his jaw. "Then we need to get there. Fast."

Chapter 3

H124 hefted open the hatch, peering up at the welcome night. Above, stars glittered in one part of the sky, while dark clouds gathered in the west. She climbed out, eyes darting over the sand for any sign of those things. The others followed, the maglev sled taking up the rear, its small rotors whirring softly in the dark. Together they formed a grim line as they trudged back the way they'd come.

The temperature was cooler now, in the seventies, and she welcomed the break from the unbearable heat they'd experienced earlier.

As they advanced, her headlamp picked out a lump on the ground ahead—Cal's body, covered partially by windblown sand. "Are we just going to leave him here?" she asked. Her job in New Atlantic had been to remove corpses from their living pods when citizens passed away. It felt strange to just leave him in this lonely place.

Raven put a hand on her shoulder. "We can't risk one of those things coming back with his body. They could be embedded in his suit somewhere."

"What about our suits?" Rivet asked, stopping beside them. Her eyes were wide behind her faceplate.

"We'll decontaminate before we enter the vehicle." He looked down at Cal. The white of his skull reflected back in their beams, his jawbone slack as if he were still screaming. "We can't risk any of those things hitchhiking back with us on the all terrain."

Rivet gave a shudder.

They trudged on, Orion and Raven taking up the rear, the sled thrumming along behind them. She saw Orion look back over his shoulder and whisper, "I'm sorry, old friend."

The thought of encountering night stalkers while in the bulky suit sent a shiver through her. She'd barely be able to run, let alone fight. She checked her PRD, seeing how far away she was from Rowan and the waiting vehicle.

"What exactly are night stalkers?" she asked Raven. She hadn't seen them in any of the field guides she'd read.

"No one's really sure. Nothing that existed in antiquity, we don't think. They're not in any records, even those from before the Anthropocene Extinction started. They just didn't exist before."

Raven had told her about the Anthropocene Extinction, a human-caused mass die-off of animals that began many years ago and was still ongoing. It had started long ago, back before the ruined cities they now walked through had even been built, many hundreds of years before something Raven called "The Industrial Revolution."

She glanced around in the dark. Maybe Raven was right that those things in the soil kept any living thing away, even the night stalkers. Still, she hurried on.

The dark city spread out to the west, leaning towers and toppled spires, a graveyard of steel and shattered glass silhouetted against the stars. She scanned the ground around her, searching for hunting shadows creeping up on them. Her mouth went dry, but she didn't dare stop to reach into her pack for a drink of water.

As dawn started to glow on the horizon, Rowan's lights came into view, and relief flooded over her. The others were close behind, all sticking together. Then she could see Rowan himself, sitting in the driver's seat, a grin on his face as he waved at them. It was a huge vehicle, with eight giant all-terrain tires and a side-loading door that opened upward like a hatch.

Raven held up his hand, signaling Rowan to wait, and they moved to the rear of the vehicle to the decontamination area. They sprayed off their suits thoroughly, then returned to a side window.

Rowan hit the switch for the door, and they all poured in.

He moved to the back and hugged H124 through her heat suit. "I'm so glad you're okay." He went to work unlatching everyone's helmets and suits and helping them out.

Rivet hadn't said much since H124 had talked to her behind the shelves, and now she stood in silence, staring out of the windows nervously. She still didn't say anything as she stepped out of her heat suit and hung it on the wall of the vehicle in the back.

Rowan looked at all of them. "Cal's really gone?"

H124 nodded.

"What was it?"

Raven shrugged. "We don't know."

Rowan moved back to the controls and started up the vehicle. They lumbered out of there, moving slowly over the uneven terrain, getting blissfully farther and farther away from the nightmare.

H124 thought of Cal, lying out there alone, the sands creeping around him.

* * * *

As they drove silently toward the Rover camp, H124 sat up front with Rowan. The sun rose in a sky of red, with brilliant gold and orange clouds blanketing the horizon. Desolate brown mountains rose in the east, completely desertified. She watched him move in the driver's seat, his clothes stitched together from a variety of old fabrics gathered by the Badlanders: pants of worn grey canvas and a soft green material with black stitching and a black shirt with red pieces stitched together to cover the holes. It looked comfortable. She'd replaced her own old work clothes with some pieces the Rovers had made: a soft, black, long-sleeved shirt made out of something called "bamboo," and sturdy black pants with a number of handy pockets. On her feet she wore her old trusty black boots, which had begun to show signs of wear.

The temperature started to climb again, and soon the vehicle's cooling system struggled to keep them from overheating inside the cabin. She could hear Rivet crying in the back. Raven sat with his hand on her back, uttering consoling words H124 couldn't quite make out.

After two hours of jostling over broken asphalt and slogging through expanses of windblown sand, exhaustion caught up with her. She tried to fight it, but her eyes finally closed. Then Rowan braked suddenly, and she jerked awake. He leaned forward in his seat, gripping the wheel.

"This doesn't look good." He slowed down the vehicle, staring out at the horizon.

There she saw a fuzzy brown line. It bloomed higher, moving and undulating, its top edge ragged and hazy. It looked like a beige storm cloud, but on the ground. "What is that?"

"A sandstorm."

The mobile mass stretched as far as they could see to either side. Moving quickly, it soon towered before them, surging and rolling.

Raven came forward, gripping the back of H124's seat. "Can we go around it?"

Rowan sat back, gazing out of the windows. "I don't see how." He leaned over between their seats and flipped a few toggle switches. A round screen mounted in the center of the dashboard blinked on, glowing green. An arm of light snaked out from the center and started to sweep in circles around the display. The sandstorm appeared as a bright line, taking up the entire top half of the screen. Rowan studied some numbers at the bottom. "It's moving at forty-two miles an hour."

Raven gaped at him in horror. "Can this thing withstand a storm like that?"

Rowan rubbed the back of his neck. "It's been in some storms, sure. But nothing like this." He stared out at the approaching mass, searching for anything they could seek refuge near. Nothing but flat land stretched out in their immediate vicinity. "But we're about to find out."

The storm barreled toward them, a churning squall, alive and writhing.

"Will it get into the engine?" Raven asked.

"It's been specially adapted with a filter that should protect it. If I shut off the motor, it won't take long for it to heat up in here. We'll be a bag of crispy fritters."

Then the storm hit them. Visibility went from fifty feet to one. Dim sunlight filtered through the sand, growing fainter by the second. Incredible winds hit the vehicle. H124 gripped her armrest as the car rocked violently, threatening to lift up on two wheels.

A hissing erupted as millions of sand particles hit the car. The world grew darker and darker, taking on an eerie red glow. She could barely make out anything around them now, not even the hood of the vehicle.

Then darkness swallowed them, plunging them into an impenetrable black. Lights from the instrument panel glowed, lighting Rowan's face as he stared out. Powerful winds buffeted the vehicle. The hiss of sand grew to a roar.

"Make it stop!" shouted Rivet.

H124 looked back to see her cradling her head in her hands as Orion tried to comfort her. "It'll pass soon," he told her.

But it didn't.

The storm raged on and on, keeping them in complete darkness. The bellowing of the winds howled in a frenzy against the vehicle. The grating sound of sand against glass made H124 grit her teeth. All she could do was squeeze her eyes shut.

"How long can this last?" Orion asked from the back.

Raven checked the radar screen. There was no break in sight from the storm.

Rowan reached over and gripped H124's hand. They all sat in silence then, listening to the storm twisting around them, scouring the vehicle.

H124 blinked as a dim light seeped in through the windows. The darkness shifted back to the strange red glow, and suddenly she could see the car's hood. She'd never seen such a spooky crimson light, and she felt as if she'd been transported to an alien world.

Slowly the red shifted to beige, and she could now make out the ground a few feet in front of the car. But she couldn't see anything out of her passenger window. Sand had piled up, burying that side. The wind quieted and died.

Raven stood tensely between their seats, still looking out. They could now see about a hundred feet out. H124 noticed that the vehicle's brilliant green paint had been completely blasted off on the windward side. Bare metal glinted as the sun finally pierced the thick cloud of sand.

The engine still thrummed. They'd made it.

"Let's get out of here!" Rivet pleaded from the back.

Rowan tried to pull forward, but couldn't. He pressed the engine harder, but the tires just spun in the sand.

"We're going to have to put on the heat suits and dig ourselves out," he told them.

"Out there?" Rivet cried. "With those things? No way. Just push the engine."

Rowan tried again, but it was only digging them in more. "The hatch is buried. We'll have to crawl out of the window on this side."

"I can do it," H124 said, getting up. She slid past Raven, and moved to the back where her suit hung.

"You're crazy," Rivet told her. "That storm could have sprayed those things all over the place."

H124 stepped into the suit and picked up her helmet. "I'll be okay."

Rowan moved to the back too, donning Rivet's suit. Raven joined him. The three of them winnowed out of the driver's side window and stepped onto the sand.

Orion handed shovels through the window, then rolled it up again.

The sun beat down mercilessly as H124 moved to the passenger side. It was completely buried. She immediately went to work digging down toward the front wheels. Raven and Rowan took the back, shoveling awkwardly in their bulky suits.

With every scoop of sand, she dreaded finding more of the things that had killed Cal. She had almost cleared one of the front wheels when she saw them. Lifting her shovel, she tossed sand to the side, seeing grey particles squirming among the tiny brown pebbles.

She stepped back, bringing her shovel up. The section of sand at her feet erupted with the tiny creatures. They wriggled and scurried over one another, no bigger than the brown grains burying the car. "They're here!" she called to the others. But already they swarmed up over her suit. She held her breath as they flooded over her faceplate, once more drowning her in darkness.

Chapter 4

H124 held still, hoping they wouldn't find ingress to the suit.

"H!" she heard Rowan cry out. "They're all over her! What do we do?"

"I don't know!" Raven shouted, and for the first time since she'd met him, he sounded truly afraid.

"What's happening? I can't see anything," she called out to them.

"I think . . ." Rowan started to say, "I think they're leaving."

The darkness lifted a little, and H124 could once more see the tiny grey creatures swarming over her faceplate. They glinted in the sunlight as she struggled to focus on them. When only a few darted across the glass, she brought up her hand slowly. Dozens still scurried on her arm, and she studied them closely. They gleamed like silver. They weren't organic. They were some kind of metal. *Machines.*

She looked down as they burrowed back into the sand.

Rowan rushed to her. "They couldn't get inside your suit."

She stood, shocked that she was still alive.

Raven stood beside her, squeezing her shoulder. "Let's work fast," he said, and they returned to digging.

Fifteen minutes later, they'd cleared the wheels. After decontaminating their suits again, they squeezed back in through the driver's window. They shucked off the bulky suits, and Rowan returned to the driver's seat. He pushed the engine, the motor roared, and the vehicle lurched forward, rolling over the sand.

Rivet sighed loudly and hung her head. Orion nodded his thanks at them, but no one spoke. They still had a long slog to go before they reached the Rover camp.

* * * *

After five more hours behind the wheel, they pulled up at the Rover camp to find everyone rushing around. Raven climbed from the vehicle and hurried into a nearby tent. H124 followed him, seeing fear on every face. They found Onyx packing up her computer equipment. She was a tall woman with long black hair, a fellow Navajo and cousin of Raven's. She was an amazing hacker, and had been the one to save them all during the airship attack when H124 had finally found the Rovers.

"Yá'át'ééh," Raven greeted her.

She smiled, happy to see them back. *"'Aoo', yá'át'ééh."*

"What's going on?" he asked her.

"Our location has been compromised," she told them. The Rovers had been piggybacking off Rowan's listening device that he'd planted at Delta City. They all eavesdropped now on the Public Programming Control movements, including PPC troop and airship maneuvers. "They're sending in troops."

Raven rocked back on his heels, watching everyone rush around, packing their equipment.

Rowan joined them and squeezed H124's hand. "Where will everyone go?" she asked.

Raven cracked a rueful smile. "Sanctuary City. It's our stronghold, and the media can't find it. But we don't have time to join the others there now. We need to get to the east coast."

James Willoughby appeared as Raven rushed away. He was back in his impeccable suit, his black hair freshly styled. She'd gotten used to seeing him in casual wear around the Rover camp as they'd healed from the airship crash. Now he looked every inch the stylish PPC exec. "H," he said, moving quickly to her. "I'm glad I got to see you before I left." He gave her an affectionate pat on the shoulder.

"Left?" She felt a pang. For the last few weeks they'd been spending a lot of time together. She'd learned so much about how the PPC maintained its power, and how they kept the citizens enthralled. But more than that, they'd talked of their lives, and she felt bonded to him. He was the one member of the PPC they could count on, their source of inside knowledge, and he'd been a powerful ally. She'd grown attached to him.

"I've contacted the PPC and explained that my airship crashed, and that I've been recovering. They have no idea that I helped you. I pitched them a new show, too, to sweeten the deal. They've been struggling. The

British Entertainment Corporation City has installed some new, very powerful transmitters, and citizens in New Atlantic are able to pick up their shows. We've been having some infrastructure problems as a result." H124 knew that to keep the media streaming, citizens had to periodically enter codes and commands into their consoles. These in turn managed the city's infrastructure, though the citizens weren't aware of it. If they were watching BEC City's programming, then all their efforts would go toward maintaining that city instead of New Atlantic.

"They've arranged an airship to pick me up," he told her.

She raised her eyebrows.

"Don't worry. It's nowhere near here. And everyone's packing up, anyway."

She took his arm and led him away from the others. "You can't go back to New Atlantic."

"Why not?"

"When we were at the radar facility, we were able to see the fragments. Get an accurate idea of their size and where they're going to hit. I'm sorry, but New Atlantic is going to be completely destroyed."

Willoughby rocked back on his heels. "What?"

"In a very short amount of time, too." She told him about the spacecraft and how they had to retrieve a section of it on the east coast before the impact. "You can't be anywhere near there."

"What should I do?" he asked, blinking.

"Can you go to Delta City?"

He looked down at her. "I can't . . . that place . . ."

"You could work for the PPC there, gathering intel. One of the sections of the spacecraft is there. We could really use your help to infiltrate the city. In the meantime, you could work undercover to convince the citizens to leave. If we're unsuccessful in altering the course of the main asteroid, it's going to be a direct hit on Delta City. "

Willoughby swallowed. "What about the people in New Atlantic?"

"We can try another pirate broadcast. You could reach out through your channels, and warn people to leave the city."

He pursed his lips and nodded. "I can't believe this."

"I'm sorry," she told him, clenching his arm.

"I'll go contact the PPC airship, tell them I want to be routed to Delta City instead. And I'll think of a way to warn people in New Atlantic." His faraway gaze fell back on her. "You take care of yourself. Don't take any unnecessary risks."

She thought of crossing the desert, of the things that had eaten Cal. Of the night stalkers and megastorms. There was nothing now to her life *except* risk. "I'll be careful. And you take care of yourself in Murder City."

He hugged her, kissing her on her forehead. "Back into the lion's den," he said, and turned away to join the throng of rushing people.

As the Rovers shifted around camp, H124 spotted Gordon sitting nearby, examining some charts. The elderly man—whom H124 had guessed to be in his late eighties, but never asked—wore his usual flannel shirt and worn pair of overalls. He spotted her and got up, smiling. "How are you feeling?" she asked him.

The aviator had been badly injured in the airship crash too. The medpod had fixed all his broken bones, but she knew he still ached just like she did. "Better and better every day," he told her with a smile.

Across the room, she saw Rowan answering a call on his PRD. Concern washed over his face as he nodded and talked quietly. She heard someone say, "You've been away too long as it is. They aren't your people. We are. We need you, Firehawk."

The words stung her, and she didn't want to eavesdrop. Raven came back into the tent and waved Rivet and Orion over to where H124 stood with Gordon. "We'll need a way to cover that distance to the east coast, and fast," Raven told them.

Gordon glanced around at them. "What's the mission?"

H124 told him about the spacecraft pieces, and how the one on the east coast was in danger of being destroyed.

He lifted his chin. "I'll take you."

Raven raised his brow. "But your plane. It's gone. And we don't have any others near here."

Gordon stood firm. "It wasn't my only one. I've got access to a few, stashed around in different places. My friend's got a little jet that can get to the east coast in no time." His twinkling eyes rested on H124. She felt herself smiling. They'd been through hell together and shared a concrete bond. "It'll have to be a small group if we're loading a piece of this spacecraft aboard. I can only take two people. And it'll be dangerous. That part of the coast is lashed with storms this time of year. Bad ones."

Bad storms. They'd been through that together too. "I'll go," she said.

"And so will I," Raven offered.

"That's two," Gordon said.

Rivet exhaled, the relief clear on her face. "I can take the schematics back to Sanctuary City and figure out how it's going to fit together when we get all the pieces."

Raven nodded. "Great."

Orion cleared his throat. He looked relieved as well. "And I'll keep an eye on those fragments. You're going to be cutting it pretty close. That thing could hit while you're out there." He thought a minute, then added, "I can send the data to your PRDs. Let you know when it's getting close to impact."

"Fantastic," Raven told him, extending a hand to Orion. Raven shook it. Rivet did the same, shaking H124's hand. As she and Orion walked away, Rivet looked over her shoulder, giving H124 a sad smile. "Good luck, H," she whispered.

Raven turned to Gordon. "Where's your other plane?"

He grimaced. "I hate to say it, but it's back on the other side of the Rockies." H124 thought of their terrifying ordeal, trying to cross a pass in the mountains during a violent snowstorm. She shivered.

Gordon brought up the location on his PRD's map, and turned so they could see it. Raven almost laughed. "We just caught a bit of luck!"

"What do you mean?" she asked.

"We can get really close to this location using the old I-70 freight hyperloop."

"The what?" Gordon asked.

"Before the megacities, supplies and food were transported across the country on huge trucks. It required a lot of petroleum and emitted a lot of pollution as the country's population continued to climb. To work toward a cleaner future, some inventive entrepreneurs suggested the use of hyperloops, giant steel tubes in partial vacuums that could move pods with passengers or freight. Only a few were built, mainly along high-traffic corridors, like this route through the Rockies. Ironically, even the oil companies built one going up north to transport equipment and personnel for oil and tar sands extraction. We use that one to travel to Sanctuary City. We found them a couple decades ago and repaired them, so there are a few places we can travel to quickly. There used to be one along the west coast, along the route we just followed. But as sea levels rose, it got flooded. It was destroyed."

Wonder crept across Gordon's face. "Fascinating."

H124 glanced at Rowan across the room as he said goodbye and switched off his PRD. He joined them. "I'm afraid this is where we part company," Rowan told them, stepping aside as a woman carrying a stack of equipment hurried past. "My people have picked out a good location for our new settlement, but I need to go out there and help shield our communication, set up some proximity alarms in case the PPC goes in silent and we don't have advance warning. I think they know we're listening in by now, but it'll still take them some time to find the device I planted."

H124 felt a punch in the gut at the thought of his leaving. First Willoughby, and now Rowan. She felt like she was back outside New Atlantic, when he'd walked off into the night, leaving her to hike to the weather shelter alone. She swallowed hard. "Of course. We understand," she heard herself say.

"To be honest, they're getting pretty mad at me. I'm supposed to be their go-to tech person, and I've been a bit remiss."

Raven held out his hand. "It's been for a good cause. We really appreciate all the help you've given us."

Rowan took his hand and shook it. "Thanks for fixing us up after the crash." "Of course."

Then Rowan took H124's hand and led her away. Around them people hurried with equipment and boxes, rushing out to a common meeting area from which they could evacuate the camp. She felt pressed, wanting him to stay, wanting to go with him, to be in two places at once, finding the spacecraft parts and helping him with his new camp. He touched her cheek gently and opened his mouth to say something, then closed it. He clasped both her hands. When he looked up again, she felt that same longing in his gaze that she'd felt once before. "Words fail me . . . this whole thing has been . . ." He trailed off. "This whole thing has been the most powerful experience of my life. I feel terrible leaving you, especially when we're getting closer to finding a way to stop this thing."

His hands were warm around hers. "I understand. You have to make sure everyone's safe." She glanced over at Gordon, who had pulled out an E6B—what he called a whiz wheel—that the Rovers had found for him. It was an analog flight computer, and he was already calculating their upcoming path. "But I'm in good company. Gordon says only a couple of us could have gone anyway."

He sighed. "I feel like I'm being called away to plug a leaky bathtub when a tidal wave is on the way."

"But if we're successful, your people are going to need a safe home. If the PPC finds them and kills them before that . . ."

He nodded. "I know." He pulled her to him, wrapping his strong arms around her. She breathed in his familiar scent of exotic spices, the rain scent of his clothes. "You take care of yourself," he whispered into her ear.

Then he pulled back, took her head in his hands and kissed her deeply. She felt an electric surge in her stomach and allowed herself to melt into the kiss, to grip his back, reveling in the sensation of their bodies pressed together. When he pulled back, she whispered, "You do the same."

He released her hands and turned away, hurrying through the crowd to his all-terrain vehicle. Before he climbed in, he turned, just as he had that first night outside New Atlantic, and raised a hand, his face full of emotion. She held up her hand as well, the pang growing in her as he swung up into the driver's seat. And then he was pulling out of the Rover camp, and she became aware once more of the crowd around her, shouting and running.

She helped a few people carry boxes full of ancient books and maps out to the rendezvous point, then stood there, blinking under the bright sun as she watched Rowan drive off into the distance.

"You ready?" Raven's voice cut into her reverie.

She collected herself. "Yes." She surveyed the frightened Rovers. "Will they use the hyperloop to get to Sanctuary City?"

"Yes. And we'll catch the one toward Gordon's plane."

Gordon approached them. "Got the route almost calculated. We should get out of here before those media bastards show up."

She took his arm. "Right."

Raven waved them over to a dirty four-wheel drive jeep that had been charging all day in the sun. "Get in. We can drive to the hyperloop from here."

She and Gordon piled in. The older man clapped his hands together. "This is going to be fun!"

* * * *

Raven drove them about thirty miles out, bouncing along rough ground in the jeep, winding up and down small hills. Winds tore from the west, sending up spiraling dust devils that meandered across the terrain before dissipating.

They entered a patch of forest that had died long ago. Some skeletal, sun-bleached trees still stood, lonely sentinels with bare arms stretching out plaintively. Raven steered the jeep between thick fallen trunks, and their progress slowed. She wondered how the other Rovers fared, if they'd all gotten out in time. As they bounced along, she scanned above for any sign of a media airship. She was grateful to see only a blue sky, with dark storm clouds forming in the west.

As they passed a group of large solar panels, Raven stopped the jeep. He hopped out and walked over to them. He entered commands on his PRD. When he finished, he gave a thumbs up. She'd seen other Rovers use that same "all is well" sign with each other, and decided that she liked it. He returned to the jeep, and they motored along for another mile before he stopped again.

Raven brought up a window on his PRD and entered a command. She startled when she heard the grinding of gears, a loud clank, and watched two massive doors creak open in the ground before them. She hadn't seen them until now. Scrubby vegetation grew on their surface, disguising them completely.

The doors swung straight up, revealing a dark rectangular hole. Raven switched on his headlights, and drove down into it. H124 turned in her seat to watch the doors close slowly behind them. With another clang they sealed, and the darkness engulfed them.

Raven drove on, his headlights illuminating a large ramp leading down to a flat area. Several other cars were parked at the bottom. He pulled up next to one of them and cut the motor. The cars all looked to be solar-powered, though down here in the dark, their batteries would die. Then she saw that they'd all been plugged in. As they climbed out, Raven unwound a small wire from the back of the jeep, and led it over to a power contact point in the wall. It adhered with a click.

"This way," he said, removing his backpack from the car. She slung her own on her back. Switching on their headlamps, they followed Raven down a walkway. Temperatures here were cool, the tunnel musty and disused. She stifled a cough.

As they descended a metal staircase their footsteps echoed in the cavernous tunnel. At the bottom stood a wall with a round door. Raven typed something into his PRD, and the door hissed open, revealing a tubular vehicle with over a hundred seats and a large area where freight could be strapped down. He ducked inside, and they followed. Gordon took the place in. "Well, I'll be . . ." The door hissed shut behind them, and H124 took a seat up front, shrugging off her pack. Gordon sat next to her.

"How fast does this puppy go?" Gordon asked.

"Over 700 mph."

Gordon gave a long, low whistle.

Raven sat down and entered more commands into his PRD. "Here we go."

H124 heard a hiss, and something gave off a loud peal. The pod shook slightly, then grew still. She felt a gentle acceleration, and the ride went amazingly smooth. "And we're off," Raven said.

Gordon chuckled as he gazed around the pod. "Hell of a thing." He swung his legs in his seat, grinning. H124 couldn't help but crack a smile watching him.

"We should get some sleep. It's a long haul ahead of us," Raven said.

H124 sighed. Sleep. She felt like she could sleep for a week. She'd only grabbed an hour or so on their drive back from the radar facility. Her eyes burned with exhaustion.

She rolled up her new jacket, one she'd picked from the myriad choices in Sanctuary City. It was a knee-length black jacket with red and purple sections on the back, made out of a sturdy material that felt like it could take a beating. Raven had watched her, amused, as she had selected new clothes to replace her old worn ones, going not by aesthetics, but feeling each one to see how durable the fabric was. Now she made a pillow of her jacket and moved to one of the empty rows, stretching out. In moments she was out.

* * * *

She woke to Raven gently touching her arm. "We're here."

Groggy and disoriented, she sat up. Gordon stirred a few rows behind her, rubbing his eyes and yawning. He gave a big stretch, and stood up.

This time the door at the front of the pod hissed open. They trudged out, feeling the lack of sleep.

This end of the hyperloop looked just like the one they'd entered from. They climbed up a set of grated stairs. At the top, another assortment of cars waited. Raven selected a jeep and detached its power cable, which auto-retracted into a small hatch in the jeep's side.

They all climbed in, and Raven brought up a window in his PRD. "Let's just make sure no one's up there." As H124 looked over his shoulder, he connected to a series of topside cameras. She could see the high, impressive silhouette of the Rocky Mountains in the distance, their details obscured by what looked like a grey layer of haze or smoke. The land above was dry and barren, and dust blew along the ground. Stands of long-dead, blackened trees fanned into the distance. There was no sign of life or movement.

Raven started up the jeep. H124 insisted Gordon take the front seat, and made herself comfortable in the back. They drove up the steep ramp, gears clanking as the gigantic doors swung open. They stopped with a clatter, and Raven eased the jeep out of the tunnel.

Again the doors swung shut to their rear. H124 looked back to see them concealed perfectly in the ground. She studied the area, trying to spot the cameras, but saw only an assembly of boulders and the skeletal remains of the ancient forest. She could have walked right over the area and been completely ignorant of the hyperloop.

Gordon brought up his map, sharing the location data to his jet with Raven. "We're only twenty-four miles away," Raven said, grinning. "Not bad at all!"

She smiled as they motored off in that direction. Behind them loomed the massive peaks of the Rockies. They hadn't made it last time they tried to cross those mountains. She pushed away memories of the crash, the little plane that was torn apart, Gordon's terrible injury, and the unbearable cold.

They bounced along in silence, taking in the scene. To their south lay an abandoned town, which they drove through, motoring down broken streets. Most buildings no longer stood, but were lying in piles of rotted wood. A tall steel sign leaned at an angle. It had probably once advertised the location of a lodging or restaurant. At the top of its high pole was a circular enclosure, but its innards had long since broken and fallen out.

On her right, strange pillars stood in a row beneath a rusted and sagging overhang. She'd seen these things all over the roads when she'd driven west in her solar-powered car. Nearby, a tarnished sign with a winged red horse leaned against a fallen building. At the far edge of town, the remains of a single edifice still stood, its southern wall collapsed, the roof long since gone. The barely legible lintel above its door read "Wagon Wheel Saloon."

Gordon brought her attention to the front of the car. "What's that?" He pointed at what looked like a small dust storm five or so miles in the distance. It was nothing like the immense squall they'd encountered on their way back from the radar facility, and at first she was relieved it was so small. Then she spotted objects moving in the dust, speeding toward them. Raven slowed the jeep, and she pulled out a pair of diginocs from her pack.

Standing up in the back of the vehicle, she gripped the roll bar with one hand to steady herself, and raised the nocs to her face. A roaring mass of cars thundered toward them, tall spears mounted on their front grills and bumpers. Even from this distance, she could see bulbous shapes impaled on the spikes. Human heads, she realized, with streaming ribbons of blood-soaked hair.

Savage-looking men and women stood in the back of the trucks, fists raised, yelling at their compatriots in neighboring cars. One man held the severed head of an enemy, waving it around violently, his face a mask of rage.

"Death Riders," she breathed. "And they're headed straight for us."

Chapter 5

The dust cloud grew closer.

Gordon gripped the dashboard. "What do we do?"

Raven looked over his shoulder. "Have they seen us?"

H124 turned around, noting the dissipated remnants of their own dust trail being carried away on the wind. It was nothing compared to the plumes the Death Riders were kicking up. H124 studied them again with the nocs. They were veering slightly to the right, and most of them seemed to be focused on each other, as well as a certain point in the distance. "I don't think so."

"We need to hide," Raven said. He gripped the wheel, coming to a stop. "The doors to the hyperloop are too big. If we swing those open now to hide in there, they'd spot them. We can't risk them finding it."

"Isn't this area riddled with old uranium mines?" Gordon recalled.

"You're right." He brought up the map on his PRD and waved through it. "There's one not far from here."

Slowly he spun the jeep around, moving just a few feet at the time to avoid kicking up a dust trail. The progress was agonizingly slow. He drove down an embankment, and the Death Riders disappeared from H124's view. Raven drove along an empty wash, where the ground was uneven and bumpy. She jostled around in the back.

The jeep climbed up the embankment on the far side of the wash, and once again H124 could see the Death Riders' cloud of dirt. She turned around, kneeling backward in the seat, and watched them through the nocs. One armored van was mounted with a fifty-caliber gun in a crow's nest, a woman wheeling it around, ready to fire. Red paint covered her face in a complex geometric pattern. H124 zoomed in, noting that the paint was uneven and caked, clumpy in some places. It wasn't paint, she realized. *It was blood.* The woman bared her teeth, chanting something with the others, her mouth streaming with fresh scarlet.

Raven lurched over a bump, and H124 momentarily lost sight of them. "How's it looking back there?" Raven asked her.

She retrained the nocs on them. The Death Riders were still focused on some point in the distance. "So far, so good." She looked ahead. Raven was steering them toward a dilapidated old mine, decrepit timbers bracing the entrance. The dark, four-sided aperture was barely big enough to accommodate them. Raven inched the jeep inside, and the cool darkness enveloped them.

They could hear the Death Riders' engines now. H124 jumped out of the jeep and stood at the mine's entrance, just out of sight. The dust cloud behind the riders was thick and churning, and H124 realized they were dragging objects behind the convoy. She zoomed in, spotting chains that dragged large lumps, rocks maybe, or bundles of material. She zoomed in a little more, and saw that one of the lumps had long snaking projections, flailing and whipping this way and that. She realized with horror that they were arms and legs. Then a screaming head came into view, the man's skin scoured off in large patches from being dragged, a chain wrapped tightly around his torso. Seeping holes riddled his chest.

She saw two Death Riders standing in the back of their trucks, pointing down at him. Each held a bow and arrow. One drew back on his bow, and H124 could see something bulbous at the tip of the arrow as he nocked it. As the other Death Rider pointed at the helpless victim, the second one loosed the arrow. It lodged inside the man's chest. Seconds later, he exploded in a crimson spray, and mounds of flesh flew skyward. Only his legs remained, bouncing away into the dirt, as the chain dragged on bare ground.

H124 lowered the diginocs, gasping for breath. When she looked again, she saw that the other lumps being dragged were bodies in various stages of dismemberment, some nearly whole corpses, others mere torsos. The two men with bows high fived each other, grinning as the severed legs vanished into the distance.

"What are they doing?" Raven asked, joining her. He pulled out his diginocs just as Gordon walked up to them, holding his own pair. Together the three watched as the Death Riders' path veered slowly, on a course that would soon intercept their location.

A wind kicked up, mercifully covering their tracks in the dirt.

"Do you think they saw us?" Gordon asked. "Is that why they changed direction?" She heard his dry swallow.

"I don't think so," she told him, her heart hammering.

Scanning the procession, she spotted a vehicle with a large, flat top. Three Death Riders stood atop it, strapped beside a man tied to a stake. A fenced-off area had also been built on top, with flames licking along its length. H124 didn't want to see, but something compelled her to keep staring. As they watched, a woman took a long knife and sliced off the man's calf. His mouth opened in a scream, drowned out by the engines. She stuck the muscle over the fire, searing it, then threw it to her comrades, who devoured it eagerly. H124 felt sick as she saw the exposed bones on the man's arms, where they'd already carved away flesh.

"Oh, god," Gordon breathed.

Now the Death Riders thundered close, so much so that H124 could feel tremors in the ground. Small pebbles and soil fragments sifted down through the entrance of the mine. She backed away, out of sight, the others doing the same.

The rabble was going to drive right over the hyperloop doors, coming dangerously close to their location.

H124 retreated farther into the mine, backing up until she bumped into Raven. He brought his hands up and clutched her shoulders. Gordon stood a few inches away. She could hear his quick and shallow wheezes.

The dull thunder soon became a clamorous roar as the combustible engines drew near. They passed over the hidden hyperloop doors, giving them no notice. H124's breath stuck in her throat as the first Death Rider reached the wash by the mine, his car screaming down the embankment and up the other side.

Then dozens more poured into the arroyo, like beetles swarming over a carcass, their engines deafening and sharp. They streamed up the far side of the embankment, passing within a hundred feet of the mine entrance.

Raven's hands tightened on her shoulder and she pressed back into him. Gordon eased back, moving alongside her. She gripped his arm.

The Death Riders became a steady stream of cars and trucks, each mounted with decaying bodies, spitted and spiked, with tattered streamers tied to their antennas. The booming noise began to shift as the bulk of the Death Riders drove off to the north. Then came the last few vehicles, dragging the mangled corpses.

The dust cloud drifted into the mine, the clamor faded to a dull roar, and the vibration died. They were gone.

H124 realized she was holding her breath. Gordon gripped her hand, and Raven peered out of the entrance. "I think we're clear."

Gordon exhaled and slumped against the jeep.

H124 clapped his shoulder. "That's two times we've been lucky with them."
Raven turned in the mine doorway. "That was a little too close."
Gordon looked up at him. "Let's just hope they haven't found my little
jet and stripped it to pieces, or this'll be a real short trip."

They waited another half hour to be sure their enemy was well out of
sight, and resumed their trek.

* * * *

Forty-five minutes later, they pulled up outside an abandoned airstrip.
It looked like it hadn't been used in more than a century. All the buildings
had collapsed, and the methane refueling pump had exploded sometime in
the past. The south end of the compound had been torched recently. Soot
and dirt covered the fallen buildings.

"Your plane is here?" Raven asked, downcast. "I don't think it could
have survived."

As Raven stopped in front of the ruined methane pump, Gordon
climbed out and walked along the central airstrip, where planes had once
taxied into their respective hangars. He studied the ground carefully, at
times stopping to bend over, hands on his knees, peering intently at the
runway. A few times he kicked and lifted away debris—fallen metal
sheets, shattered cement blocks with protruding rebar. Approaching a
large piece of crumpled aluminum, he picked up one corner and dragged
it aside. Beneath lay a small hatch, barely visible, flush with old asphalt.

Gordon entered a command on his PRD, and the hatch ground open,
sliding to one side. "Wait here," he called to them.

He climbed down into the opening. H124 and Raven waited, expecting
Gordon to come back out. But he didn't.

Just as she started to worry that something had gotten him down there,
a great boom sounded to their left. She snapped her head that way, seeing
the side of a building move. Its fallen walls and roof pushed upward, sheet
metal and siding sloughing off to one side. A huge metallic chamber came
into view, rotating as it rose, pushing away debris. She could hear the
whirring of a motor as the chamber broke through the rubble, revealing a
wide freight door on the far side.

The new room clicked into place. Moments later the freight door lifted,
its motor unbearably loud. As the door raised, a small white jet came into
view. Gordon sat in the cockpit. When the door opened completely, she and

Raven jogged over and started dragging away debris. The little jet, some thirty-three feet long, taxied out, stopping on the main runway.

Gordon climbed down from the cockpit. "Isn't she a beaut?" he asked, chuffed. "It's a modified Eclipse 500. And still in pristine condition. Plenty of methane left down there, so she's refueled. Just need to do a pre-flight check and we can go."

"This is fantastic," Raven said, impressed.

"My friend took good care of her."

"Where is he now?" H124 asked.

The smile left Gordon's face. "He was taken a few years ago."

"Taken?" she asked.

Gordon didn't look at her, but placed his hand flat on the plane's fuselage and looked down. "The Death Riders got him."

"I'm so sorry."

"Me too. He was a good man." He turned away, wiping his face on his sleeve. Then he met their gaze. "He'd be happy to know his jet helped in a mission like this."

"We're grateful to have it," Raven added.

Gordon went on to perform his pre-flight check and maintenance, going over the length of the plane with various tools he pulled from a chest in the cockpit.

H124 constantly scanned the horizon for any sign of the Death Riders. But their luck held. The sun set. She was grateful for the dark, which masked their presence. By the time Gordon was ready, she'd seen no dust cloud announcing their approach.

"You kids ready?" Gordon asked, tucking a dirty red rag into a pocket in his overalls.

They circled to the side of the plane as Gordon unfolded a small stepladder from the fuselage. Inside, the Eclipse was posh, with blue velvet seats, a sleek bar, and matching cabinet space. She sank into one of the seats, placing her pack next to her. Raven did the same.

Gordon fired up the engine, taxiing down the runway. She stared out as they lifted off, watching the shrinking scenery in the gloom, a patchwork view of dry, barren land.

He banked toward the east, and before he'd even leveled out, her lids were drooping from exhaustion.

Chapter 6

As they flew over the east coast, drawing closer to the spacecraft section, dawn was breaking. She turned sleepily in her seat to stare out the window. They could see a storm in the air, a monstrous swirl of churning grey clouds. It brewed to the southeast, where the sky was completely socked in. As winds buffeted the Eclipse, Raven clutched his armrest. H124 tried in vain to suppress memories of the previous time she and Gordon had ventured through weather like this. She gripped her seat as they veered toward an old airstrip. "Not long now," Gordon told them.

They dipped below the clouds, a shock of turbulence rattling the plane, and the ground came into view. Miles of crumbled asphalt and toppled buildings lay scattered across a desolate landscape. She saw no greenery, just the beige and grey of an ancient industrialized area. The old streets lay clogged with debris: rusted cars, bricks, cement blocks, and a score of decayed items she couldn't even make out.

They'd entered the coordinates on their PRDs for Lockhardt Aeronautics, the facility tasked with building one part of the spacecraft. As she took in the ruined scene below, with all the toppled structures and choked streets, she bit her lip. What if it had long since been destroyed?

Her PRD beeped, and she looked down to see that Orion had sent them a countdown for the impact time of the fragments. It overlaid her map, revealing the areas where damage would occur. She waved through the map, reading what the effects would be if they were present at the site of Lockhardt Aeronautics when the fragment hit. The readout read:

At the time of impact, this location faces the following dangers:

Maximum radiation will impact you 320 milliseconds after impact
Irradiation duration will be 1.15 minutes

Thermal Effects:
Thermal exposure will be 3.41×106 Joules/m^2
Third degree burns over entire body
Trees ignite
Grass ignites

Seismic Effects:
Greatest shaking will occur 10 seconds after impact
Richter Scale 7.0

Air Blast:
At your location, air blast will arrive 2.53 minutes after impact
Wind velocity will be 128 m/s = 287 mph
Sound Blast will be 97 dB

Damage To Surroundings:
Collapse of multistory buildings
Shattering of glass windows
Any trees will be blown down

Raven brought up his own PRD and flipped through the data.

"This is helpful," she said to him.

He gave her a rueful smile. "Yes. Now we can know the exact time we'll meet our doom by fire and shattered glass."

She gave a small laugh. Moments later his PRD beeped again. "Great!" he said, reading the message. "I'm sending this to you, too." The message was from someone named Nimbus. "Nimbus is our meteorologist. She's up in Sanctuary City. She's the one who's been keeping track of methane and CO_2 levels in the atmosphere. She's also got a fleet of buoys in the Atlantic and eastern Pacific that measure sea surface temperatures. So she's got a pretty good handle on hurricanes."

"Hurricanes?" The term wasn't familiar.

He pointed out at the storm. "It's one of the main reasons the first megacities were built along the coasts. As the earth heated up, sea surface temperatures rose, creating ideal conditions for larger hurricanes to form.

Instead of using methods that would have cut global warming, they used stopgap measures like building more levees, but these were just destroyed over and over again. These towns were eventually abandoned for the first environmentally shielded megacities."

H124's PRD beeped, and she opened the forwarded message. Data streamed into her map, generating an image of the hurricane, its predicted path and wind speed. She monitored the wind speed churning around the storm's center. "251 mph winds?" she asked, jaw slackened. She remembered the storms she'd survived on her way out to find the Rovers. She'd thought *those* were bad.

"Winds won't be so high if we steer clear of the eyewall," he told her, indicating the spinning area near the clear center.

Wind speeds did vary along the breadth of the storm, but still hovered above 100 mph in most places.

"That's a monster brewing out there," Gordon told them. "I haven't flown out this way in a long time. It's all gotten worse."

He circled the old airstrip, full of cracks and broken asphalt. The wind tossed the plane around as if it were paper. She gripped her armrest as he dipped low, blasted by a sudden gust. They raced toward the ground, the shattered cement looming up beneath them. She gritted her teeth as the wheels touched down. They jostled to a stop.

Raven looked at his PRD, checking the coordinates of the facility. "It's not far from here. We'll have to hurry. We only have eight hours until the first fragment hits."

"I'm going to refuel and come back when you signal me," Gordon told them.

She unbuckled her harness and leaned over, gripping Gordon's arm. "Will you be okay?" she asked him, thinking of the harrowing times they refueled before.

"Right as rain. At least there aren't Death Riders out this way."

Given their recent encounter, she could picture them all too well, racing toward her and Gordon as they tried to refuel at a remote airstrip, glistening skulls mounted on their cars, the bloodthirst plain in their faces.

She hugged him and hopped out. "Take care of yourself."

"You, too, kiddo." He smiled warmly.

Raven grabbed his pack with the collapsible maglev sled out of the back. The rain was already pelting them. She grabbed her own pack, filled with a water bottle and filter, her multitool, some MREs, goggles, and an extra set of dry clothes. They donned their raingear as the wind picked up, and she watched as Gordon turned the plane and taxied down the old runway, lifting off in the opposite direction.

Catching his long black hair whipping around in the wind, Raven pulled it back and fastened it with a cord. Consulting their PRDs, they headed off in the direction of the facility, the wind so loud they could barely hear each other.

By the time they drew within a few miles of Lockhardt Aeronautics, the wind was howling, and the buildings groaned. Rain pounded on their backs. The streets started to fill with water, washing in trash and rotted material that triggered H124's gag reflex. Old poles that had once held signs were now permanently bent from scores of storms that had battered the coast. Winds picked up, tossing more debris. She heard glass shatter on a neighboring street, the final gasp of a building that couldn't withstand another storm. Water sloshed at their ankles. She leaned into the wind, checking her PRD. They were within two miles of the location.

She wondered what condition they would find the building in, and hoped they'd followed protocol and built the section underground. Maybe subsequent generations had built on top of the original structure, consigning it to oblivion, which meant it might still be there, buried, like the university she'd discovered under New Atlantic.

The wind tore at her rain parka, soaking her hair where it blew free from the hood. She tucked the strands behind her ears, shielding her eyes from the stinging gusts. Raven moved behind her, his clothes flapping violently against his body as he gripped the straps of his backpack.

The storm churned inexorably toward them, moving north, the rain lashing so hard it stung her skin. The surge raised the water above their ankles, and it began to seep into their boots. Detritus washed in with every new wave, and finally she rummaged through her pack for a scarf to tie around her nose and mouth to filter out the stench.

The sky grew dark as they hiked on, and the terrain grey and dim. The winds bellowed around her, and her ears popped from a sudden pressure change. She staggered to stay upright, the wind rippling her skin in waves. She couldn't see anymore, so she pulled the pair of goggles out of her bag and struggled to put them on. Raven did the same.

Wind gusted down her throat and up her nose, and she could barely breathe. Raven called out to her, but the wind stole his words away; she could only see his mouth moving. He pointed to a steel railing sticking out of a broken sidewalk, a bent sign pushed all the way to the ground under the force of innumerable storms.

As trash and debris flew around her, a shard of metal swirled out of the gloom and hit her side. She threw up her arms, protecting her head as another rusted chunk of sheet metal sailed by, barely missing her. The storm surge intensified, forcing them to wade through calf-deep water.

As she struggled on, a sudden gust lifted her off her feet. She landed hard on her back, splashing down in the filthy brown water. The gale propelled her along, pushing her through shattered glass and broken bits of masonry.

Raven tried to run to her as the rain lashed down in sheets, but he was blown off his feet too, slamming into the brick facade of a crumbling building. For a moment he lay there, unmoving, and H124's mouth went dry. She flipped onto her stomach and tried to elbow-crawl over to him, but the wind forced her back, rolling her along the street. She grabbed a metal pole and held on. The gust weakened, and she seized the opportunity to jump up.

Raven staggered up, rubbing his head. She hurried over. Once again he pointed to the railing. They fought against the gale, leaning in that direction, unable to make more than a few inches of progress. Keeping her hood up was hopeless. The rain slapped and beat against her skin, needles in her ears. Raven took her arm as they battled their way toward the railing.

Lightning flashed, illuminating the tumult in a flare of bright silver, and for a brief instant she saw the droplets suspended in the air. A tortured whine sounded to their rear. They turned to see a building looming precariously over them.

Raven snatched her arm tightly and propelled them forward. They grabbed on to the life line of the sturdy railing, steadying themselves. She looked down to see a refuse-choked stairwell leading to a tunnel. A small hole in the wreckage at the base of the stairs would just barely allow them access if they crawled. Raven went first, using the railing to pull himself down. He hunched down and pulled a stone aside, then stuck his head into the dark opening. She watched as he crawled inside. Seconds later, he stuck out his head and yelled something she couldn't hear. Again the building behind her whined and shuddered. She peered over her shoulder, watching it topple over in slow motion.

Clutching the railing, she whipped herself into the stairwell just as one of Raven's arms snaked out through the opening. She grabbed his hand, and he pulled her through as the building crashed down behind her, spraying stones through the stairwell with a godlike roar.

The sudden muffling of the storm made her ears ring. She struggled to her feet. She was soaked. At least the water was lower here, only ankle-deep.

Raven switched on his headlamp, shining it back the way they'd come. The narrow hole in the debris was now blocked. "We're not going back that way," he whispered. "Let's hope this tunnel is still open at the other end."

Above them the hurricane roared and slammed against the street, shaking the ceiling and raining down tiles and dirt. She also switched on her light, and they walked along the tunnel until they reached another staircase. They descended, turned a corner, and stopped at the top of a long, grated staircase. Each step had metal grooves. A decayed rubber banister ran the entire length of the stair. They started down, her boots clinking on the grate. On both sides hung old advertisements. Most of them were too dusty or moldy for her to make out much, but she read a few lines:

"Be part of our Friends and Family Package! Upgrade to 12g!"

"Share your company with the world. Ad packages start at only $9999!"

"Time for retirement? Be smart! Our advisors are standing by today!"

At the bottom of the stairs they entered a long platform, where crumbling pillars held up a bare ceiling. Tiles had covered it once, but now most of them lay broken and dusty on the floor. In front of them a large tunnel meandered off in both directions. Raven consulted his PRD, then pointed to the left.

They descended a small set of stairs and stepped into the tunnel. At their feet, strange steel tracks led away into the darkness. They started down them slowly as they stepped over wooden crossbeams. "What is this place?" she asked.

"People used to ride down here on electric trains, moving around the city."

"Trains?" The word was unfamiliar.

"Vehicles capable of holding hundreds of people. The trains moved from station to station, picking people up and dropping them off."

"Why did they get on and off?"

"What do you mean?"

"Where were they going?"

"Jobs, dates, concerts, social engagements, family events . . ."

She stared at him, and her headlamp made him squint. She didn't know what "concerts" were, or how you could go to a date on a calendar. But she knew what family was, and envied those people who knew their parents or siblings. "You mean they lived in a city, but were free to roam around, to spend time with other people?"

"Yes." He studied her for a moment as she took it all in. "Things were different for you, huh?"

She exhaled. "Very."

Raven looked down at the tracks, stepping around a large chunk of ceiling that had given way. "For me, too. I spent my childhood on a mission, traveling with my parents, stocking weather shelters and tending to experimental forests." He tucked a wet strand of hair behind his ear. "Since they were killed, repairing things has become my new goal. It's hard to imagine an entire city full of people able to go about their leisure, to see musicians play and visit with friends. Add to that the destruction of everything else . . . the forests, the rivers . . ." He took a deep breath. "We don't know what we've lost."

They walked on in silence before she asked, "What's a concert?"

He cracked a smile. "It's when a bunch of people gather to hear a musician play."

She nodded, still having no idea what he was talking about. "What's a musician?"

He stopped and faced her. "You serious?"

"Yes."

"Someone who performs music."

She thought back to her life in New Atlantic. She'd heard the term "music" before, when she was little. Before she'd been moved to corpse cleanup, she cleaned the living pods of citizens. Piped into the living quarters were strange, magical, lilting sounds. Sometimes they were dreamy and atmospheric, other times full of energy.

"I think I know what music is. I may have heard it before, a long time ago."

He appeared stunned. "I had no idea, or I would have played you some." Wind whistled through the tunnel. "I'd play you some now on my PRD, but I think we'd have a hard time hearing it."

"How do you go to a date? Aren't we always going to a date, every time the day changes?"

He wrinkled his brow in confusion, then burst into laughter. He caught himself, and cleared his throat. "Excuse me. It's not that kind of date. It's a term for when . . . well . . ." All of a sudden he got awkward, and his words trailed off.

"When what?"

He rubbed the back of his neck. "When two people want to spend time together alone."

She thought of Rowan kissing her, and recognition dawned. "Oh. I see."

He adjusted the pack on his back. "I don't suppose you've had many of those in New Atlantic either."

"Never in New Atlantic." Her eyes met his. "What about you?"

"When I was younger, traveling with my parents, there were a couple of people. One was a Badlander."

H124 knew how that felt. "Oooh . . . dangerous!"

"Tell me about it. Her father hated me. We had to sneak out to see each other."

"What happened?"

He fidgeted with his pack's straps. "After my parents died, I felt like my whole world had turned to ashes. To lose them for such a senseless reason . . . I spent weeks just sitting in a weather shelter, staring at the wall. I couldn't bring myself to eat. I felt like I was underwater, and time slowed to this agonizing crawl. It was an effort just to breathe. I hadn't just lost my parents, but my belief that we could change things, that we had any ability to do good on this planet. The weeks turned into months, and instead of things starting to heal, the reality of them being gone just set in all the more. I saw her a few times, but I guess she didn't understand the depth of my grief. She still had her parents. She wanted the same fun-loving me she'd gotten to know. And I guess that part of me was gone. We drifted apart. I haven't seen her in years."

"I'm so sorry."

He looked at her appraisingly. "Must have been tough for you, living that isolated life, not even knowing your parents?"

"It was. I've always felt this ache inside me, this longing, but I didn't know what it was. Now, being with you all, meeting Rowan and Gordon . . . I realize that it was companionship."

"I wonder what's worse. Never knowing your parents at all, having terrible, abusive parents, or having loving parents who die prematurely."

"They're all terrible."

"Yes."

They walked on.

He looked at her from the corner of his eye. "Huh. I've never told anyone about that."

The hurricane was raging on above, and the ceiling continued to rain down in scattered fragments. A sudden wind tore through the tunnels, as if a debris-choked egress had suddenly come free ahead. Her eyes streamed with tears. A loud boom erupted overhead. Something massive had hit the ground. The entire tunnel shuddered, and H124 brought a hand to her chest. "What was that?"

"Probably another building falling." Raven checked his PRD. "We're getting closer. We'll have to switch to a different tunnel, though, one going east to west."

Their boots squished on the ground. Water was starting to seep into the tunnels. "You mean . . ."

"We have to go topside."

They reached another platform, and climbed the stairs up to the street entrance. It was hopelessly blocked from a cave-in that probably happened decades ago. Moss grew on the exposed rock.

They turned back, traveling down another stretch of tunnel to a third station. This time when they climbed up to the surface, they saw a crack of dim light filtering through a pile of fallen ceiling.

"I think this'll work."

They went to work hefting away chucks of tile and cement. They levered out the bigger pieces using lengths of rusted rebar. Wind shrieked through the hole as the aperture grew wider. When it was big enough for them to crawl through, the wind tore at their clothes. She put her goggles back on, and watched Raven disappear through the jagged opening.

Then she was crawling through herself, back out into the lashing storm. As they emerged from the stairwell, the wind blasted her in the back. Raven grabbed her hand just as the wind sent her off her feet. Though it was still day, they could barely make out anything before them. Dark, thick clouds hung so low she couldn't see where the lashing rain ended and the clouds began.

Raven tried to hold on to her hand, but then he went over too. She looked at her PRD, trying to make out the wind speed. One hundred sixty mph. They tumbled over, and got pinned against the base of a crumbling building. Water rose around them, foul-smelling and cold. Raven shouted to her, trying to point to a neighboring street, but the wind tossed his arm away. Wind rippled their skin. She had to keep her mouth shut, lest it be forced open. Her throat was so dry it hurt.

Rain slashed at them, plastering their hair to their faces. He shouted something else she couldn't hear.

The force of wind against her was unbearable, like a thousand knives pricking her all at once. Sand, glass, and other debris pummeled past. She felt a stinging cut on her cheek as the jagged edge of an old metal sign screamed past.

They had only a block to go, but H124 didn't see how they were going to make it.

Chapter 7

Crawling on their hands and knees through the sloshing water, H124 and Raven struggled to cross the street. She could see another railing leading to a tunnel. A building on their right moaned, and she looked up to see it leaning dangerously, its bricks being torn from its facade and tossed into the wind. As it shuddered she tried to crawl faster, but each time she picked up an arm or leg, she had to fight against the gale to plant it down again, often losing. Their progress was agonizingly slow, and when she heard the building groan and fall, she braced herself to be crushed beneath it. She kept crawling, kept fighting, keeping Raven in sight, then looked up to see the edifice collapsing just behind them. It came down with a dull rumble and a howling of the wind. The street shook as it hit, bruising her palms and knees.

They had only a few feet to go. Raven reached the railing, lacing his fingers through the metal. He turned and stretched out his other hand for her. She grabbed it, his skin warm against the cold rain. She was surprised at his strength as he pulled her up close to him against the forceful wind. She gripped the railing and took a deep breath, every bone in her aching.

Sometime in the past, a building had fallen over the entrance, and rubble now blocked it completely. Holding on to the railing, she reached out with her free hand to start clearing away bricks. But a sudden gust at her back sent her sprawling onto the pile of rubble. Sharp, broken corners cut her hands and knees. Raven grasped her arm, trying to pull her up, but she could feel the bricks shifting beneath her weight. As her stomach pitched downward, the bricks swallowed her. Her hands sunk into the mess as she struggled to get out. The whole thing gave way with a shudder, and she fell down, arms flailing, bricks falling on her head and back. She slammed down hard on the floor. Raven landed beside her.

She curled into a fetal position as the rest of the bricks cascaded down on top of them. Rain kept lashing at her face. She wiped the brick dust out of her eyes, and saw that the dam of bricks had fallen free—the opening was clear.

Raven shifted beside her, brushing crumbling mortar off his face. Piles of red dust littered the floor. They stood, wiping themselves off as the wind pushed on them from above.

"That went faster than I expected," he said, flicking a broken chunk of brick off his shoulder.

She laughed. "I knew just where to apply pressure."

He grinned. "Brilliant." After he'd made sure the sled in his pack was undamaged, they made their way into the darkness of the new tunnel.

They descended to another platform and hopped down onto the rails, this time going east. She checked her PRD. It was six hours before the fragment was due to hit.

"Raven," she said, wiping the rain out of her eyes as it dripped down from her hair. "How can we possibly move the spacecraft section to safety out there?"

"I've been thinking about that. We'll wait for the eye of the hurricane to pass over, and move it then."

"Doesn't that mean we'll be out there, exposed to those winds in the eyewall if we don't make it in time?"

"We have to risk it." He brought up a series of old maps that had been scanned into his PRD. "Looks like there's an old commuter train tunnel that runs due west. If we can enter it while the eye is passing over, we can have Gordon pick us up at a station beyond the edge of the hurricane."

She knew he was thinking the same thing, but she said it aloud anyway. "What if we can't make it that far before the fragment hits?"

Raven remained silent.

They hurried faster now, moving down the main tunnel, branching off at different service tunnels. As they made their way through the dark, another fear came to her. She glanced around in the gloom. "Are there night stalkers down here?"

He shook his head. "Probably not. They don't seem to live this far east for some reason. We're not sure why."

H124 thought back to her escape from New Atlantic. She'd slept out in the open that first night, and hadn't encountered those things until she was farther west.

At last they reached another platform. A tile marquee still survived on the wall above, though some of the letters had fallen off and shattered. It read: *Loc.ha.dt Aer.na.tics.*

"They had their own station?" she asked.

"Guess so. This company was probably a huge draw to the city back then."

They took the stairs two at a time, and found the entrance only partially blocked. Water poured in from the street above. They only had to remove a few stones to squeeze through. She stuck her head through the ingress, holding her breath as the water cascaded down her face. Pulling her body through, she gasped as she emerged from the waterfall, only to have the wind rob her of her breath. To her right she saw the remains of Lockhardt Aeronautics, a marquee above the door now reading only "AERO—TI—." It had once sported a large glass-enclosed lobby, she guessed, but now all of it was exposed to the elements.

She stepped out, and the wind immediately sent her off balance. Gripping the railing around the stairwell, she moved hand over hand to get closer to the building's door. Raven moved as she did, and she let go of the railing, letting the wind lift her toward the entrance. She tried to stay upright, but instead tumbled head over feet through the framework that had once held the glass. She sloshed through brown water. The wind shoved at her, pinning her on the opposite side of the lobby, cold water seeping all around.

As Raven let go, she watched him fly through the entrance, slamming against the wall next to her. A metal door stood to their left, still intact, so they strained toward it. Raven's hand closed around the handle, and as soon as he pushed down, the door flew open, pulling him with it. H124 managed to stand, letting the wind urge her through the door.

It took both of them to get it closed again.

The sudden absence of wind was shocking, and her skin tingled and ears rang. The gale shrilled through the cracks around the doorframe. She could hear it tearing at the building around them.

With the door shut, the stench of mold assaulted them. The room was knee-deep with water. Decaying plaster, drywall, and black, molded ceiling tiles floated on its surface. The musty smell was so intense she pulled the scarf back up over her face. They seemed to be in an old room filled with workstations. Several desks stood furred and black with mold, with a few chairs sticking out of the water. Raven studied his PRD, and pointed to their left. Wading through the water, they tested each step for weak areas in the floor, avoiding several spots where water spiraled downward as if there were a drain. Ancient insulation, now black and tattered, floated around them.

They moved through a series of rooms as the building shuddered against the wind. Coming to a flight of stairs, they opened the door at the top. "Down here," Raven said. They descended several flights, opening the door at each floor to explore, but found most rooms to be the same, full of old desks and workbenches, rusted tools, and collapsed ceilings. Finally, three flights down—now deep underground—they entered a gigantic workspace. Machines lay scattered about, with all manner of tools she didn't recognize. Water seeped through the ceiling in places, pooling ankle-deep on the floor.

The space was hollow and resonant, and she couldn't shake the feeling that she was trespassing. She could almost feel the ghosts of the men and women who had worked here, laboring on a worthwhile project designed to save the planet. Now their tools lay scattered and unused. She could imagine their disbelief when the project lost funding, when they walked away from this workroom for the last time.

Inside stood a round, self-contained room with glass walls. White suits with helmets hung on hooks beside the door. And in the center of the room stood a device that still looked pristine.

They entered the room, and approached the object. This was it—the spacecraft section. She recognized it at once from the schematic in the binder she'd found. It was square and metallic, covered in places with gold foil, with areas of complex wiring on the exterior. An antenna extended from one side, and there were panels with strange inputs. It stood nearly three feet tall and two feet wide.

"How long before the eye passes over?" she asked.

Raven checked. "Forty-five minutes."

"We're cutting it close."

He pulled the mag-lev sled from his pack and turned on the four copters that formed its base. The little propellers moved around the room, calibrating themselves to each other to form a perfect rectangle. He unfurled the horizontal portion and placed it over the copters, where it levitated easily.

Next he unpacked a translucent skin.

"What is that?" she asked, looking at the unfamiliar membranous material.

"It's a clean skin, an electrostatic shield that also keeps off bacteria and other pollutants. It'll protect the craft." He draped it over the spacecraft section, then entered a command on his PRD. In an instant the skin shrank to the exact proportions of the craft.

Now that it was protected, he ordered the maglev sled over to it. It hovered out, snaking levers in under the craft and slowly lifting it off the table. Raven pulled out a tarp, and together they covered the craft, cinching it tight as an added layer of insulation.

He checked his PRD again. "Once the eye comes, it'll be faster if we take the streets than moving at right angles in the subway tunnels." Raven took a deep breath. "Here we go." He entered the "follow" command to the sled on his PRD, and they hurried out of the small glass room. Even down here, she could hear the storm raging.

She moved to a table where a number of drives and disks were stored on a little shelf. She stuffed them all inside her pack.

They climbed to the ground level of the stairwell and waited for the eye to pass over, taking a seat on the top step. The howling wind screamed overhead. She kept checking her PRD to see when the fragment was going to hit. Four hours. She tried not to think about the effects of the impact where they now stood—their bodies catching fire, windows shattering everywhere, the building collapsing on top of them. Her soaked clothes clung to her skin, and a chill set in.

"You okay?" Raven asked.

She nodded, though she felt quite the opposite. Her fingernails had turned blue. She forced a smile, listening to the winds tear the building apart. Her teeth chattered.

"We're going to make it," he said. When she didn't answer, he lifted his arm. "C'mere. You're freezing." She looked to him, seeing that he was inviting her closer for warmth. Beneath his jacket, his clothes were warm and dry. She shrugged off her own wet jacket and scooted over on the step, leaning into him. He put his arm around her, pulling her close. Her face felt warm against his bare neck.

"This is quite an adventure, huh?" he said.

"Better than my old job." Warmth started to spread through her body.

They sat there in silence, and she became all too aware of his nearness, his scent. She was so unused to being near other people that it still felt strange and new. She watched rain drip off the ends of his long hair. Much of it had come loose from the cord he'd tied it with.

Outside the raging winds started to fade away abruptly. Soon they found themselves in an eerie quiet.

"This is it!" Raven said. "The eye!"

They jumped up, and she slung on her coat. Hurrying through the stairwell door, they rushed through the foyer and stepped out under a clear, blue sky. The grey eyewall was visible above them, staggering and tall. But directly above, the air was clearer than she'd ever seen.

Once they reached the street they ran toward the commuter train station. The streets were choked with so much rubble and clutter that at times they had to scramble over debris piles and around great heaps of jagged glass. Cold water swashed against their legs as they struggled to make progress.

As they scrambled over a pile of bricks blocking one street, she looked up and realized they were moving counter to the eye's path. The terrifying hurricane wall was turning toward them, and their time in the eye was cut mercilessly short. Behind them the maglev sled glided smoothly along the ground, the buzzing of its copters strangely comforting.

She took the opportunity to call Gordon.

When his face flashed up on her screen, a sense of relief washed over her.

"How you doin' out there, kid?"

"It's been a breeze," she answered.

"You ready for me to pick you up?"

"Yes!" She flipped through her display to the image of the hurricane overlaid on the map, and gave him coordinates for a place beyond the edge of the storm where he could land.

"I'll be there. Might take me a bit to circle and find a good landing spot."

"Thank you."

"You be safe."

She ended the transmission, and the roar of the hurricane grew. As the storm churned toward them, she could see things tossed in its depths: scraps of old cars, poles, signs.

Just ahead she saw what remained of the commuter rail station. A sturdy stone building, surprisingly intact compared to those nearby. A chiseled sign in the lintel read, "Garden State Train Station." She hoped the stairs wouldn't be blocked. As they ran, her breath came in gasps, and a stitch caught her side. She still wasn't at a hundred percent after the airship crash. Her heart plummeted when she saw that the top of the stairs was blocked. A building had crashed down long ago, its eroded bricks strewn about the entrance. They didn't have time to dig it out.

"Oh no," Raven breathed.

H124 jogged around the side of the stairs, running along the block until she came to a partially buried circular covering. "Here!" she called. She recognized these openings from her flight from New Atlantic.

Raven ran over, and they cleared the few stones blocking the cover. Together they managed to lift the heavy disc, revealing a utility ladder below. She climbed down first, with Raven close behind. The sled reoriented itself, and floated down through the hole. She climbed back up, grabbed the cover, and hefted it back into place with a clang.

Raven took a moment to catch his breath, hands on his knees. "How long till impact?" he asked as she reached the bottom of the ladder.

She checked. "Three hours and twenty minutes."

He whistled and cracked a smile. "Plenty of time."

They hurried downstairs to the platform and found it in shambles, with tiles and bricks spilled out onto the tracks. Some antique clothing and vestiges of an aged shantytown were scattered just inside the westbound tunnel. A sad collection of mold-covered tarps and fallen tents surrounded a central space. There was also a rusted grill, and beds set up on old cinder blocks. Something white stuck out of the bottom of one of the tents, and as they stepped around the rubbish, H124 knelt to study it more closely.

She jerked back. It was the remains of a human foot, all bone now, picked clean by detritivores in some distant age. She felt sick. She quickly moved past it, swallowing down rising bile. She saw more ivory fragments around the makeshift camp—a skull, someone's finger bones, part of a leg. It had been nibbled through, the marrow long since dried up, or perhaps even eaten.

She wondered how long these remains had been down here, entombed and undisturbed, and what had driven the people to live here in the first place. Camping on the tracks meant that the commuter trains weren't running anymore by that point. Had they hidden down here because of the intense storms, or were they fugitives from New Atlantic? She thought the technology of the camp was far older than that of the megacities.

A short way down the tunnel, they found an old maintenance crawler still attached to the tracks. Its battery had long since died, and its steel wheels had rusted to the rails. "This would be a lot faster than walking," Raven said, kneeling down beside it.

He leaned into it, trying to rock it on the rails. She helped him, throwing her weight into it. With a loud crash it came off the track and landed on its side. They hefted it back onto the rails, then tried to push it. It was sluggish, and the wheels squeaked. It hadn't moved in a long time. But it would work.

The crawler had been fitted with a manual hand crank in case the battery died. They each took one side, climbing onto the crawler. They pushed and pulled, and the wheels shed more of their rust, and began to move faster. Before long the crawler was speeding briskly down the tracks. The sled glided along smoothly in tow.

She consulted her PRD. "We've lost a lot of time. We need to be in the air if we're going to escape the tsunami when the first fragment hits."

Raven glanced around the cavernous gloom. "This place will fill with water." Right now there was only an inch or so of water pooling on the floor. Once it hit, they'd drown for sure.

They picked up the pace, operating the hand crank as fast as they could. The crawler wound down the track, passing station after station. They fell into a rhythm, working in silence. The little sled thrummed along behind them.

As they moved farther west, they passed more shantytowns, and more skeletal relics on the tracks. It appeared as if scavengers had scattered their bones.

The miles churned by slowly, and her arms started to ache. She could tell Raven was starting to suffer, too. Soon her muscles were trembling from fatigue, but they pressed on with ragged gasps.

Then Raven burst out laughing.

She looked up at him, her arms threatening to give out. "What is it?"

He just kept laughing, shaking his head all the while.

It was infectious, and soon a smile broke out of her, and a small chuckle to boot. "I have no idea what's so funny."

He wiped a tear from his eye. "Neither do I. I think I'm losing it," he managed to say through his wild cackling.

She couldn't even look at him, it was so contagious. Instead she checked her PRD, one hand on the crank. "We've got one hour and twenty minutes to go."

"Let's hope Gordon found fuel, and is waiting."

Slowly the laughing fit came to an end, and they moved along the tunnels in silence. Eventually they reached the rendezvous point, their arms rubber and useless.

"This is it," Raven said, double-checking their coordinates.

Leaving the crawler behind, they climbed up to the platform, and took the stairs to the ground floor. The train station roof had fallen through, and sunlight streamed in through the jagged, exposed walls. H124 shielded her eyes. Even though thick clouds hung across the horizon, the sudden glare was intense. She searched the sky for Gordon's plane, listening.

A low thrum met her ears, so she looked to the east where dark clouds gathered. The thrumming grew louder, and she expected to see the little Eclipse 500 appear against the clouds. But it didn't, and the vibration grew so loud she could feel it in her chest. She remembered that feeling, and gripped Raven's arm. "Airship," she whispered.

Raven's eyes went wide, and together they scanned the sky. The deep thrum seemed to come from everywhere at once, the airship's engines drumming in her ears. She saw something flicker to the right. Then a sleek PPC airship descended through the clouds. She'd seen what they could do—entire hillsides vaporized in an instant, scores of people incinerated on the spot when they tried to flee. She knew Raven had witnessed them too, when they had set his parents on fire.

"What are they doing out here?" she asked him.

"They do routine patrols close to the megacities, taking out any rogue transmitters that might interfere with their broadcasts."

Feeling panic rise within her, she searched the clouds for any sign of Gordon. "If Gordon comes now, they'll shoot him out of the sky."

Raven shot her a wary gaze. "I know."

She sprinted back toward the commuter train station, leaping over rubble and shattered glass, and brought up her PRD's communication window. "Gordon!" she cried the moment his face appeared on her display. "There's an airship here. Don't land."

He frowned. "I'm nearly at the rendezvous point." She could hear the distant sound of the jet's engines now. "You only have twenty-two minutes before the first fragment hits."

She waved her display to the pertinent screen. "I know. After that, we'll only have a few minutes before the ejecta hits us."

"Then the tsunami. I need to come in and get you."

"Give us a chance to deal with the airship." She reached the cover of the station, and jogged down the stairs. It was then she realized Raven wasn't with her, "I'll call you back," she told Gordon, ending the call. Cautiously she moved back up the stairs and saw the airship lowering over the ruined cityscape. If they didn't already know they were here, they would soon enough.

Where was he? She sprinted back down the cracked street, weaving between rusted hulks of ancient vehicles. And then she saw him, standing in the same spot, staring up tearfully.

The airship thundered toward him. It had spotted them.

Chapter 8

"Raven!" H124 called out when she reached his side. "We have to get to cover!"

He didn't seem to hear. He just kept staring at the airship, jaw set, his entire frame shaking as tears streamed down his face. She touched his hand. "They've seen us."

His every muscle went taut, and his hands balled into fists. Above them the airship drew near, homing in on their location.

"Raven!" she cried, shaking his arm. He gave no indication that he was even aware of her presence. She spun in front of him and gripped his shoulders. She couldn't break his vacant stare. Finally she brought her hands to his face, forcing him to look at her. When his dark eyes met hers, she felt a visceral hatred, a white-hot fury so intense she shivered. "Raven, they'll kill us. They could fire at any moment. You know what those things are capable of." She cradled his face. "Raven!" He blinked, and finally he saw her. "We have to get to cover."

He brought up a hand and touched her fingers. Then he grasped her hand, and they sprinted back to the train station. The airship wheeled in the sky, descending, a massive, gleaming asteroid of its own.

Raven ran slowly at first, stumbling, then found his footing and tore with her across the desolate streets. They started down through the tunnel, but his grip on her hand tightened. "No, wait—if they fire on us when we're down there, we could get trapped." The sled slid along behind them, matching their speed. They passed the train station, and he pointed to a recessed doorway in a building that was still largely intact. "There!"

They hurried over as the airship rounded the street corner behind them. There was a chance it hadn't seen where they went. When they reached the door, Raven commanded the sled to pull in next to them, out of sight. It was evident that the door had once had glass, but now the metal frame stood empty. They moved inside. He brought up Onyx's hack, hands shaking as he waved through the display. His dexterous fingers flew over the controls.

"What are you going to do?"

"I'm going to break into their comm system. Try to convince them that they're in danger. If they're still out there when the fragment hits, the airburst will probably down them."

H124 thought of the crew of the airship, likely quite small—a pilot, and maybe a weapons officer. They followed orders just as she had done all her life, never questioning what she was working for or toward. "Will they listen?"

"I can try. If not . . ."

She waited for him to finish, but he didn't.

"If not?" she prompted.

He met her gaze with that same look of agony and contempt smoldering in his eyes. "I'll take it down." He gestured toward the sled. "This is too important."

Her PRD came up suddenly, with Gordon's face on the display. She clicked on it. "Gordon?"

"I'm in trouble up here. That airship wasn't alone. I've got one on my tail."

The nearby aircraft slid above the street, passing their hiding spot. Raven raced outside once it had gone farther down, H124 hugging close.

"Hang on!" she told Gordon. The jet was louder now, so she followed the sound to pinpoint his location. The low clouds brushed the top of his tail, and another glint revealed a huge ship descending right on top of him. "We don't have time to talk to them!" she urged Raven, gripping his elbow.

He set his mouth in a grim line. "I agree."

His fingers flew deftly through a number of screens, and H124 clenched her jaw as the airship started the low thrumming she knew all too well. It was about to fire on Gordon, and when it did, nothing would be left but a few chunks of charred metal. Raven entered a series of commands, and the airship tipped violently to one side, sweeping well past Gordon and screaming down toward the ground. Raven halted it about hundred feet from impact, spun it around, and shot it off into the distance.

He turned his attention to the other airship. "Get out of sight!" H124 urged Gordon over the comm link.

Raven hacked into their comm system. "I'm in. I see their designation." He entered a few more commands. "Crew of the airship L435," he said, reading off its serial number. "If you want to live, you'll get clear of this area. A piece of space rock is about to collide with the earth. You don't want to be airborne when it happens."

H124 thought of themselves being airborne. They had to get away before the first airburst hit, but now they were cutting it too close. They needed to be at least sixty miles out or it could bring down the plane. She glanced at her PRD. Looking at the data Orion had sent, she studied their location as it related to the impact. A red circle denoted the thermal radius of the blast, and how close they'd have to be to feel the thermal effects, such as catching fire. A glowing yellow-orange circle marked the extent of the airburst, from a deep orange where it could topple buildings, to a paler yellow where glass would shatter. She didn't relish being in the remains of this crumbling city when the airburst hit them, followed shortly by a second when the other fragment impacted.

The airship pilot didn't listen. The machine reversed its course, backtracking to their location. The deep vibration hurt her ears as it closed in, but the pilot still didn't know exactly where they were.

"Airship L435," Raven said again. "Do you acknowledge?"

"Get off our comm link," growled a man's voice.

The low thrumming grew, and a glaring flash erupted around them. A deafening boom filled their world as the airship fired on the buildings immediately to their right. A concussion wave blew H124 and Raven off their feet, sending them sprawling into the street. What had been several blocks of crumbling masonry and bricks was vaporized in seconds, leaving only a smoking crater.

Raven rose steadily. She could feel hatred washing off him. He brought up his PRD and hacked into the airship's navigation system, shooting them high into the sky, then bringing them down at a screaming velocity. This time he didn't stop a hundred feet up. He drove the ship straight into the crater, where it crumpled and smoldered, a wreck of fiery, twisted metal.

She saw his chest heaving, his jaw trembling with rage. He stared out at the wreck, tears streaming down his face. She was about to reach out to him when a distant tremor met them. The other airship had returned.

He switched over to control the second airship, reversing their engines and entering a location for them to travel to hundreds of miles to the west.

She contacted Gordon. "Okay!"

They heard his jet approach, watching as he landed half a mile away. Racing down the old streets, they didn't slow their pace until they reached the plane. Raven commanded the sled to enter, and then they both piled in. Gordon started taking off as H124 slid the door closed.

She looked at her PRD. "Seven minutes till impact," she told them. They had to get those sixty miles out to escape the majority of the airburst. Even that far out, it would rock the plane, hitting them just minutes after impact.

Gordon pushed the jet down the road, the wheels bumping over countless cracks and ridges from years of frost-heaving. At last the plane went airborne, and H124 buckled in as he pushed the engines.

They climbed so fast that her head pressed back into the seat.

Raven stared out, watching the crashed airship recede from view. Then he closed his eyes, and gripped the armrests.

The jet raced away as Gordon pushed the engines to their limit.

She checked the impact time. "It's about to hit." She strained against inertia to look out the window and to the east. They were too far away to see the incoming fireball over the horizon, but she was compelled to look anyway. She looked back at her PRD. "It's hit."

The jet raced over the terrain, Gordon climbing higher. The engines roared in the confines of the cabin. H124 braced herself against the seat. Four minutes later, the airburst hit.

The jet's windows shattered, showering them with broken glass. A searing pain erupted in her ears, and she swallowed to equalize the pressure, which had dropped in the cabin. She grabbed her backpack as it flew off the seat next to her, before it was sucked out. The tarp covering the spacecraft piece tore off, and whipped out of a side window before they could seize it. The sled shifted, and the craft wrenched free. As it toppled by her, she grabbed it, clenching it with both arms. Raven leaned over and seized the other side. Together they held firm as the violent pressure threatened to fling them out of the plane. Her seatbelt cinched hard across her lap. The air felt thin, and every breath was agony.

Gordon lowered the plane. "The air pressure should equalize soon!" he shouted above the wind. "I'm slowing the plane and bringing us down to 10,000 feet!"

At last the pressure diminished, and H124 felt her weight return to her seat. She and Raven set down the spacecraft piece. Wind still whistled through the broken windows, but it was bearable.

"Everyone okay back there?" Gordon called.

"Yes," she answered. Then she looked at Raven. "We are, right?"

He pulled hair out of his eyes. "Somehow." Blue skies lay ahead. "We did it, didn't we?" He leaned back in his seat with a triumphant exhale. "I can't believe it."

She couldn't help smiling. "We have the first piece."

Chapter 9

Carston was not having a good day. He'd just been bawled out in the producer's office for his latest failed reality show. He thought he'd really been on to something this time—a show about what scarves to pair with what media streams. But hardly anyone had chosen to watch it.

And right now was the worst time. BEC City had upped its signal strength, and now many citizens were tuning into it instead of New Atlantic's feeds. And that meant that their task windows were seeing to maintenance in BEC City. Infrastructure was compromised in New Atlantic now, and other than offering fresh new streams, the producers didn't know what to do to combat the competition.

Carston let out a breath as he sat down in his swivel chair, turning to face the city below. He lived and worked on the seventy-sixth floor. But he'd gotten this promotion twenty years ago, when he'd been a hot new director rising up from the PPC ranks. He'd had fresh new ideas, real game changers, back then. He'd risen quickly.

But he hadn't had a hit in more than six years, which his producer Langstrom had so delicately let him know just now by launching a glass sculpture at his head. He had ducked though, and it had shattered against the wall, kindling her ire even further. Did she expect it not to break? It's not like *he* threw it. He'd never liked that sculpture on her desk anyway, a sort of abstract grotesquerie that had always looked vaguely like an angry pickle, making it very hard for him not to snicker every time she was in the middle of bawling him out.

He didn't want to think about how the meeting had ended. He'd left her office, thoroughly chastised, then realized he'd left his PRD on her desk.

He'd doubled back to get it, and found two Repurposers leaving her office, with that unnerving look of sadistic anticipation on their faces.

Had she ordered him to be Repurposed?

He'd hurried back to his office without retrieving his PRD. Now sweat beaded on his upper lip, and he loosened his tie. He stood and approached the window, surveying the endless streets. They were clean and empty, a vision of order and control. He liked working here. He'd gone to Delta City once for a conference, and had been horrified by the ugly sights sprawling out from the PPC Tower there, the starving rabble climbing over one another like mice eating their own kin when left too long in a cage.

Something in the sky caught his eye, a bright light high above the horizon to the far right. He watched as it brightened, streaking down through the sky, flaring up so luminously he had to squint. It was coming his way. Beyond the atmospheric dome, the grey ocean waves surged and churned, their small whitecaps tossed by the wind. He could see the tops of ancient buildings sticking up out there, and had often wondered how old they were and who had lived in them.

The light flashed down through the sky, a trail of fire in tow, and vanished beyond the skyline. He'd never seen anything like it. But he had other things to worry about. He sat back down, eyes burning, and cradled his face in his hands. He had to come up with a smash hit. Something that would make up for his string of failures.

He made himself a drink and returned to his seat, fishing his older backup PRD out of his desk. He brainstormed ideas into it. He was so damn tired. He'd barely slept, worrying he was getting the axe. Now he had to worry if the Repurposers would pay him a visit when he was of no further use.

He closed his eyes for a moment, leaning his head back.

Then he jerked awake. He wasn't sure how much time had passed, maybe just a couple minutes, perhaps more. But he'd drooled down one cheek. The whole building was quaking, and the windows pulsed and hummed. Wiping his face, he rose from his chair, and turned to the window.

What he saw astounded him. The sea had receded, so far back that those mysterious ancient buildings he'd marveled at for years were now completely exposed. He could see the old roads between the buildings, now buried under layers of wet sand. Beyond the buildings stood a giant statue of a handsome woman holding a torch. She leaned to one side, splotched with grime.

He grabbed his diginocs from his desk, focusing on the scene before him. Something grey was moving out there, beyond the unearthed buildings. Something massive that spanned the horizon as far as he could see. It grew and grew, towering over the old structures, a living wall surging to the heavens.

He was transfixed. It was a wave, he realized, roaring inland, armed with all the water it had sucked up.

It barreled toward the coast, inundating the ancient city once again. A corroded building toppled under the water's weight, crashing down beneath the wave.

The waterwall rushed toward him. It was going to hit New Atlantic. He gripped his desk behind him, heart pounding, not sure what to do. His first thought was to call Langstrom. He lifted his old PRD, brought up the communication window, and waved through the floating display until he came to her. The connection went straight to her messages. She probably didn't want to hear from him right now. He wondered if she were looking out at this, too.

The window before him vibrated. The building continued to shake, but the glass didn't shatter. He stared out. The wave would short out the atmospheric shield, and all that water would get in. Citizens trapped in their life pods on lower floors, not looking out the window, would all die. Then who would enter the commands to keep New Atlantic running? It was bad enough his media stream hadn't been getting enough followers. If there weren't any followers at all, he'd surely get the sack.

He had to do something. He ran out of his office, taking the elevator back up to the producer's floor. Racing down the corridor to her office, he passed another director.

"What's the fuss?" the man asked him.

"Huge wave's about to hit New Atlantic!"

The man just looked confused, so Carston ran on, reaching her office at the end of the hall.

He pressed the doorbell, but she didn't answer, so he started pounding on the door. Finally it hissed open. She sat at her desk, looking up at him with disgust. "You're not doing yourself any favors," she said.

"Turn around!" he demanded.

"What?"

He ran over to her chair and grabbed her hands, trying to pull her up.

"Have you lost your mind?" she snapped, yanking her hands from his.

He pointed to the colossal wave beyond her window. It was now past the ancient city, looming over New Atlantic. It had breached the shield wall, so that the new wall filled their view as it rolled toward them, grey and foreboding.

Then it hit.

The building shook and swayed. Langstrom gripped her armrests, mouth agape.

He could see things in the water beyond the window: debris, twisted metal, rusted pipes, parts of ancient vehicles that had once littered the ruined city off the coast. A long, rusted I-beam surged forward, its tip cracking hard against the building below.

"No, no, no, no!" cried the producer, leaping up. She ran from the room. Carston followed her, wondering if the higher-ups had some kind of shelter. "Put out a message!" she cried to no one in particular. She reached the stairs and tore up a flight, Carston in tow.

At the top she banged open the door and flew down the hall to one of the hundreds of transmission rooms where they broadcasted their media. She burst through the door, panting. Carston followed her in as the entire building tilted and groaned. Elsewhere he could hear glass shattering.

In the small, windowless room, a startled broadcaster looked up from his console, his face masked in sweat. "What's going on? Why is the building moving?"

"Tell all the citizens to take cover. We could lose everyone! New Atlantic will fail! We'll never be able to replace all those people in time."

The broadcaster turned back to his console, started to enter something on the floating display, and paused. "Tell them to take cover *where?*" His face was bewildered.

The producer opened her mouth to speak, raised a brow, then shut it again. The ground shifted beneath her feet, and she lost her balance. Carston caught her elbow before she fell. "I—I don't know," she said, gaping up at Carston. "I don't know where anyone can take shelter."

The electricity flickered and went out, sending them into a pit of darkness. Carston gripped a table as the building moved again, and before long his eyes adjusted to the dark. He could make out the forms of his two colleagues, frozen where they were.

Equipment slid off tables and shelves, crashing all around. Every time the building rocked Carston thought it would crash to the ground and kill them all.

But the swaying subsided. The building stopped moving.

They all exchanged confused looks, as if in disbelief that they still were alive. Then came a flicker of hope, and relief.

"I'm getting to a window," said Carston, hastening out of the room. Langstrom followed close behind. He rushed down the hall to a conference room, and opened the door.

Light flooded back into their world. Huge windows spanning the entire far wall overlooked the city. The water level was dropping, now dozens of floors lower. As the waters receded, he stared in horror at the destruction below. All of the citizen housing from here to the edge of the atmospheric dome lay in ruins.

He withdrew the diginocs from his pocket and scanned down below. Debris from living pods floated in the grey water: bedding, ruined doors, light fixtures. Then he saw the bodies. Scores of them, limbs flung out, surging out to sea.

One person was still alive. He flailed in the water, mouth caught in a scream, trying to grab on to anything. He found a floating table and held on desperately, but the surge was too powerful, and it ripped him away from his salvation. Carston could see an edifice right behind him. Still the man cried out and flailed, trying to swim inland. His head went under, and the water gushed around the building's edge. Then he saw the man again, head above the waves, fighting the current as hard as he could. But it was all for nothing; the water slammed him against the building, with all the force the surge could deliver. The man stopped moving, and sank down into the grey depths. Carston didn't see him again.

He didn't know it would be like this, watching those people die.

Langstrom joined him at the window. "We made it," she breathed, incredulous.

He turned to her. "Not everyone. People are dying down there."

She looked at him, a cruel gleam in her eye. "Yes, but *we* made it."

He turned back to the window, stunned by the nightmare below. The light grew brighter, forcing Carston to squint. For a moment he couldn't figure out where the glare was coming from. Then terror sank his heart, and he lifted his eyes to the sky. He swallowed hard, and his jaw lost its ability to close.

A second ball of fire streaked across the sky, coming directly at them. It didn't arc beyond the horizon the way the first one had. It stayed high, coming in so fast that it grew into a colossal blazing orb before his very eyes.

This one wasn't going to land in the sea.

He backed away from the window, toward the door, his heart hammering as the fireball took up his entire view. All he could see was flame.

Langstrom screamed.

The windows burst, blowing them back. Carston slammed into the far wall, and all the air left his lungs. He felt his bones break. An immense heat greeted him, burning his hair, his skin, his lungs. Next to him,

Langstrom's clothes caught fire where she lay, crumpled in a broken mass against the wall.

His whole world was fire. The building went up, giving way to a molten hell . . . and vaporized.

New Atlantic was gone.

Chapter 10

It was slow going to Sanctuary City. In the east, the sky had taken on an unusual red. With the Eclipse's windows shattered, Gordon had donned H124's goggles as he piloted, keeping at a low altitude below 14,000 feet.

H124 dozed on and off, waking up now and again, eyeing the terrain below. Gordon landed to catch some sleep before they could press on, and night enveloped them on a dark stretch of broken road. They took turns watching for night stalkers, then continued their flight after dawn.

Brown, caked earth stretched as far as she could see, the beds of long dried-up rivers evident in the dust. In a few places she could spot the borders of old farms, square patterns in the dirt. Towering dust devils spiraled around the ruined landscape. She was awake as they flew over sprawling Delta City, so she peered down through its atmospheric shield to the jungle of skyscrapers below.

Finally real sleep took her. She awoke a few hours later and looked out, noting a vast green blanket below. At first she thought it was some kind of chemical spill, but as the plane lowered, it proved to be a forest of trees—not the skeletons of a bygone age, sun-bleached and white like the ones she'd seen when she first flew with Gordon, but a living, vibrant woodland stretching to the horizon.

She was in awe. Amid the trees, great patches of grasses grew, with other bits of color scattered throughout.

Raven joined her at the window. "We're getting close to Sanctuary City."

"What are those?" she asked, pointing to a patch of yellow.

"Wildflowers. That's a meadow." He pointed to a wide, glinting ribbon winding through the trees. "See that?

She nodded.

"It's a river. We were able to rehabilitate an old riverbed, make it flow again. Long ago, the river had been dammed upstream from here, as a power source for an oil field."

"What's an oil field?" She couldn't take her eyes from the verdant scenery. Gordon lowered the Eclipse 500.

"A place where fossil fuels were extracted. From what we understand, there was a wildlife refuge to the north of here. It was the last sanctuary for a number of species—caribou, musk ox, polar bears. We've found evidence that people tried to save it. It was one of the last natural places that hadn't been developed."

"What happened?"

"Protections for the wildlife refuge were lifted, and the oil companies moved in. There was evidence that a handful of people fought to the bitter end to prevent it."

"What kind of evidence?"

His mouth became a grim line. "Their corpses. They'd been killed, buried in shallow graves near one of the old oil rigs. We think this happened around the time of the water shortages, just before people started moving into the megacities after the great die-off." She'd read about the great die-off. Drought, megastorms, shortage of drinking water, intense air pollution, coastal flooding, all leading to numerous conflicts across the globe. Ultimately, a great many people perished.

Her brow creased. "I don't understand. Why not just use another energy source? Why kill for one that was running out anyway?"

Raven crossed his arms and shrugged. "Now that's the million-dollar question."

She stared back out as the little jet glided gracefully over the treetops. "Where is the city?" she asked.

He smiled, and relaxed his arms. He pointed ahead, to where trees dotted the grassy landscape. "This is it."

"Sanctuary City . . . is a forest?"

"A living, breathing ecosystem. We've managed to bring back some of the animals who lived here. This all used to be treeless tundra, with ice frozen in the soil. Not a lot could grow up here. But as the earth warmed up, biomes moved northward. These rich, pine-forested areas used to grow much farther south than this, but now it's too hot and dry for a forest to thrive where it once did. So the pine forests shifted north."

"How do you protect yourself against the PPC? I mean, if they did come up here?"

"They don't know about the hyperloop that the oil companies built here. If the PPC did come up this far, they'd have to come by air or land, and we'd see them coming long before they arrived. Cal has an extensive radar setup here." He caught himself, but she could see his grief for his friend consume him. "It's actually an old one he retrofitted. It had been used during a war long ago, when people feared invaders would come from the continent directly to the west of here."

Her eyes widened. "There's a whole continent right next to us?"

He nodded. "And the north of it is largely uninhabited. Endless desert advanced over much of it when things warmed up. The continent is vast, and the weather extremes were too much for people to continue living in the central region. Most moved into megacities or . . ." He didn't finish.

"Or?" she nudged him.

"Perished."

She pointed out the window, to what appeared to be giant white blankets tethered to the ground and flapping in the wind. "What are those things?"

Raven sat down beside her, following her gaze. "Our wind sails. It's one of the ways we generate electricity." She saw that they were curved and billowing. *Wind catchers.*

A little farther out she saw enormous hunks of metal, rotating on vertical bases. "And those?" she asked, pointing.

"Wind turbines, also for power. We have to take special precaution with those."

"What do you mean?"

"Some of the creatures we've brought back up here are vulnerable to turbines like that. Having the rotors spin on a vertical axis rather than a horizontal one helps. We light them with UV during the night. One of the creatures that's at risk is bats."

H124 remembered the pictures of them in the cavern beneath Delta City. She'd looked them up since she came to stay with the Rovers. "I've seen photos of them," she said.

"They were susceptible with some of our earlier designs. But bats don't tend to fly as much in high winds. We only have the turbines kick on in gusts above 6 mph, so the blades aren't spinning when the bats are out. We barely lose any energy, and they remain safe. We also have these emitter boxes that broadcast ultrasonic frequencies between 1 kHz and 100 kHz. It essentially jams the bats' echolocation abilities, so they avoid the area." He pointed west. "And you can't see it from here, but we also use solid state wave energy."

"What's that?" she asked, still staring down at the distant turbines.

"It's way out in the ocean. We have electricity-generating floats out there. The power is transmitted here through a network of underground cables. It's clean, boundless energy from the motion of the waves."

Gordon descended, passing close to the trees. She saw places where they were interspersed with layers of other foliage along tiny green hills. She gestured toward them. "What are those plants between the trees?"

"All kinds of food. Barley, kale, peas, beans, apples. Growing them in rows with trees provides shade, and prevents erosion. It's a great way to recharge groundwater. We call it stratified agroforestry."

She gazed out in wonder. The whole place felt so vibrant, so alive, even from the air. She couldn't wait to land, to feel all that lush soil beneath her feet. She could only imagine how good the air would smell.

Then she saw something that robbed her of her breath. In the distance, out on a wide, flat, grassy plain, dozens of creatures roamed in a cluster, grazing on vegetation. She pulled out her diginocs. "What are those?"

Raven grinned. "Perhaps our biggest accomplishment. Thousands of years ago, all kinds of grazers roamed this land—mammoths, woolly rhinos, saiga antelope, elk, caribou. Back then it was full of grasses, willows, and sedges, not shrubs and trees. Permafrost lay beneath the grass, locked up in the soil. It was a huge carbon sink. Then humans came, hunting most of the animals to extinction. The landscape changed without the grazers. Trees spread across the area, soaking up sunlight and heating the soil. Vital areas that used to sequester carbon melted, releasing methane and CO_2. The entire region transformed. So one of the first things we did up here was de-extinct as many grazers as we could. We're hoping to return it to the grassland it once was."

She watched as the creatures snatched up vegetation. Some were slender with strange snake-like noses, while others dug up the earth with massive antlers that looked too heavy to lift, long, snaking appendages sprouting from their heads.

"Those," he said, smiling, "are saiga antelope and caribou."

The antlers gleamed in the late afternoon sun. They moved together as a unit, with some smaller, younger caribou frolicking among them.

"We also revived woolly rhinos and musk oxen, moose, mammoths, and Beringian bison . . . Since we've brought them back, the original floral composition has begun to return. It's been amazing to observe."

"Where is this de-extinction lab?" she asked. "I have to see it!"

"I'll give you a personal tour," he told her.

She grinned, and the seeds of hope bloomed inside her. If the Rovers could do something so miraculous, revive extinct species and create a safe, thriving habitat for them, then maybe there was hope for all the remarkable animals she'd seen in books. If only she could see them out in the world.

Then she thought of Raven's parents and the PPC and what they'd done to the experimental forest in the east. Somehow the PPC would have to be convinced to let more of these places exist. "Raven," she said, hating to bring up such a sad subject, "how do you protect this place? I mean, after what happened to the forest outside New Atlantic . . ."

He stared out the window. "We use a sort of cloaking technology. Any electromagnetic signals we use in the city are shielded from going beyond the forest. This way the PPC won't pick up any transmissions. Sometimes they send out unmanned scouting drones to various locations, but so far Onyx has been able to hack them, hiding our location. But mostly, the PPC doesn't venture this far north or west. They stay south, in cities like Delta City and New Atlantic. When the PPC built the megacities, this site was too remote. They built on top of existing power grids like nuclear and coal fire plants, geothermal ones, too. There wasn't an established electrical grid or infrastructure up here, so they didn't bother."

She leaned her head out the broken window, watching the caribou dip out of sight. She felt the jet's landing gear clunk beneath them as it emerged from the belly of the plane.

"Is that an honest-to-goodness airstrip up ahead?" Gordon asked Raven.

The latter moved to the cockpit, scanning the area. H124 joined them. Ahead lay several landing strips with hangars on either side, not only intact but pristine. "Yes!"

Gordon set them down gently on the smoothest airstrip she'd ever experienced. As they glided to a stop, she looked down at the pavement.

"We've done a lot of rehabilitation on this strip," Raven told her, noting her interest. He turned to Gordon. "I think you're going to like the collection of planes we've amassed."

"Amassed?" Gordon said, turning in his seat as the engines powered down. "I like that verb. How many you got?"

"Twenty-two, last time I checked," Raven replied.

Gordon whistled. "Hot damn." H124 was used to cracked cement and rusted rooftops. These hangars were gorgeous. Lush, green vegetation grew on the roofs, each sporting a unique design.

"They're living buildings. As are all the structures in Sanctuary City. They also generate more power than they consume. We call them 'net positive buildings.'"

"They're incredible," H124 said. Gordon lowered the jet's stairs, and she deboarded.

The hangar nearest her trailed with vegetation, a verdant display spilling over its sides.

Then she turned and saw Sanctuary City. Graceful buildings stood sentinel in a forest. She found herself drawn to it, stepping away from Gordon and Raven before she even realized her feet were moving.

She wound her way through the trees, approaching a two-story structure with tinted windows and a garden on its roof. Inside people milled about. A creek ran right into the building and out the other side. She spotted solar panels on top, tucked amid the rows of plants. A long, graceful pea vine snaked down the sidewall, sporting fresh green pods. She walked to it, caressing the delicate plant. Raven walked up beside her, the maglev sled hovering in tow, carrying the spacecraft section. He picked one of the beans, and handed it to her. "Go ahead."

She lifted it to her nose. It smelled sweet. She'd never had unprocessed food before. She took a small bite, and the sudden burst of sweetness made her grin. Then she laughed.

"What is it?" he asked, peering at her curiously.

"It's the best thing I've ever tasted!"

He picked another pea pod. "Have another."

This one she savored even longer, breathing in its scent and enjoying its sugary taste. Her life hadn't been very happy or contained many good moments, but right now, tasting her first pea, gazing around at the living city with Raven standing beside her and the spacecraft piece hovering nearby, she felt pure, unadulterated joy.

"This is incredible," she finally managed to say.

He gestured toward the sled. "Let's drop this off with Rivet, and I'll give you the full tour."

She nodded. They walked between the buildings, life teeming all around them. Flowers of every hue grew in patches of sun and shade, and she watched a small, winged creature with yellow-and-black stripes land on one of the blossoms. She rushed over to it. "What is that?" she wanted to know.

"Canadian tiger swallowtail," he told her. "A butterfly."

"Look at the colors on its wings!" She saw a long black thread uncoil from its head and dip into the flower. "Is that its tongue?"

She could tell he was amused by her curiosity. "Yes, it is," he said

She knelt down, coming to eye level with the delicate creature. So innocent. Pure. Hope swelled within her.

She saw Raven walking away. Reluctantly, she got up and left. She followed him through the city, passing Rovers who kept greeting him. She'd never seen such colorful, creative clothing. Each Rover looked completely unique, wearing jackets, pants, flowing robes, and shirts in a myriad of colors. Each item looked more like a piece of art than mere functional clothing. They passed one woman who wore a long flowing scarf that depicted a mountain landscape, while her shirt and pants were a deep shade of patterned green, almost like peering into a forest. The woman smiled at H124.

They passed a shaded stand of tall green poles, leaves snaking off them. Raven gestured to them. "That's bamboo. What your shirt is made out of."

She approached one of the stalks and ran her hand across its smooth surface. "Amazing!"

At last they reached a one-story building. The same creek wound through it, and it too had dark glass. "Why is the glass so dark?" she asked him, as they entered through a door.

"It changes throughout the day. It's dark at the height of the afternoon. In winter, the glass would appear clearer this time of day, so it could soak up the heat from the sun. But for now it's dark, growing lighter only as dusk approaches."

She reached out, and found it warm to the touch. They then passed over a small footbridge, and descended a stair.

"Most of Sanctuary City is underground," he told her. "It's one way to minimize our footprint. Not to mention, the underground sections are self-sustaining. If the PPC ever found us up here, we could take shelter below."

They approached a lab marked "Engineering." Inside she saw Rivet leaning over a table, studying schematics spread out before her.

She turned as she heard them enter. "Raven! H!" She smiled, and started to greet them, then paused, her eyes drifting to the maglev sled in fascination. "You found it!" She veered over to it, examining the device it bore, as well as the clean skin draped over it. "Incredible . . ."

With a few commands on his PRD, Raven steered the maglev over to Rivet's work table. The sled's levers emerged, gently maneuvering the craft onto her work surface.

Rivet circled the machine, examining every inch, comparing it to the schematics. "I'll get to work right away," she said, turning her back on them and readying her tools. She didn't even realize when they left.

"Tour?" Raven asked H124.

"Please."

"First I'll take you to my favorite area." He led her down the hallway, through a warren of underground passages. At the end of a long corridor, they came to a double door marked *De-Extinction.*

The doors slid apart as they approached. The space beyond was cavernous. Shelves spanned every wall, and polished white tables ran its length.

A pair of technicians labored at different work stations. Raven stopped midway down the center table. A large glass box waited there, full of small, membranous sacs of every size. He checked the display next to the box. "This is an incubator," he told her. "Let's see who's ready to come out."

He scanned a nearby list, and read an entry: "LC143 *Ovibos moschatus*—Muskox."

He donned a pair of sterile gloves, and opened a small door in front of one of the sacs. He gently lifted it out, and shut the door.

With nimble hands he pulled away the sac, parting it along a neat seam. Fluid drained out into a bin on the table, and Raven removed the sac completely, placing it on a large tray with similar sacs already opened.

H124 stepped closer. Resting in Raven's arms was a brown, furry, hooved creature. It lifted its wobbly head as Raven wiped a viscous fluid off it, then examined it closely. "Hello, little fellow," he said in a soft voice.

It made a bleating sound. Raven moved it to another case lined with cushioned bedding. He set up a tiny feeding tube full of white fluid, and the little muskox immediately began suckling it.

They both clustered around, watching it feed. Raven beamed. She'd never seen him so happy.

When he was sure the muskox was taking to the food, he faced her. "This is my favorite place. My mom developed a lot of this technology. When she was younger, she set off to travel through the country, see what parts might be suitable for species reintroduction. She met my dad at another Rover camp, and they fell in love. After they had me, we traveled around, restocking weather shelters and tending to the experimental forests and sites that the Rovers had planted over the years. It wasn't until . . ." He looked back at the muskox. "Until after I lost them that I came here for the first time. A group of Rovers found me and took me in. I pored over my mom's notes, not to mention she'd taught me a lot about de-extinction when I was young." He cracked a smile. "The first animal I ever brought back was a raven. She'd told me all about them, how smart they were, and resourceful. A lot of Rovers choose their own names when they get to be adults. But my parents named me Raven, and I wanted to keep it."

"It suits you."

He stared down at her with a bittersweet expression. "Thank you."

She looked back to the incubator and display. "How does it work?"

They walked back over. "We've collected DNA for decades. Some samples are centuries old. We find DNA from specimens in old museums and labs. Also discovered a few cryogenic facilities over the years."

"Cryogenic?"

"A long time ago, if people didn't want to die, they could pay to have their bodies frozen. Some of these labs also preserved the remains of animals that were going extinct in zoos."

She wrinkled her brow. "What's a 'zoo?'"

"Place where humans kept animals. At first it was just to entertain people. They kept animals in cages."

"That was entertaining?"

"Some people thought so. As more animals became threatened, zoos started collecting the last surviving members of species, hoping that by keeping them safe, they could preserve the species, and eventually reintroduce them once a suitable habitat was secured." He scanned the list. "But habitats weren't protected, and many of these creatures went extinct. Even the last living zoo animals eventually died of old age. But since we have their DNA, we can grow them all over again in these little amniotic sacs. The goal is to restore a thriving, healthy ecosystem."

"Is it working?"

"Well . . . it's not ideal. It would have been better if these creatures' habitats weren't fragmented in the first place. There's been a bit of trial and error. A lot of these ecosystems have been drastically changed, and it's taken a lot of research to figure out how they're supposed to be."

She walked back to the baby muskox, watching him drink.

"Do you have any opossums?" she asked.

His face softened. "That's a very specific request."

"I knew one once."

"As a matter of fact, we've revived and reintroduced them to a couple forests east of Delta City."

H124 wondered if the one she'd helped was one of those.

She moved to the DNA display. "May I look?"

He stepped aside. "Of course."

She scanned the names of available samples:

Beringian bison *Bison priscus*
Gray wolf *Canis lupus*
Woolly rhinoceros *Coelodonta antiquitatis*
Wolverine *Gulo gulo*
Woolly mammoth *Mammuthus primigenius*

Sea mink *Neovison macrodon*
American pika *Ochotona princeps*
Musk ox *Ovibos moschatus*
Vaquita porpoise *Phocoena sinus*
Mountain lion *Puma concolor*
Caribou *Rangifer tarandus*
Tasmanian tiger *Thylacinus cynocephalus*
Grizzly bear *Ursus arctos*
Polar bear *Ursus maritimus*

She advanced the screen, reading off a number of bird species:

Golden eagle *Aquila chrysaetos*
Common raven *Corvus corax*
Passenger pigeon *Ectopistes migratorius*
Great auk *Pinguinus impennis*
Dodo *Raphus cucullatus*

Then she moved to a screen labeled "Osteichthyes":

Devil's Hole pupfish *Cyprinodon diabolis*
Coho salmon *Oncorhynchus kisutch*
Lahontan trout *Oncorhynchus clarkii henshawi*
Atlantic salmon *Salmo salar*

The lists went on and on, screen after screen. She swallowed, sick that so many creatures had vanished from the earth.

"This is our overall databank," Raven told her. "We share it with several other de-extinction labs around the world."

"There are more of you?"

"Not a lot. But we have other DNA storage facilities around the globe. When we can, we de-extinct creatures in their native habitats. But so many of those places have been fragmented and destroyed that in many places we can't rewild them, so we haven't tried to bring them back. Then there's the PPC, with its megacities. They take pleasure in destroying experimental forests. Nature seems to challenge their sense of power. They just don't see the bigger picture. In other places, extensive, unsustainable agriculture has caused extreme desertification, and the land can't uphold its original ecosystem."

He moved to another terminal, and brought up its display. "That reminds me. I've been thinking of those things we encountered . . . the ones that killed Cal."

She moved to his side.

He brought up an image of what appeared to be a tiny insect, then enlarged it. She saw that it wasn't an insect at all, but a composite of plastic and metal. "What is it?"

"They were called agrobugs. Before they were developed, farmers used poisonous chemicals to kill insects that fed on their crops. But it backfired. The pesticides got into the ecosystem, killing natural pollinators like bats and butterflies. Their populations plummeted. So the agriculture industry devised these agrobugs that would serve as both pollinators and pest control. The first few batches stopped functioning after only a couple seasons, so they built them to repair themselves, eventually to replicate autonomously. And so they spread, eating not just the pests, but the crops themselves. Then they moved on to destroy any living thing in their path; breaking down organic matter was their best means of replication. Before long they were grazing land, killing cattle . . . Fertile lands had to be abandoned."

He brought up an antiquated map of the country, zeroing in on a section near the west coast. "This was once the most fertile land in the west. They called it the Central Valley. This is where the agrobugs really took hold." He switched to a current view. The Central Valley was underwater. "As sea levels rose, the lowlands flooded. I think the agrobugs were pushed out, moving south and west to where we were with Cal." He shifted the map nearer to the coast, where the radar facility stood. "Most likely they've been surviving out there, destroying any living tissue they encounter."

H124 shuddered, recalling the horrid way they swarmed over Cal.

Raven shut off the display, gaze cast downward. "It's something I didn't even consider when we planned the trip."

"You couldn't have known."

He exhaled, and checked once more on the muskox. "Ready to continue with the tour?"

She nodded.

He took her through the rest of the city, showing her chemistry and biology labs as well as food preparation areas where they made the MREs they stocked in the weather shelters.

Then he showed her to her quarters, a roomy space with open windows that allowed plenty of light. A bookshelf stood in one corner, and in the other, a bed covered in soft blankets. It looked like heaven.

"Why don't we get some rest, and tomorrow we'll plan how to retrieve the next spacecraft section from Delta City?"

"Sounds good." Once he left she turned to the bed, excited to sleep as long as she wanted. Her whole body ached with cuts and bruises.

* * * *

The next day Raven stopped by her quarters, and they made their way to a communal dining area. She dove into her fare, tasting a number of dishes for the first time. She ate a salad with things called quinoa, kale, and beets—all strange-sounding, but no less delicious. The latter was the most gorgeous shade of red she'd ever seen.

Her PRD beeped and she looked down at it. A stream of numbers came up, filling her display. The string grew so long it started scrolling down. She frowned. "What is this?"

Raven leaned forward, the same message coming up on his PRD too. "We don't know. It's been happening for the last few months. The numbers come in. They're always the same. We have some people trying to decode it, but no luck so far. We don't know where it's coming from or from whom." He closed off his display after saving the numbers. He leaned forward. "We've been calling it 'the phantom code.' It only happens when we're in Sanctuary City."

She saved the numbers too, and shut down her display. "Spooky. I wonder what it is." She finished her tea and leaned back in her chair, watching the trees dance beyond the windows. The entire building drank in light, and everything took on a golden hue.

Soon they made their way to Rivet's office. She was still poring over schematics, moving between the craft and another worktable.

Moving to a quiet corner, Raven brought up a map of Delta City on his display. He and H124 studied it. The location of the ancient aerospace facility was on the western side of the city.

"How would we get in?" Raven asked.

"If Willoughby's there, he could help us." She called him on her PRD. He didn't answer, so she left a message. She returned to the map. "Before, we were able to enter through these huge tunnels that vented out CO_2." She looked for the nearest CO_2 vent, finding it some fifty miles from where they needed to be. It was too far in such a dangerous place. They'd be killed.

She glanced around at the other Rovers. Two people clustered around Rivet where she stood scrutinizing the diagrams. A few more passed in and out of the Engineering lab, carrying supplies.

"Have you been inside Delta City before?" H124 asked Raven.

He shook his head. "I haven't been inside any of the megacities."

H124 bit her lip.

"What is it?"

"Do you have any fighters?"

Raven leaned back in his seat. "You mean are there any Rovers who specialize in combat?"

She nodded.

He ran a hand through his hair. "I'm afraid not."

She thought back to the nightmare of Delta City, or "Murder City," as the Badlanders had so aptly named it. They'd barely made it out alive. She released a heavy breath. "We'll have to rely completely on stealth, then."

"It's bad in there?"

Memories of the crush of bodies came back to her, the shoving and grabbing, the cry for Badlander blood, the teeming masses dragging them down. She studied the overlay again. With the nearest vent that far away, they'd have to travel quite a way into the city.

"Have *you* been to this part of Delta City?" he asked, leaning forward to soak in the detail.

Her PRD beeped. Willoughby was calling her back. "Hello!" she greeted him.

"H! Sorry I missed your call. Had to get somewhere where I could speak privately."

"Where are you?"

"When the airship picked me up, the PPC gave me orders to check out a few of these abandoned satellite sites where the old transmitters used to be. Seems that BEC City has really been cutting into their feeds, and they want to build some stronger transmitters."

"So you're not in Delta City?"

He shook his head. "Not yet. What did you need?"

"A way in."

He screwed his face up. "Sorry. I'm not there yet."

"No problem. We'll find a way in."

"I'll contact you when I'm there. Oh—I have to go." He looked over his shoulder, and hung up quickly. She caught a glimpse of a PPC airship pilot to his rear before the transmission ended.

"Well, we're out of luck there," she told Raven. She thought a minute, then said, "Rowan might have been to that part of the city. I'll call him. Maybe he knows a better place to get in." She brought up the comm window on her PRD. When he answered, she lit up at the sight of his face.

He grinned. "Hey, H."

"How's it going down there?" she asked him.

"We're a long way from being done. But things are shaping up. I meant to call you earlier, but things have been crazy here."

"No problem."

"How did it go retrieving the first part of the craft?"

"Piece of cake," she said, a phrase she'd heard him use in the past, though she had no idea what "cake" was.

Raven laughed, and Rowan noticed him. "I take it this isn't a social call."

"We need to access part of Delta City, much farther west from where I've been. We wondered if you had any ideas. It's an area that doesn't have any CO_2 vents nearby."

He bent his brow. "What part?"

She sent the coordinates to him, and he consulted his map. "This is a much older part of the city. The infrastructure's really run down. It's basically been left to rot."

"What about crossing from the nearest vent?"

He scrolled through the map. "It's way too far. You'd need a vehicle, and you'd be torn apart." He looked up at her. "Who are you going with?"

"Probably just Raven and me."

Rowan's mouth parted somewhat. "Just the two of you."

"We got the first piece together."

He narrowed his eyes. "Weather is one thing . . . Murder City is something else."

She leaned forward and lowered her voice. "We're not exactly teeming with fighters here."

"Damn. I can't leave until I get everyone set up here. But I think I know someone who can help. He's not far from that location either."

"Who?"

"Byron. Call him and tell him I thought you could use the Silver Beast."

"Byron?" She hadn't spoken to him since the Badlander camp had been attacked after their harrowing escape from Murder City. Though she'd started out his prisoner, they'd ended up forming an uncertain alliance in the end.

"Yes. I think he can get you in," Rowan went on.

She thought of Byron's reluctance to help before, and seriously doubted he'd drop whatever he was doing to come out and help her break into a city where desperate, starving people cried out for Badlander blood in exchange for food.

A man ran up to Rowan and spoke into his ear. "I have to go, H. Contact Byron. Tell him I said if he doesn't help you, I'll come down there and kick his ass."

H124 felt a pang of disappointment. She'd hoped Rowan would know a good way to infiltrate the city that they could use immediately. As he ended the transmission, she and Raven exchanged glances.

"Who's Byron?" he asked.

"This Badlander who kidnapped me, stole my car, and used me to infiltrate Delta City."

He pursed his lips and nodded, unsure of what to say. "And Rowan thinks this guy will help?"

"By the end we were sort of friends."

"Sort of? Can you trust him?"

"I'm not sure if I can trust him exactly." She thought of Byron and his comrades—Astoria with her bloodthirsty grin and readiness with a knife, as well as her sweet-natured twin brother, Dirk. "But they're fighters. And they might know another way in. I'm sure they'd been inside Delta City before they captured me. They must have a way that doesn't involve using the TWRs in the CO_2 vents. Maybe this Silver Beast thing."

Raven frowned. "Or they used other workers who they buried in shallow graves." He swallowed. "Or ate."

She couldn't tell if he was joking. Only then did she wonder how lucky she'd been getting away from them. "It's worth a try. I did save his life."

"That's got to count for something. Call him."

She brought up the comm window. Using the Badlanders' encrypted message system, she put out a call for Byron. She had no idea where he was now. For all she knew, he was off rebuilding a different Badlander camp, or breaking into some PPC facility to steal weapons.

She brought up her beeping PRD. Byron's face filled the floating display, his long, dark blond hair falling about his shoulders, his face rough shaven, his eyes twinkling with mischief. "H!" he said, the corner of his mouth turning up. "I wasn't expecting to hear from you. Don't tell me your mission to save the world's landed you in trouble again."

She couldn't help but smile back. "Hey, you were the one who got me in all that trouble last time, if you remember."

"Our lark into Murder City was a blast! Would you trade that experience for anything?"

"In a heartbeat." She still had nightmares about the people grabbing her arms and legs, calling for their deaths. She dreaded the thought of going back into that chaos. "But since you bring it up, I need to get back in there."

His mouth formed an uneasy circle. "You want . . . to get back into Murder City . . . ?" He made a face. "If you're looking for a good vacation spot, I can recommend some much nicer locations."

"Thanks all the same, but I have to. We need something in there to avert the asteroid."

"Still trying to save the world? I think 'H' must stand for 'halo.'" She didn't know what a "halo" was. When he saw her puzzled expression, he added, "It's what angels have, you know?"

She didn't.

"It's these glowing rings that . . . and angels are these . . ." He sighed. "You can't get in through a CO_2 vent?"

"The closest one to where we need to be is fifty miles away."

"Damn." He glanced behind him, where she could see Badlanders milling about, some drinking, others standing around a massive bonfire and daring each other to jump over it.

"Rowan mentioned something about a Silver Beast?"

He laughed. "Oh, did he? So it's Firehawk who's put me up to this?" He shook his head good-naturedly. "We could use the Beast, but it's dicey. It's much safer to use the TWRs." He said it like "*twirs*." TWRs, or theta wave receivers, were installed on most locks in the megacities. Workers like H124 could mentally send signals for them to open or close, and it's how they'd gotten in through the CO_2 vents in the past. "But fifty miles . . . that's a suicide mission."

"We'll take the alternate way."

"You keep saying 'we.' You didn't actually find the Rovers, did you?"

She grinned. "I did. And we're making progress."

He shook his head in disbelief. "I didn't think they were still out there. Thought they were just a myth."

Raven leaned into view. "Hello. Myth here."

Byron grinned. "I'll be. You did it, Halo."

She sent him the coordinates of the old aerospace facility. "This is where we need to go."

"What is the Silver Beast?" Raven asked.

"It's a mobile transmitter. We use it to make pirate broadcasts, targeting the citizens who maintain the atmospheric shield. They get distracted, the shield goes down in places, and we get in. But the PPC is quick to notice and zero in our location."

"We'll take it," H124 said. "How soon can you meet us outside the city? Are you close to it?"

"Did you hear me when I said that the Beast is also a surefire way to get attacked by PPC troops? I can get you in, but getting out might be a different story."

She didn't say anything.

"Nothing dissuades you, does it?" When she still didn't answer, he said, "Okay. I'm relatively close. I just need to check the Beast over. Make sure it's got a full charge. Send me your coordinates, and I'll get back to you with an ETA." He laughed under his breath. "Ironic that now you want *me* to get *you* into that place."

"At least I'm not kidnapping you and stealing your solar-powered car."

"I love that car."

"I'm going to need it back one of these days." The Badlanders had held onto it after their escape from Murder City.

"After you save the world?"

"Exactly." She smiled. "Thank you, Byron."

"I owe you, Halo. You did save my life." He gave her another rare smile and said, "See you in a bit," and signed off.

Raven turned to her. "About us not having fighters." He gestured down the hall. "We do have weapons, but we rarely use them. Just things we've stockpiled, old guns we've come across, things like that. You're welcome to take a look."

She nodded. They headed down the hall and entered a spacious room with weapons stored in wall racks. She saw traditional guns that fired projectiles like bullets and pellets, a handful of flash bursters, a few beautifully preserved swords, and a collection of energy weapons designed to immobilize. They both selected energy rifles, adjusting the settings just shy of lethal. They could always dial them up if they got in any real trouble. Which H124 suspected they'd have no shortage of in Murder City.

Raven checked over his weapon, then slung it over his back. "Looks like now we just need to find Gordon. I wonder if he's picked out his next plane?"

Out on the airfield, they found Gordon in absolute bliss. He was running his hand over the fuselage of a red plane with double wings. Several other planes were parked nearby. He turned when he heard them.

"Isn't she beautiful?"

She took in the plane. "Sure is."

"She's a Model BH Travel Air biplane." He turned and opened his arms wide as he took in the sight of all the well-preserved planes. "Isn't this place amazing?" He grinned. "And come take a look at this!"

They followed him as he hurried toward one of the hangars. He swung open the door, revealing a strange aircraft with a see-through cabin and a seat with pedals. It looked to be human-powered, with no combustible engine. "It's a Gossamer Albatross. Can you believe it?" He hastened to another hangar. "And look in here!" He pushed open the doors to reveal a plane that didn't have wings. Instead it sported a flat, circular body with two propellers near the front. "It's a Vought XF5U Flying Flapjack! These have an almost near-vertical takeoff! Seems to be in pretty good condition, too. I've been tinkering with the engine. There's even a flying wing in another hanger!"

Raven laughed. "Glad you're enjoying it!"

He clapped his hands together. "So where are we off to?"

"Delta City," Raven told him.

Gordon's smile faded. "Oh. Yippee."

"Once more unto the breach?" she asked him. She'd heard Rovers use the expression.

"Apparently so," the pilot said, stuffing a rag into his back pocket.

"Did you pick out a new plane?" Raven asked.

Gordon slapped his hands together, louder this time. "Boy howdy." He narrowed his eyes and pointed a warning to both of them. "And this one's not getting wrecked. You hear?"

Raven made a slight bow. H124 held up her hand and swore an oath, "We will do our best."

"You better. I'll get it ready. Meet me back here."

She and Raven returned to their quarters and packed up some gear. They stuffed MREs, water bottles, and filters into their packs. Raven got a new maglev sled and clean skin, and then they headed back to the airstrip.

By late that morning they were off in a 1928 Lockheed Vega, banking east toward Murder City.

Chapter 11

They flew for hours, and soon Gordon was soaring them over dry, dusty plains. Already H124 missed the lush green of Sanctuary City. She watched him steer the plane, gazing out over the horizon, completely in his element. She felt bad that her quest had already cost him two planes; this was now his third.

"Love how this baby handles," Gordon said, grinning. As they flew, the amber dome of Delta City came into view, stretching across the horizon.

Gordon circled and landed beyond the streams of glistening fecal matter that emanated from Delta City. Raven looked at his PRD. "Do you have an ETA from Byron?"

She called him, learning that they wouldn't be there until early the next day. "We'll have to make camp here tonight, then," Raven said.

Gordon wished them luck. "I'll find a refueling station and wait to hear from you." He gripped her hand affectionately as she deboarded. "You be careful."

"I will." They climbed out and watched him wave and taxi off, bumping along the uneven ground. Then he rose into the sky and she squinted, watching him go.

In the ensuing silence, she and Raven stared up at the dome. Her eyes teared from the reek of urine and methane. The shiny rivers of stool meandered off into the distance.

Nothing grew here, no grass, nor a single tree. Trees were rare enough, she'd found, but in this ruined ground, they didn't stand a chance.

She turned to Raven. "Shall we try to get some sleep?"

He glanced around. "Definitely. Just wish it weren't so pungent here."

They selected a hill about a mile away, high enough to be free of waste matter, and laid their jackets out as makeshift sleeping bags. At least they were somewhat elevated above the river of refuse, though that didn't stop the smell from creeping up the hillside and assaulting them. She wiped off her squishing boots, then kicked them off, consigning them to a patch of dirt a dozen yards away.

She looked up again at the dome, then down at her PRD. Quiet moments like these made her heart race even more than being inside a hurricane or infiltrating Murder City. In them she could feel the inexorable march of time, feel those chunks of space rock hurtling ever closer. Sitting there doing nothing made her panic. Every minute spent like this was one they might desperately need later as they assembled the spacecraft.

"You look worried," Raven said, stretching out on his jacket a few feet away.

She nodded.

"I think we did pretty good in that hurricane."

She managed a smile. "So we did."

"We can do this." He watched her for another minute, then gazed upward and closed his eyes.

She shifted her weight, trying not to think of the horrors that awaited them tomorrow.

* * * *

H124 jolted awake, sitting bolt upright. The first light of dawn glowed gold in the east. She snapped her head to the west, where she heard a noisy mechanical pounding. The only thing she could make out was a cloud of dust, and something moving within it.

Raven sat up next to her, sweeping his long hair out of his eyes. "What is that?" He stood up, and pulled a pair of diginocs out of his pack. He focused them, looking immediately perplexed. "Looks like a giant robotic animal."

"What?" She stood up and borrowed the nocs. Through the dust she saw a massive mechanical quadruped powering across the terrain. Four figures rode on top of the creature, headed straight for them. It glinted in the sun.

"The Silver Beast," she breathed, handing back the nocs.

As the behemoth drew closer, one of its riders stood and waved. Byron wore his usual worn green jacket and black jeans, his long, dark blond hair tied back. His green eyes twinkled mischievously in his tanned, fawn-colored face. Two others figures rose as well, and H124 couldn't help but grin. One, nearly six feet tall, was unmistakable with her red-and-black mohawk and facial tattoos covering her sepia face. Astoria. The other, just as tall, but slightly stockier, had long black-and-purple dreadlocks that framed his dark umber features. It was Astoria's twin brother, Dirk. The last person, a thin man with a weather-worn beige face, blue eyes, and a blue-and-blond twin 'hawk, drove the Beast.

"Hello!" H124 yelled, waving back.

The Beast came to rest at the bottom of the hill, and the four riders climbed down a metal ladder. Byron gave her a warm hug, nearly cracking her ribs. Dirk followed suit, and Astoria gave a standoffish wave, though her usual gruff manner was familiar and welcome. They were all covered in dust, each wearing guns strapped to their waists.

"This is Raven," H124 told them. They shook hands all around.

"So you're a Rover?" Dirk asked him. "We didn't think you guys actually existed."

Raven smiled. "Turns out we do."

Byron gestured at the thin man. "This is Chadwick. He runs the transmitter. Built it himself."

H124 bowed her head. "Thank you so much for helping us."

He gave a shy smile. "When I heard what was at stake, I knew it was the least I could do."

H124 appraised Astoria. "And you two? I definitely wouldn't expect you to come with us."

Dirk hooked his thumb at his sister and laughed. "You mean you wouldn't expect *her* to come."

H124 grinned. "Okay. Yes. Astoria."

The fighter shrugged. "Seemed like you guys could use me. Especially this loser," she added, punching Dirk in the shoulder.

He rubbed it. "Thanks."

"So what's the plan?" H124 asked.

Chadwick cleared his throat. "I fire up the transmitter. Get a broadcast going, targeting the media streams of the citizens who maintain the shield. Then you guys get in."

"Sounds good," she said. "Let's do it."

As they all checked their gear, Chadwick climbed back up into the Beast. The whirring of gears attracted H124's attention, so she looked up to see him raising a huge antenna. "You best be off," he told them. "I'm starting my broadcast now."

And so they headed toward the shield wall, H124 looking back over her shoulder. "Thank you!" she called out, waving. Chadwick waved back.

"We'll have to be really careful once we get inside," Byron warned them. "This part of the city is highly unstable."

"What do you mean?"

"This section of the city used to run on nuclear energy, but the plants failed years ago. They decided to try geothermal, tapping deeper and deeper down into the crust. The bedrock fractured and shifted. It affected some old fault lines, and earthquakes started to occur. Buildings fell faster than they could be rebuilt. Finally they just gave up, leaving the infrastructure here to run at a bare minimum. This whole place might fall down around us."

Raven unpacked the maglev sled from his pack, and powered it up. "We can use this to raise ourselves above the wall."

Byron turned toward the sled. "I'll go up first. Get the lay of the land." Above them, a hole appeared in the shield, just big enough for them to slip through. The transmission from the Silver Beast was working.

Byron climbed onto the sled's flat surface, commanding it to lift him up the enormous retaining wall. He hopped off at the top. H124 followed him with her eyes, shielding them against the sun as she did. He walked through the hole in the shield and out of sight. A minute later he returned. "Come on up." He sent the maglev back down, and one by one they rode it to the top of the wall.

Astoria was last. "I can't believe I'm following you damn fools into this."

"We're grateful to have you," H124 told her.

Once they were inside the shield, H124 looked back to see the mobile transmitter moving away, its powerful legs stomping across the terrain. Behind them the shield flickered and came back on, its orange glow restored.

Before her stretched the sprawl of Delta City. Byron was right—the buildings here were in shambles, many with missing walls and some collapsed outright. It didn't look as bad as the ancient, ruined cities she'd crossed through on her journey, but it wasn't far behind.

After they rode the maglev down the wall to street level, Raven packed it away. Dirty, starving citizens squatted in alleys and slept in spaces under fallen slabs of concrete. A woman in soiled, tattered rags looked up at them from where she crouched. Eyes full of fear, she struggled to her feet, and hurried off. When the others saw the Badlanders coming, they also slunk away, dragging their filthy blankets. Recalling the eager mob from her first visit to the eastern part of Murder City, H124 worried they'd be back in larger numbers.

"They're probably amassing reinforcements," Astoria growled, reading H124's mind. "There'll be about a million more of them in a minute, dragging us down and clawing at our faces."

"Let's get a move on," Byron said. "Which way?"

H124 consulted her PRD. They headed in the direction of the aeronautics facility.

As they passed down a quiet street, they came across a living pod building that lacked an entire wall, with gaping holes to the outside. H124 was amazed to see citizens still inside, working on their floating displays, watching media and entering commands as if nothing were wrong.

On the ground floor, one person sat on his couch, his attention not once leaving the floating display, even as they walked by. His eyes were dark and sunken, his body so emaciated she wondered how he was able to function. She backed up, and noticed the occupant in the living pod one floor up. She too was thin and starving, her arms mere skin stretched over bone. Yet she continued to enter commands on the display, completely zoned to the entertainment channels before her.

"It looks like these citizens aren't getting fed," H124 said, gesturing toward them. "They're starving."

"Maybe the PPC has abandoned them, too," Byron said.

She walked toward the man on the ground floor. He still didn't notice her. As she got closer, she saw that he was watching a reality show. Two women sat around a table, comparing bracelets:

"The emoticon on your bracelet is so much better than mine."

"I know. The crying wah-wah face is the best. But if you get enough points, you could get one, too."

"But then I'd be just like you."

"I know!" They both tittered happily.

The man's pod was filthy. Workers hadn't cleaned it in who knew how long. She walked closer.

"Hey," she said to him, stopping at the edge of the ruined wall. He didn't look up.

"What are you doing, Halo?" Byron asked, aghast.

She turned to him. "We can't just leave these people like this." She went back to the man. "Hey. Can you hear me?"

Nothing.

She stepped through the wall and into the pod.

"What the hell are you doing?" Astoria yelled. "We don't have time for this!"

H124 heard footsteps crunch in the debris behind her. Dirk joined her. "Is he even aware of us?"

On his screen, one of the women said, "We could both get the wall and have little stars forever!"

"They don't even make sense," Dirk said.

"Willoughby told me that they aren't even real people, that it's all computer generated, with words and plots that are strung together randomly."

The other woman on the screen said, "Don't even tell me about the walrus. We all went to the corner that time." The women laughed again.

H124 walked up to the man and bent over him.

She put her hand through the shimmering display, and finally he noticed them. His mouth came open, and he stared up at his guests. "Who . . . ?" he started to say.

"Hey," she said. "Are you okay?"

He blinked, his face vacant.

"When was the last time you ate?" she asked him.

"What?" the man asked. Already his attention was returning to the reality show. He entered a few commands on the virtual keyboard. He had completely forgotten about H124.

H124 leaned to the side, seeing the glowing power conduit below his headjack. It wouldn't detach him from the network, but his display would shut off. She reached down and pressed it. The shimmering display vanished, and the man let out a gasp. He tried to stand, but fell back down on the couch, his eyes watery and wide.

"What . . . ?" he said again. He gazed around the room, mouth open in terror. "*Where did it go?*" he cried in a cracked voice.

"Take it easy," Dirk told him, reaching out to touch his arm.

The man shrank away, touching his headjack, fumbling for the display switch.

"Wait," H124 said, catching his hand before he could switch it back on. "When was the last time a drone delivered food to you?"

The man pushed her away. "I don't know." He shoved feebly at her hand, and switched the display back on. In moments he was back to watching the show, the two characters now showing off anklets to each other. "Only two thousands credits!" one of them cried gleefully.

She heard the familiar sound of a food delivery drone outside, and stepped back out of the living pod. Two buildings down, a single drone delivered food cubes to another building of living pods. In New Atlantic, there'd be a fleet of drones, not just one. There was no way it could carry enough cubes to feed even a single floor of a building. Once it left, she waited for it to come back, but it never did.

"They must be providing the bare minimum to keep these people alive," Dirk observed, watching the sky where the drone had vanished.

H124 looked back at the starving man. At least the people in the street knew what was happening to them. They fought for food. This man was completely unaware he was starving.

Raven joined them, peering in at the thin man. "I don't see how these people can live for long like this."

Out on the street, Astoria put a hand on her hip. "Are you bleeding hearts ready? Let's get this thing and get the hell out of here."

They continued on, following the blinking arrow on H124's PRD map. She took the lead. Finally she reached the location. To her disappointment, the building there had collapsed, leaving a pile of rubble on the spot. But if the engineers had followed protocol, the spacecraft section would be deep underground.

"It's got to be down here," H124 said, waving them over. Raven was the first one to reach her. They began lifting away debris.

Suddenly she went off balance, and sprawled into the street. For a second she couldn't figure out what had happened. Then Raven fell over, too, his back striking a cement block. The street groaned as a wave shook through it. One block over, a building moaned and toppled, sending up plumes of dust.

"What the hell?" Astoria cursed, grabbing on to a rusted street sign.

"It's an earthquake!" shouted Byron, as the tremors grew more intense. They rolled through the ground, and all around edifices jarred upward.

"Take cover!" Raven yelled. "This whole block could come down!"

H124 struggled to her feet, searching for a sturdy object she could hide under. But the entire area was ancient and crumbling, with only a few doorways still standing. Another violent wave shimmied beneath her. She staggered, then lost her footing. Completely off balance, she careened toward a jagged piece of rusted rebar sticking out of the cement block in front of her. Byron caught her just in time and pulled her to the side. The street bucked upward, sending them sprawling. She landed on top of Byron, who shielded her with his arms as a shower of bricks rained down. One struck her shoulder. Her world continued to shake violently, the ground rough and unforgiving, its glass shards and broken rock digging into her knees and elbows. Byron held onto her as glass shattered and masonry crashed down around them.

She gritted her teeth and covered her head. Byron rolled over, guarding her with his body, one arm across her back, the other over her head.

A huge crack tore open the street, jagging away into the distance. Soil and trash fell into the fissure.

The trembling lessened, then stopped altogether.

"You both okay?" Raven called from the other side of the street. Byron uncoiled himself from her and got up, extending a hand. She took it, and he swung her to her feet. Across the street, Astoria and Dirk were brushing themselves off as they stepped out from a pile of rubble. Raven had fallen some fifty feet away, dangerously close to the crack.

"That was a close one," he said, brushing dirt off his pants.

Astoria looked angrier than usual. "This whole thing is crazy. If the people don't kill us, the city itself will."

"This isn't too bad," Raven told her, in an attempt to lighten the mood. "You should have seen what H and I went through to get the first piece. We'll get through this no problem. It's just a little bit of shaking."

Then another earthquake hit.

"Why did you have to say that?" Astoria shouted, falling off balance.

The trembling threw H124 toward the jagged rend in the road. It widened, issuing a foul, rotten odor.

"What is that?" Astoria asked with a wrinkled nose.

H124 fell down hard on her hands and knees. She moved away from the widening crack, and Byron did the same. The concrete bumped painfully against her knees. A building two blocks down gave a final gasp before it collapsed, shooting up a billowing cloud of dust.

H124 felt like the world would never stop shaking. She gripped the road amid the settling dust, and shielded her head. The dry, bitter taste of dust filled her mouth. Finally the shaking stopped.

She was about to stand up when another quake hit.

The living pod structure across the street lost its front wall, which separated and crashed down. Inside, she could see citizens looking vaguely startled, peering out for a moment at the street. One even walked over to the open wall and stared out. But the floating display still shimmered in front of him, and he couldn't help but look back. A few more stood up, approaching the open wall.

Then the tremblor dissipated. In unison, all the citizens returned to their couches and the entertainment flashing before them.

H124 helped Dirk up. He'd banged his knee and head pretty good, and H124 could already see a small bump forming along his hairline. He rubbed his knee as his sister joined him. "You can't even fall down right," she cursed at her brother. "You'd probably hurt yourself eating a bowl of rice." Still, there was concern in her eyes.

H124 returned to where the facility lay beneath their feet. The earthquake had shifted debris, covering all the progress they'd made. She bent down, pushing aside old stones and bricks, lengths of copper pipe and tangles of wiring.

They all worked in silence, though H124 could feel the hostility radiating off Astoria.

At last they uncovered a dark hole leading to a cavernous space below. H124 pulled out her headlamp and switched it on, aiming the beam into the darkness. She vividly remembered finding the other hole beneath the living pod building in New Atlantic. Here a mound of debris made a rough ramp leading down. Raven pulled two ropes out of his pack and affixed them to a metal pole embedded in the ground. H124 grabbed hold, and swung her legs over the edge. Testing the stability of each section as she stepped down, she made sure the whole pile wasn't about to collapse beneath her.

Raven followed, also switching on his lamp.

Byron grabbed a rope and lowered himself down after them.

"Where are you going?" she heard Astoria bark, and looked up to see Dirk starting to descend as well. Astoria grabbed his jacket, dragging him back into the light. "No way. Let them kill themselves if they want to. I'm not crawling down there after your ass."

"They might need our help."

"You're going to need my help in a minute when I send you sprawling," she threatened.

Dirk continued to hold on to the rope. "They're newbies here. They need our expertise."

"A reality check is what they need. This whole plan is crazy."

"But it's our best chance. This thing hits," he added, pointing up at the sky, "and we're all gone."

She exhaled in disgust, then peered down into the void. "Fine."

H124 watched as Astoria and Dirk joined them on the ropes.

As she moved, she glanced over at Raven, his hair dusty and dusky. His eyes met her in the darkness.

"Once more unto the breach," he said quietly, and they descended.

Chapter 12

One by one they lowered themselves into the dark, and the beams from their headlamps created erratic shadows on the walls. The floor immediately below had collapsed, so they went straight through to the level beneath that. Here another hole in the floor allowed them to pass through to the sub-levels. Five floors down, they could still look up and see the sky. H124 worried that the spacecraft piece, having been exposed to the elements, would have long since rotted away, or been picked clean by Murder City denizens.

When they got to the sixth subterranean floor, their feet set down on solid ground. Though the flooring felt weak, there were certainly no holes big enough to allow them to pass to the level below.

They walked along the damp floor and headed down a darkened corridor. It ended in a solid steel door with an ancient keypad next to it.

H124 reached out with her mind, but found no theta wave receiver to open the door.

Though power was still functioning in this quarter, the keypad appeared dark and dead. She took out her multitool, and popped off the keypad cover. Beneath lay a tangle of wires of different colors, its innards furred with mold.

"This is old tech," she told them.

Dirk came forward. "Let me see." He pulled the wires out gently, sorting them in his nimble fingers. "Can I have that?" he asked H124, gesturing to her multitool. She handed it to him. He cut a few wires, stripping the cracked, degraded insulation off them, and twisted them together. "Someone hand me the UV charger for a PRD." Astoria came forward, detaching her UV charger and handing it to him. He connected the newly stripped wires to it, and the lights blinked on for the keypad. He touched two wires, and the door came open with a rusted shriek.

"Wow," Raven said.

Beyond, the reek of mildew hung in the air. A long hallway with offices on either side led to another steel door.

Dirk hacked that one, too, then another that led to a stair.

They descended to the floor below, where Raven checked the schematics again. "This should be the right level. It's toward the middle of the floor."

They wound along a series of labs, some with tools still strewn on their worktables. Just like the one near New Atlantic, this place looked like workers had dropped their tasks in the middle of the day and simply walked away, their work unfinished. She saw ancient computers like the ones she'd found in the university beneath New Atlantic.

Dirk hacked one more door, which admitted them to a vast warehouse. Their boots echoed. In the center of the room stood a glassed-in enclosure identical to the one they'd found on the east coast. White, helmeted suits hung on the exterior. Inside, the spacecraft section stood, complete and wondrously pristine. H124 felt like cheering.

"Is that it?" Dirk asked, circling the small glass room.

"That's it," Raven told him. He slung off his pack and unfurled the maglev sled, letting it orient itself.

Then he and H124 entered the room, and Raven draped the clean skin over the craft. He maneuvered the maglev over to it, and it used its levers to work its way under the craft and lift it onto the sled. They had one more section to retrieve before Rivet would be able to piece the spacecraft together. The progress eased H124's mind a little.

They carefully covered the section with a tarp. Then H124 did a circuit of the room, stuffing anything that looked useful into her pack. She found a binder full of the circular disks and grabbed it, along with a handful of what Raven called "drives."

Moving in silence, they retraced their footsteps back to the ropes.

At the series of ruined floors, they used an ascender to climb back up, one at a time. Dirk and Astoria went first, followed by Byron. When it was just H124 and Raven at the bottom, he said, "You were right to trust them. They've really come through for us."

She smiled. "Thanks."

They climbed the ropes together, the light around them growing brighter as they neared the surface.

Byron's voice shouted down. "Climb fast! We have company up here!"

"What?" H124 asked.

"PPC troops. They're making their way down the street!"

H124 and Raven climbed faster, their boots slipping on the loose rubble, the maglev humming along behind them. When she reached the top, Byron stuck his hand through the hole. H124 took it, blinking in the sudden brightness. She turned to help Raven climb out, the sled following close behind.

Down the street she saw a troop transport hovering slightly above the pavement. She'd seen them before in New Atlantic, shuttling PPC troops around the city. Several troopers marched alongside it. They hadn't spotted H124 and the others yet. The soldiers stopped at a building, and went inside.

"Guess we're not going back the way we came," Dirk said.

"I knew something like this was going to happen," Astoria growled.

H124 took in their surroundings. To their left stood a largely intact building of living pods. "This way!" she said. They all sprinted down the street, staying low and keeping piles of rubble between them and the troopers' line of sight.

"We need to get off the street," Byron said.

"There," she said. They sprinted to the living pod's exterior door, finding it locked with a theta wave receiver. H124 stilled her mind, sending the unlock command to it. The lock clicked, and the door slid open. "Hopefully we can escape a block over through here," she told them, running down the hall. At the far end stood another locked door. She commanded the TWR to open it, and hesitated in the open entryway, checking the street beyond. She didn't see anyone.

"This way!" She sprinted across the street to another building, a kind she recognized from New Atlantic. It was a laundry and maintenance building, though it had been shut down long ago. No low thrum of machinery reached her ears. Using the TWR, she let them into the ground floor, which was large and empty. Only old dryers and washing machines lined the wall, covered in a thick layer of dust. They ran across the warehouse space, pausing at a large docking door on the far side with a small window mounted in it. H124 peered through. Checking her PRD, she saw that they now stood about six blocks from the edge of the city and the atmospheric shield.

Byron stood next to her, catching his breath. When he saw how close they were, he contacted Chadwick, giving him the coordinates. He didn't respond.

They waited tensely in the shadows. Byron tried again, but still got no response. He looked at them all, eyes wide in the dark. "This mission might be over sooner than we thought. The troops may have found him."

Then Chadwick's voice came over Byron's PRD. "Sorry about that," he said. "I had to move and stay silent. An airship was out here, patrolling the perimeter."

"Do you think they know we're in here?" Raven asked.

"I don't think so." His face shimmered on the display. "I think it was just routine. But I've got the coordinates of where you're coming out. I'll start a new broadcast now."

"Thank you," Byron told him. He signed off. Byron checked the street beyond and said, "Let's go."

They moved through the blocks quietly, using the TWRs to move in and out of buildings undetected. As they stepped out to cross a street, H124 stopped. Two blocks down, a transport waited in the middle of the street. A PPC trooper was loading citizens into it.

H124 studied the insignia on the transport. "I recognize that symbol. It's for the food processing plants."

Dirk raised a brow. "They're taking them to be fed? Well, that's good at least."

Raven put a hand on his stomach, and took on an ashen hue. "Are you sure that's what they're doing? Why wouldn't they just have food delivered? Why bring the people to the processing plant?"

Dirk's eyes shot open. "You mean they're going to use them for . . ."

Raven grimaced.

Byron glanced around, staying low. "I think they've been cleaning this place out for a long time. The more they can consolidate, the less energy they'll have to expend to keep the infrastructure going. They're abandoning this part of the city."

"But couldn't they just move these citizens to the east?" Dirk asked.

"They already have more people than they can handle there," Byron said.

The PPC trooper loaded in more weakened citizens as they arrived. The faceplate on his helmet was down, his demeanor unfeeling. He watched them file in, shoving an older man who stumbled as he tried to climb the ramp into the transport.

The citizens' shimmering displays still glowed in front of them. More troopers joined the first, stepping away from their street patrol. They passed the citizens from one soldier to the next, the people in their care barely aware of what was happening. Videos just kept flashing in multiple windows, allowing the citizens to watch more than one show at a time.

"We have to do something," H124 said.

"No way. Not this again," Astoria mumbled.

"What could we do?" Byron pointed out. "They outnumber us."

"But they're carting them off to be killed!" H124 said.

"Better them than us," Astoria put in.

H124 spun to Dirk and Raven.

"I'm with you," Raven told her, "but I don't see how we can get them away."

"What about a distraction?" H124 said. "We draw the troopers away, then steal the transport."

"And then what?" Astoria said. "We fly them off to Never Never Land where they can live happily ever after?"

"We have Chadwick hack a bigger hole, one that can accommodate the transport, and we fly them through it. We take them back to Sanctuary City," H124 suggested.

Astoria's face flushed with anger. "I am *not* risking my neck for a bunch of jacked-in zombies."

"They won't be, once they unplug," H124 pointed out.

"You saw that guy you approached," Astoria went on. "He panicked when he wasn't getting his media feed. Those people can't survive without it."

H124 felt anger well up inside her. "You don't know that." She glanced around at her companions. "So we're just going to let those people get carted off and die?"

Byron exhaled sharply, and broke his silence. "God damn it, Halo." He shook his head. "You are the craziest fool I've ever met. You can't save everyone."

"Maybe not. But we can save these people."

Exasperated, he pulled out his diginocs. "The transport's a JLK352 model. I've driven one of those before."

Astoria watched him in disbelief. "You're actually considering this insanity?"

"I can create a diversion," Dirk offered. "If we run over to a neighboring alley, I can draw their attention."

"And then what. Get killed?" his sister snapped. "What a plan."

Dirk grinned slyly. "I'm better than that, and you know it."

"I know you're a whiz at math. And jury rigging things. But this?" She looked at the others. "And what about our glorious mission? Are we going to risk the craft getting damaged just to save a few checked-out citizens?"

H124 stared over at the maglev, hovering a few feet behind him. "You're right." She turned to Raven. "Can you get out of the shield ahead of us with the sled?"

Raven hesitated. "And just leave you all? No way."

H124 gestured at the spacecraft section. "This is more important."

Raven glanced at them all, then sighed. "Okay. But I don't feel right about it."

H124 handed him her pack with the disks and drives in it.

Byron turned to Raven. "Take off now. Let Chadwick know to hack a bigger hole. When they load the last person in, we'll strike, then catch up with you."

Reluctantly, Raven turned, hurrying in the opposite direction. H124 watched until he disappeared safely around a corner, the maglev gliding along in tow.

Byron bent low, whispering. "Remember, no guns. This has to be quiet. We don't want to draw more soldiers."

Dirk grinned. "Here we go." He slunk over to a pile of debris, then when the troopers weren't watching, vaulted over it and rounded the building on the far side of them.

"Goddamn it," Astoria cursed, taking off after her brother.

Byron and H124 headed west, hunkering low. A patrolling trooper came into view, checking a neighboring street. They approached him quietly from his rear. Byron picked up a piece of rebar, and got closer. As the trooper rounded the next corner, Byron ran up behind him, slamming the rebar down hard on his shoulders. The trooper stumbled, Byron took the opportunity to rip off the man's helmet, knocking him on the head. The trooper slumped to the ground, unconscious.

They peered around the corner to the transport. There the five troopers had taken no notice.

Byron rummaged around in his pack. He pulled out a rectangular block, pliable and black. "Take this," he said, handing it to H124.

"What is it?"

"An explosive." Then he handed her a sleek cube, which had a red light on it. "Just stick this little box into it and press the button. Then get clear. When Dirk distracts them, let 'er blow. That should draw the troopers in opposite directions. Once they split up I'll steal the transport."

He took off, approaching the vehicle.

H124 gripped the explosive, slinking low to keep out of sight, moving quietly along a parallel street. When she was two blocks west of the troopers, she took shelter behind a fallen slab of concrete.

At the far end of the street she could see Dirk and Astoria creeping along behind the other trooper. Astoria grabbed his shoulder, wheeling him around. She thrust a powerful blow to the man's throat, and he stumbled back. Then Dirk appeared, giving H124 the thumbs up. He shouted, "Some citizens are escaping! Over here! We need assistance!"

Two troopers jerked their heads in their direction, then wielded their flash bursters and took off toward them. But three remained behind, loading the last citizen inside. They started to close the door.

Finding a good spot in the center of the street, amid a mess of crumbling bricks, H124 set down the explosive. Following Byron's instructions, she stuck the small black cube into the putty, and pressed the tiny red button. Then she bolted, taking shelter behind a building.

The explosion shattered the silence, and the brickwork became a barrage of projectiles. The three troopers ran toward her.

A block to the north, Byron closed the distance to the abandoned transport. H124 continued west, racing between buildings to keep out of sight. She could hear the troopers' boots slamming on the pavement, drawn to the explosion.

She ran around a corner just as Byron slid into the driver's seat and started up the transport. It lifted above the ground, and he wheeled it around, picking up Dirk and Astoria at the end of the block. She waved them down, and climbed into the passenger seat. Byron raced toward the rendezvous point. Up ahead, she could see the hole in the atmospheric shield now wide enough to accommodate the transport.

Checking over her shoulder, she saw Dirk and Astoria sitting with the citizens, the latter bunch completely oblivious to the fact that the transport had just been hijacked. They all watched different media streams on their floating displays, checked out as usual. Dirk studied them in fascination, while Astoria sat with her arms crossed, looking straight ahead. "We better not get killed," she growled.

Once they reached the debris ramp, they saw Raven standing on top of the retaining wall, the maglev hovering beside him. He waved them on with a grin. Then he stepped through the hole, standing next to the craft on the maglev to lower himself.

They were almost free.

Suddenly all of the citizens' floating displays shut off.

The light in the transport dimmed. H124 turned as the passengers lifted their heads all at once, eyes narrowing on the Badlanders. They stood up, shambling toward them. She put a hand on Byron's shoulder. "Something's wrong."

The citizens shuffled toward Astoria and Dirk in a daze, then lunged forward, pinning them down. Astoria unholstered her revolver and fired it in the narrow confines of the transport, the ear-splitting series of blasts deafening H124. Citizens fell back, splattered with red, seeping holes in their foreheads and necks. After six shots, the gun clicked on an empty chamber.

"Reload me!" she called to Dirk, but he was too pinned down to take her gun, and he couldn't even free his arms to get to his own. H124 watched as crimson arcs sprayed above the tangled mass as Astoria's knife flashed. "Get them off us!" she cried out.

H124 unslung her energy rifle. She couldn't hit any of the citizens without the electric charge carrying through their bodies and into Dirk and Astoria. Instead she brought the butt of the rifle down onto the thronging mass's heads. But already half the citizens had crept forward, moving between her and Byron. He floored it, speeding toward the debris ramp and the hole in the shield. He pulled out his 9mm from a hip holster and handed it to her. But before she could fire, hands grabbed her, dragging her down, bony bodies swarming over her. She shoved them away, struggling to see out the front window. They were a hundred yards from the hole. "Damn it!" he cursed. The bodies kept coming, grabbing Byron now and dragging him from the pilot's chair. They were thin and feeble, but there were too many of them.

The transport crashed to the ground. Through a mass of squirming elbows and legs, H124 saw troopers running toward the transport, flash bursters aimed at them. The atmospheric shield above flickered and glowed, the hole now gone. Then the transport door slid open, and a blinding flash filled her world. An electrical surge snaked through her body, every muscle jittering in agony. Her teeth clamped shut, and darkness swallowed her.

Chapter 13

H124 stirred, waking slowly and groggily. For the briefest of moments she didn't know where she was, and then, alarmingly, *who* she was. Then it came back to her—the transport, the swarm of citizens, the blast from the troopers' flash bursters. She lifted her head, finding that she had been sleeping on Byron's shoulder, his arm around her.

She awakened more fully, pulling away. His eyes were closed, and he mumbled something as she stirred, taking in their surroundings. They lay on the cold cement floor of a cell, rusted metal bars caging them in. There was no bunk or food or water.

She and Byron were alone. Astoria and Dirk were nowhere in sight. She sat up straighter, and at last Byron woke. "H," he breathed, disoriented. "You woke up. I was getting worried."

"Where are we?"

He scanned the area with narrowed eyes. "I don't know. I haven't seen anyone. I woke up about an hour ago to find us sprawled on the floor. You were shivering."

"Where are Dirk and Astoria?"

"I haven't seen them." The place smelled old and dank, and she could hear water dripping somewhere. Rising on wobbly legs, she moved to the bars and peered out. Other cells stood along a narrow corridor, all empty. The place sounded vacant.

Tall, narrow windows stood high along the far wall, but decades of grime and mold coated them, letting in only the most feeble light.

She tested the bars and rattled the door.

"Tried that," he told her.

She bent down by the lock. "Can we pick this?"

"If we had something slender."

She realized then that all of her pockets had been emptied, her PRD and multitool removed. She moved to the old hinges and gripped one of the pins, trying to jimmy it upward. It was stuck fast.

Kneeling, she examined where the bars had been sunk into the cement. Some of the floor had decayed a bit here, so she gripped one of the bars and shook it fiercely. It barely moved. She tried to chip away at the cement with her fingernails, but just ended up scraping her fingertips.

"Do you think we're in that food processing facility?" he asked.

She thought of the sprawling, sterile buildings where they made food cubes in New Atlantic. There, the food was made from soy that was harvested from gardens on rooftops. Here in Murder City, all bets were off. "If so, it looks nothing like the ones in New Atlantic."

"Unless they're holding us till they process the citizens, then plan on hauling us over there."

Just in case an unseen TWR was in the door, she closed her eyes and concentrated, reaching out to connect with it. But she sensed no receiver. It was an analog lock, old and simple.

A few cells down, on the same side as hers, she heard someone stir, then gasp in panic. "Astoria?" cried Dirk's familiar voice. "Astoria!"

"Dirk?" H124 said in a soft voice.

"Are you and Byron over there?" Dirk asked.

"Yes."

"Astoria's here on the floor, but I can't wake her up. Where are we?"

"I don't know," she answered.

Byron joined her at the cell door. "Don't panic," he told Dirk. "H didn't wake up right away either."

"Astoria?" he said again, and H124 could hear her shifting on the floor.

"What the hell?" came her gruff voice. H124 couldn't see them at all, but thought they were probably three or four cells down, with the way their voices echoed off the cold stone.

She heard Astoria stand up, rattle the cell bars. "What the hell is this?" The noise reverberated in the empty space. Then it grew quiet. "Where are Byron and that soft-hearted PPC-attractor?"

"Here," Byron called down to her.

"Damn it! This is why we don't help worthless zombie motherfuckers! Their minds aren't their own. Those jacked-in assholes couldn't have a single original thought if they wanted."

H124 turned to Byron. "Is she saying that the citizens were controlled? Made to do that?"

His eyes looked hesitant. "We've never really understood the depth of influence the PPC has on people who are jacked-in."

H124 thought of the eerie way they'd all moved in unison, the way all their screens turned off at once. The citizens hadn't done that themselves. She hadn't seen any of them reach under their ears to switch their displays to sleep mode.

"See what your bleeding heart has gotten us into this time? We're fucking rats in a cage here."

She heard Astoria punch one of the bars, then Dirk adding in a calm voice, "Let's just figure a way out of here."

A door on the far side of the room clanged open. It was around the corner at the end of the cell row, so H124 had to crane her head against the bars to see.

Her blood turned cold when she saw four Repurposers round the corner. The familiar black uniforms, long sweeping coats, and red and black lightning bolt insignias on their upper sleeves made her mouth go dry. A worker had once told her that she shouldn't fear the Repurposers if they came for a visit, that they were good and the lightning symbolized a bolt of inspiration. Repurposers offered the gift of innovation to a person's mind, he'd said. But now she truly understood the dark truth about them. They devastated your brain, scrambling and destroying it in an effort to make you compliant.

They stopped in front of Astoria's cell, their pale, cruel faces smirking beneath the brims of their black hats. The lead one pulled out a flash burster and fired it into the cell. She heard Astoria cry out, then fall silent. The blast hadn't been very bright, probably not enough to knock her out, but enough immobilize her.

"Leave my sister alone!" Dirk cursed. One fished out a key, and they let themselves into his cell. As the last Repurposer stepped inside, he turned, black eyes locking on H124. She backed away from the bars, bumping into Byron.

"Repurposers," she breathed. She heard the other cell door slam shut.

"Don't you dare touch my brother," they heard Astoria say, feebly.

And then Dirk started to scream, a primal, keening wail. H124 backed away in horror, slamming against the wall, the panic welling within her.

"H," Byron said, grabbing her by the shoulders. She blinked, tearing.

"I'll kill you bastards!" Astoria shouted, and another bright flash lit up the space. H124 heard her fall, still cursing them. "You're dead!"

"Tell us what we need to know, and we'll stop this," she heard a Repurposer say, only he hadn't asked them any questions.

Dirk screamed again, and H124 heard the terrible sound of the repurposing tool whirring to life, its bone saw spinning.

"Don't you dare touch him!" Astoria bellowed, and another flash illuminated the gloomy space. Astoria cried out in pain.

"We have to do something!" H124 shouted. She ran to the bars again, shaking them, checking the wall for any loose cinder blocks. There was nothing. She pounded a fist against the wall.

Everything went quiet in the neighboring cell. She heard that door creak open. Pressing her forehead against the cold bars, she watched as two of the Repurposers dragged Dirk away. Moments later, the other two emerged with Astoria, who hung limp between them, feet dragging behind.

They disappeared round the corner, where the heavy door there slammed shut. She spun to face Byron. "They'll wipe them! Or kill them!" She thought of the Menials—silent, almost robotic people who had been wiped and told to perform a simple, repetitive task. "This can't be happening!" She gripped the bars again, rattling them, crying out in frustration. "Damn it! I shouldn't have tried to save those people! Why did I do that?"

Byron placed a hand on her back. "This isn't your fault."

"It damn well is! She told me no good would come out of it. I should have listened to her!"

"Astoria never thinks anything good comes out of anything." He took her by her shoulders, and gently turned her around. "Don't do this to yourself. We have to find a way out."

The door opened, and the Repurposers entered again, this time marching toward her cell.

A white-hot rage welled up inside her. She reached out with her mind, trying to find any TWR out there, something she could connect with, unlock. Some machinery she could start up to create a diversion. Anything to distract them and make their escape.

She squeezed her eyes shut, backing away from the bars, mind searching. Then she connected with something, a receiver of some kind, but different from any controls she'd operated for incinerators or door locks. She felt around for its status, feeling that the device was on. She sensed its proximity. If she could make whatever it was malfunction, distract the Repurposers, maybe Dirk and Astoria could make their escape.

She reached out, giving the device two simultaneous signals that it would be unable to process. She told it to turn on and off at the same time, putting every ounce of mental energy behind the command.

One of the Repurposers cried out in pain. She opened her eyes to see his eyes go wide. He grabbed his head, screaming, and collapsed. The other three turned, bending over him. "He's dead," one of them whispered.

The lead Repurposer slowly pivoted his head, locking eyes with her in the cell. Then he turned toward his fallen colleague. "Remove him," he commanded the others.

All three filed out, dragging their dead comrade.

Byron squeezed her arm. "What just happened?"

She blinked, relaxing her neck muscles, feeling her mind detach from the receiver. "I don't know . . . I think I might have killed him. He had something in his head, some kind of receiver."

"Holy hell!" Byron said, clapping her on the shoulder. He grinned, the hope flickering in his eyes. "Can you do that again?"

A wicked smile came to her face. "I sure as hell hope so!"

With the Repurposers gone, they went over every piece of the cell, again unsuccessfully. The outer door clanged open again. Already H124 reached out with her mind, feeling for another receiver like the one she had discovered inside the Repurposer. But she didn't sense anything. Five soldiers marched around the corner, all wearing the anonymous black fatigues and helmets with opaque face shields. They drew their flash bursters, and aimed for the cell. She drew back as they unlocked the heavy door and swung it wide. The soldiers filed in, grabbing H124 by the arms and dragging her out.

Byron rushed forward. "Leave her alone!"

A soldier in front knocked him aside, sending him sprawling against the wall. Byron got up, wiping blood from his lip. H124 kicked and struggled as they lifted her off the floor and out of the cell.

"Let go of her!" Byron shouted, rushing one of them before he had the chance to relock the cell door.

He grabbed the soldier, yanking the keys out of his hand. Byron brought up his palm, dealing a savage blow to the soldier's chin. The man crumpled, neck snapping back.

One of the soldiers turned to Byron, reaching for his flash burster. Byron made for him, kicking the man's hand. The gun went skittering across the floor. "You're not taking her!" He dove for the gun, getting off a shot on another one of the troopers. H124 bucked, throwing off one of the men, then spun and punched another in the throat. He gagged and choked, grabbing his neck as he staggered backward.

The last solider gripped H124's arm, but she shoved him away, delivering a swift kick to the man's knees. She heard the sickening snap of bone as he cried out and crumpled to the ground. Byron hit all of them with blasts from the gun. Gripping the keys, Byron rushed out of the cell, and together they bolted down the corridor.

When they passed Dirk and Astoria's empty cell, she saw blood all over the floor.

"What did they do to them?" Byron breathed.

"We have to find them."

They rounded the corner to a solid steel door.

She tested it, finding it locked. Byron rummaged through the keys, finding a likely candidate and sliding it home. He yanked the door open, and they froze.

Beyond stood more than a dozen soldiers. Byron fired the flash burster, bringing down two of them.

But the troopers raised their own flash bursters, firing simultaneously. An electric surge flooded across Byron. He fell jittering on the ground. H124 bent beside him, and saw that his flash burster was now fried and useless.

Five men rushed to grab her, once again lifting her off her feet as she kicked and punched at them. Another three came forward and snatched up Byron, dragging him back toward the cells.

"Don't you dare take her!" he screamed. "I'll kill you all! You're dead! Do you hear me? Dead!" She'd never heard such venom in his voice.

She kicked one of the soldiers in the stomach, but even as he doubled over he held fast to her feet. They carried her out of the dank jail, into the bright sunlight, and loaded her onto a transport. She fought all the way up the ramp. Once she was inside the vehicle, they chained her to a seat, slapping manacles on her hands and feet.

"Where are you taking me?" she shouted, but none of the soldiers answered. Two climbed into the front and started up the transport.

She looked out of the window as they took off, seeing that she was only a few blocks from where they'd been captured. They glided over debris as they navigated through decrepit streets.

Then the transport rose, climbing higher until they were sailing over the tops of buildings. They were headed north.

She gazed down at the terrain below, watching as the buildings went from crumbling and abandoned to more contemporary and well kept. Above them, the orange shield glowed, lending a familiar light to everything below. She'd grown up with that unnatural light. Outside, she'd seen blue skies and forests of green. This place was a living hell of squalor and pavement, nature desecrated and buried.

They continued north. She took note of different buildings and landmarks, mentally preparing a way to backtrack once she got free. The sun sank below the horizon. They flew on, taking her so far from where they'd entered Delta City that she began to despair of ever finding her way back to Byron, Chadwick, and the mobile transmitter that made her escape possible.

She bent low, trying to look out the front of the transport. Before them a PPC tower loomed into sight, its unmistakable towering stories rising so far above the surrounding city that she couldn't see its zenith, even from their altitude.

It wasn't the same one she'd infiltrated to give her pirate broadcast. That one lay to the northeast of here, she thought. But this tower looked just as formidable, the top bristling with antennae, the PPC logo glowing on one side.

They were taking her straight into the enemy's lair.

Chapter 14

She strained against the chains, looking for a weak point, but the manacles covered her hands, making it difficult to move.

The transport landed on a platform near the middle of the tower, and set down with a thump. The shock troopers yanked her out of the chair, pulling her by the chain. She expected them to take her straight to the brig level, but to her surprise, they forced her down a posh hallway, and stopped outside of an executive office.

Her heart leapt suddenly. If this was Willoughby's office, she was saved. Maybe he was in Delta City now, and had learned they were taken prisoner. Her heart thumped as one of the troopers pressed the comm button to the office. A clipped female voice said, "Yes?"

"She's here, ma'am," said the trooper.

"Send her in."

The door hissed open, and they shoved her into an impeccably decorated office. Elaborate glass sculptures stood along two of the walls, and a wide panoramic window afforded a view of the city's nightscape stretching toward the horizon. The atmospheric shield glowed not too far away.

Willoughby was not there, however, and her heart sank. Behind a desk sat an older woman. Her short, silver hair was combed stylishly, her intense blue eyes studying H124 from a pale face with high cheekbones. She rose from her seat, smoothing down a red executive suit jacket.

"Please come in," she told H124, then turned to the guards. She pointed to the manacles. "Remove those."

One of the troopers unlocked them, gathering up the heavy chain. The sudden release made her hands feel as if they'd float up to the ceiling.

"Now excuse us," she told the soldiers. They exited in silence, sliding the door shut behind them. The woman came forward, studying H124. "Forgive the treatment you received. The PPC is not friendly toward outsiders infiltrating the city."

H124 rubbed her wrists, already scanning the room for escape routes. That shield was close. If she could get out of the tower, she could try to find a nearby CO_2 vent to exit through. But first she'd have to find the others. "Where are my friends?"

"They're safe. We've brought them here in a separate transport."

"And where are they now?"

"Never mind that. It's you I wanted to talk to."

H124 thought of her pirate broadcast, and knew that the PPC capturing her like this—if they recognized her—was a death sentence. She couldn't believe she used to trust them. Her isolated life in New Atlantic was a world away now. She'd never be that naive again.

But she was surprised when the woman asked, "Do you know who you are?"

H124 didn't know what she meant, so she stayed silent.

"I mean, not the worker, but who you really are?"

"I don't understand."

"Do you have any memories of when you were a child?"

H124 did remember being in the communal child rearing facility, and had a brief flash of lying in a bed with cold green sheets, listening to a child crying a few bunks over. She recalled the rough hands of the caregivers when they fed her and when they crammed her inside the disinfecting chamber every few days. She remembered a terrible empty feeling that had haunted her even back then. But she remained silent, taking the woman in.

"Do you remember me?" the exec asked. When H124 didn't answer, she added, "I'm Olivia."

The name wasn't familiar. Nor was the woman.

"Have you ever run across a man named James Willoughby?"

H124 didn't acknowledge the question.

"I can see in your eyes that you have." She sat down on the edge of her desk and poured a glass of wine from a carafe. After she took a sip, she went on. "He's a dangerous man you should have nothing to do with." She paused. "In fact, he tried to kill you. Years ago."

Years ago? H124 didn't understand.

"You see," Olivia said, taking her wine and walking in a half circle around her. "Willoughby knew my daughter. He used to work here, in Delta City. They were both PPC execs, and had a daughter together.

"But Willoughby got bored with the media here. Didn't feel like his career could go far enough. He applied for a transfer to New Atlantic. My daughter tried to talk sense into him, but he was ambitious. He thought his ratings would climb. My daughter didn't want to go. She begged him to stay, but he only cared about his own career. They argued one night. She was higher up than he was, and could prevent the transfer. And then mysteriously, her autotransport blew up. She was killed, and their child with her. They said it was a faulty wiring, but I knew better. Willoughby left soon after for New Atlantic, free to pursue his ambitions." She approached H124, and cupped her chin. H124 recoiled from the woman's cold touch. "So you can imagine my surprise when I came up as a familial match to a prisoner's DNA."

H124 stared at the woman, mouth agape.

"You are my granddaughter," the woman told her.

This couldn't be true. Willoughby was her father? And he'd killed her mother?

She thought of Willoughby helping her, risking his life for her. Was it a coincidence that he was the one who'd come down to answer her call that first night in the PPC Tower in New Atlantic, after she'd learned of the imminent asteroid collision? Or had he been watching her before that?

"Willoughby has been a thorn in my side for years," Olivia went on. "When I heard he wanted to come back here to do a story on the asteroid collision. I thought it was all a hoax. He tried to spin it that everyone would tune in more than ever to our feeds, but I thought he was just setting up the PPC to report something that would make our ratings plummet. Just another ploy on New Atlantic's part to siphon ratings away from Delta City."

She entered some commands into her PRD, and images came to life on the floating display. At first H124 thought it was another ruined city in the Badlands, but then she started to recognize some of the structures. Everything was black and charred, and a crater of colossal proportions smoldered in the center of the image. It was New Atlantic.

"But now we know that the asteroid wasn't a hoax. You were right. We had quite an earthquake here, but we're still standing, aren't we?"

H124 peered past the display at the woman.

"New Atlantic was completely destroyed, though. It's unfortunate." H124 could tell that Olivia didn't believe it was unfortunate at all. "Our ratings have climbed again. New Atlantic can no longer cut into our feeds." The woman smirked, feeling superior.

H124 knew that fewer viewers translated to less labor for the PPC, but she kept quiet on that front, seeing an opportunity to reason with her.

"That was just a small fragment of a bigger one. That one's not going to miss you. This whole place will be obliterated."

A tiny hint of concern crept across Olivia's face. "What are you talking about?"

"The asteroid split into several pieces years ago. That little piece that destroyed New Atlantic? It's nothing compared to what's coming. And it's going fall right here, right on top of Delta City."

Olivia hesitated, studying H124 with wary eyes.

"And you've ruined your only chance at salvation," H124 told her.

"What do you mean?"

H124 figured a little bluffing couldn't hurt. "Me and my friends, the ones your troops captured? We're the only ones who know how to stop it."

Olivia was frozen. She pressed her lips together until they were colorless, and narrowed her gaze. She placed her fingertips on the table, pressing so hard they went white. "Excuse me," she said at last, and left the room. H124 heard the door lock as it closed.

She immediately began looking for a way out, rushing to the far door and trying to communicate with the TWR. But it wouldn't respond to any of her commands.

She heard a loud thumping in the walls, and the room plunged into shadow. She reached out for the nearest wall, keeping her bearings. Through the window she peered down to see the entire city block go dark. Exterior lights stopped glowing, rooftop fans stopped turning.

Then the room's floating display flickered on. Willoughby's face appeared. She realized the building was running on emergency power only. "H, can you hear me?"

Cautiously, she walked to the display, still reeling from what Olivia had told her. "Willoughby?"

"Sorry I couldn't get here earlier. I've cut into the media stream of the citizens who maintain power in the surrounding blocks. Also took down the feeds for the atmospheric shield due west of here. You can get out now if you move quickly. Your friends are on floor 114, beneath you on the brig level."

She studied his face, thinking of his past kindness. It had to be lies Olivia had fed her. Why would he continue to help her? He couldn't be a murderer.

But for now, she had only precious seconds. Rummaging through Olivia's desk, she found a multitool with a light and grabbed it. Then she hurried back to the unresponsive door and slid it open manually.

"Be careful," Willoughby told her, and the floating display flickered out. With the power off, the door was clunky and heavy, but she managed to slide it enough so she could slip through.

The door led to a narrow service hallway. H124 hastened down it until she found the stairs. She took them two at a time, rounding the landings quickly. When she was halfway down to the brig floor, she heard a door open above her.

"Down here," a man's voice said. "Sweep the staircase and rendezvous with the second team coming up."

H124 paused, listening for sounds of movement on the stairwell below. Then the steps above thundered with the trample of boots. Troopers descended.

She flew down the stairs, reaching floor 114 and slipping quietly through the metal door into the hall. A red light flashed on in the hallway, and she could hear a deep *boom* from the bowels of the building. They were trying to reboot the power, but couldn't.

She crept down the hall, manually pushing open a door that led to the holding cells. But when she emerged, she found all the cell doors partly open and empty. She listened, hearing the faint shouts of guards from neighboring floors. Whoever had been held here had escaped.

If her friends had made it out, they were likely heading for the ground floor. Instead of going back to the same stairwell that had been so close to Olivia's office, she ran to the far side of the hall and took a different stair. She sped down, the light from the multitool casting chaotic shadows on the walls as she ran. When she got lower, she could hear voices murmuring, and drew to a stop. She strained to make out who was talking, but knew they were a couple of floors beneath her on a landing.

"If we don't steal a PRD, how will we ask for a lift away from this place?" a man's voice whispered.

"We get out alive to start with," responded a woman.

H124 slipped down to the next floor to hear better.

"We don't know how long the power's going to be out. I say we make for the wall now." The gruff, lowered voice was all too familiar. Byron.

H124 raced down the last flight of stairs, and saw her friends on the landing. Pure joy swept through her. She'd never had friends like this, and the feeling of being reunited made her grin. They spun toward her, and they too broke out in smiles.

"Halo!" Byron said, hugging her. "You're all right!"

She hugged him back, then gripped Dirk's arm affectionately. She didn't dare touch Astoria, who looked likely to destroy the next person who laid hands on her. "I'm so relieved to see you all. We need to move fast. Willoughby arranged this power outage, but I don't know how long it'll last. He hacked into the feeds of the people who provide the electricity flow here, as well as those who maintain the atmospheric shield."

"We have no way to call for a pickup on the other side," Dirk said again.

Astoria crossed her arms. "We can't risk sneaking around here to steal a PRD. The power could come back on at any moment, and we still have to make our way through the streets of Murder City."

H124 moved to the stairwell door and peered out. The lobby was empty save for a single guard. It looked just like the PPC tower lobby she'd visited in New Atlantic, the first night she'd met Willoughby.

The guard had left his post to stare out the glass door at the darkened city around him. He pressed his hands against the glass, perplexed.

"There's only one guard," H124 whispered.

Astoria slipped past her, moving silently into the lobby. She slunk to the guard's rear, and wrapped her arm around his throat. She held him as he struggled to free himself. Slowly she lowered him to the floor, choking him to sleep. When he sprawled limply, she released him, jumping over his prone body. They all entered the lobby then, speeding toward the front double doors. With four of them pushing, the doors slid open a little easier, and they slipped through into the night.

The stench hit H124 at once. Rotten garbage, and a foul chemical smell, maybe methane. They headed due west, passing through the streets. Even with the atmospheric shield doing its job, the air was stiflingly hot and muggy. Above them the ubiquitous Murder City signs floated: *It doesn't matter who. It doesn't matter how.*

They reached the end of the block, then passed through an area that still glowed with lights. The power outage didn't extend this far. Up ahead the street was clogged with people. Some huddled against walls, sweltering in the heat. Others milled about aimlessly. All of them were so thin that their knees and elbows stood out like knots on a tree branch.

She knew that turning in the heart of a Badlander reaped a handful of food cubes, something these people would kill for without hesitation.

They decided to skirt around the cluster of starving men and women, moving down an alley. The smell of decaying flesh assaulted her as they passed a mound of bodies.

When they reached the next street, they could see the missing sections in the atmospheric shield where Willoughby had cut the feed. Staying within reach of each other, they jogged down the street. A few people gathered in small groups, ogling them as they ran by. They didn't want to attract undue attention, but at the same time they had no idea how long Willoughby could keep the shield open for them.

As they drew closer, H124 wondered how they were going to make it up the retaining wall. They didn't have the maglev sled to help this time. They'd need something to climb.

"Maybe we should slow down a little," Dirk said quietly. "We don't want to attract a mob." Just then, a woman who had been leaning against a wall near a heap of uncollected trash stood up. Her eyes narrowed.

They filed past her, but she fell in behind. "You Badlanders?" she asked.

They ignored her.

"I can tell you are. Your clothes. Those tattoos."

She didn't want to fight them, so H124 continued to hurry forward. She stared down each alley, staying wary.

They passed a group of three.

"They're Badlanders," the woman told them.

The others stood up, eyeing them. As H124 and the others moved past, she saw their sunken eyes, the way their clothes hung in tatters off their emaciated frames. They fell in next to the woman, trailing doggedly behind Byron, who took up the rear.

"You know how much we could get?" the woman said to her companions.

H124 knew it wasn't a lot, enough to feed them for a day, maybe two, but it was enough to make all four of them targets.

At last they reached the atmospheric shield. Though the hole was right at the top of the retaining wall, they still had no way to reach that high.

As more people filed in beside the woman, H124 knew their time was running out. Down one of the alleys, a building's facade had collapsed, its guts spilling into the street. An old gutter pipe lay on top of crumbling bricks and mortar. "This way!" H124 told them, and they veered off into the alley, moving faster.

She hurried to the drainpipe. It was rusted in places, but it would work. "Help me with this." She gripped one end of it. Byron picked up the other.

Many of the buildings along the street had toppled in antiquity, or were slowly crumbling away. But one midway down looked promising. "This way!" she urged her friends. The trailing citizens had been leery for a while, keeping their distance, but now they gained momentum as more joined their ranks. A murmur spread through them.

Above, one of the floating signs glided past: *Give a heart. Get a meal.*

H124 stopped in front of the edifice. Empty now, it had lost its front door long ago. Inside, she could see steps leading up. "In here!"

She and Byron fed the awkwardly long pipe through the door. She hurried up the stairs, Byron in tow. Outside, the people hesitated in the street, not following them in. H124 kept climbing until they were on the fourth floor.

She left the staircase and chose a room on the side facing the shield. People had been sleeping here. Dirty makeshift beds covered the floor. Her stomach lurched at the sight of some rotten meat in one corner, the putrefied remains of a human leg, partially hidden under a tattered blanket. A knife stuck out of it. Dirk hurried over, pulling out the blade.

"That's disgusting," Astoria told him.

"You'd rather we had no weapons?"

"Point taken."

The amber light of the shield glowed through a shattered window. "Help me feed the pipe through to the shield," H124 told Byron. She set her end of the pipe down on the windowsill, and she and Byron pushed it out until it touched the top of the retaining wall.

Below, she heard the unmistakable sound of the amassing mob entering the building. "Don't let them get out!" she heard the original woman cry.

She wondered why they didn't want to leave with them, why they hadn't started scrambling to do just that as soon as the hole in the shield had become obvious.

But she knew if they were like her, they'd been fed lies about the outside world, that no one could possibly survive out there. Here, though it was deplorable, it was a familiar mode of living. And even though they were all slowly dying of starvation, it was a hell they knew. Better that than the unknown.

With the pipe in place, all they had to do was cross it to freedom.

They could hear the mob ascending the stairs, voices clamoring.

"You first," Astoria told Dirk.

He reluctantly moved to the window. "This looks precarious."

"Just climb across the damn thing," Astoria cursed.

And so he did, climbing out the window and balancing on a small ledge, until he grabbed on to the pipe. He hung from it, crossing hand over hand. As he moved, the pole rolled erratically, threatening to come off the top of the wall. Byron and H124 held it as steady as they could, and Dirk just barely made it to the other side.

After hauling himself up, he knelt atop the wall, holding the pole steady. "You next," H124 said to Astoria.

Astoria needed no convincing. She ventured out the window and onto the pipe, swinging over to her brother.

"Now you," Byron said. H124 stepped over the sill just as the mob reached the door. Dozens of eager, dirty faces pushed into the room. "Go!" Byron held his end steady while H124 swung across. She looked down to see that dozens more denizens had gathered in the street below.

"Up there!" one of them shouted, pointing at her. She glanced back as she reached the wall, the room now swarming with hungry people. Dirk grabbed her hand and pulled her up onto the wall.

"Hurry!" he shouted to Byron.

The crowd surged forward, snatching at Byron. He punched a man, then flung a woman's arm away as she grabbed on to his jacket. He dove out the window, taking hold of the pipe. Swinging onward, he reached the halfway point as the mob grabbed the far end of the pipe. Picking it up, they rolled it back and forth, causing Byron to swing wildly. He tried to keep moving, but couldn't get a good hold. Beneath him, the masses swarmed, waiting for him to fall.

Dirk held fast to his end of the pipe, but the swelling mob in the room suddenly shoved the other end off the windowsill. That end came crashing down to the street below. Dirk still held the far end, and H124 seized it too.

Byron dangled just a few feet above the crowd, who leapt up, trying to grasp his feet. He climbed the pipe, hands sliding off with every new grip; it was too wide to get a good one. He pressed his feet together on either side of the pipe, and inched upward.

The crowd grabbed the pipe, trying to shake Byron off. En masse they were too strong, and H124 could barely hold on. Dirk reached down and grabbed Byron's hand. As he pulled him up, H124 and Astoria grabbed the pipe and wrenched it away from the crowd. They hefted the tube up and shoved it through the hole in the shield wall, creating a way down on the other side.

Astoria was the first down. She lowered herself over the edge of the wall, gripped the pipe and slid down, landing upright.

Dirk motioned for H124 to go next, and she followed Astoria's example, landing in a squishy field of fecal matter and urine, the rivers of waste that oozed out of Delta City on all sides. Mercifully, she remained standing.

Dirk slid down next, followed by Byron.

They were safe. They bent over, catching their breath. H124 looked back to the top of the shield. Moments later it buzzed, and the hole sealed. They'd made it. She looked to the others. Dirk lifted his dreads off his forehead, wiping away the sweat with his sleeve.

Now they were outside, ragged and worn, with no PRDs or any way to contact the Rovers or Badlanders for a lift.

"What now?" Astoria said.

"There's a weather shelter about a day's walk from here, I think," Byron suggested.

"You think?" Astoria cocked an eyebrow.

"I'm pretty certain."

Dirk stared into the darkness. "In which direction?"

Byron scanned the horizon. "I think there's a unique-looking hill . . ." Finally he turned back to them. "It's too dark."

"You're saying we have to spend the night out here in this reeking mess?" He grinned sheepishly.

"Let's find some high ground," H124 suggested, pointing to a nearby rise. "And get away from the wall. Find some cover. We can catch some sleep and start out in the morning."

"Sleep?" Astoria said. "The inside of my nose is already seared from this stench. I don't even want to think about what it'll do to my lungs if we spend the night out here."

"You'll just have to be tough for a change," Dirk said, already flinching in preparation for the punch that landed on his arm. "Ow."

H124 led the way to the rise, covering about two miles. They crested the hillock, moving mercifully out of the thick sludge. She hunted around for some decent cover. But out here, with no trees or shrubs, it was a challenge. Then she found a place on the hill where a small landslide had broken free. An overhang remained where the dirt had slid down, and it was just big enough to shelter them beneath it. They scraped their boots off as best as they could, then laid their jackets down under the overhang.

"I'm exhausted," Dirk said as he slumped down. "Don't remember ever being this tired."

H124 lay down near him, staring out at the sky. They couldn't see any stars here. The light pollution from the dome obliterated them.

They settled into silence, and soon she heard the soft breathing of her comrades around her. It lulled her to sleep.

* * * *

H124 woke up as someone moved past. She propped herself up on one elbow, watching Byron crawl out from the overhang. For a moment, he was silhouetted against a dazzlingly blue sky. She squinted, and the glare made her tear. The sun had been up for a while.

She joined him on top of the hill, followed by a groggy Dirk. Astoria trudged up with them, still trying to scrape off her boots. Byron brought a hand up to shield himself from the glare. Sweat poured off his neck and face. It had to be a hundred and five out here in the open, maybe more. He studied the landforms around them, finally pointing to a hill with a notch in it. "There it is! The landmark. The weather shelter's roughly that way." He pointed southwest.

"Roughly," Astoria repeated, the derision dripping from her voice.

Heat waves shimmered off the ground, and the air was so hot it hurt to breathe. The acrid stench of excrement stung her nostrils.

"Let's try it," Astoria said, "if only to get out of this reeking hell hole."

H124 walked ahead of the others. As they came off the hill, her boots squished and slid in the brown rivers.

After walking in silence for a while, Byron moved alongside Dirk. "What did they do to you back in the cells?"

H124 looked over her shoulder, slowing.

Dirk closed his eyes and swallowed. "They wanted to know Badlander movements. Camp locations. Where we hide the Silver Beast. I told them I didn't know."

Astoria chimed in. "Those bastards. They threatened to kill Dirk if I didn't tell them. But I kept my mouth shut."

"Thanks for having my back, sis."

She smirked. "Figured torture would give you some backbone."

Dirk swept his arms wide. "Meet Astoria, ladies and gentlemen, the sister we all wish we had."

"Big sister," Astoria added.

"Only by two minutes," Dirk put in.

They walked on, resuming the silence. A mile out, H124 spied a vehicle shimmering in the heat. "Look!" She picked up her pace, but realized she was only kicking the stinking mess around even more, so she slowed down once again.

She hoped it was Chadwick and the Beast, but the shimmering heat toyed with her, making the vehicle appear and disappear. She started to worry it wasn't even real. Then it came solidly into view. Her heart sank. It was an old Badlander methane bottling truck. The engine and roof had been blown clean off. A skeleton sprawled across the driver's seat of the scorched interior.

When the others caught up, Astoria sighed. "Life doesn't last too long for a methane bottler."

"Must have set off a spark somehow," Dirk said, circling the truck. "It's a total loss. Looks like it happened years ago."

H124 stared down at the skeleton. To die out here alone, in this river of shit, was a terrible way to go.

They kept moving, no shade in sight, as the afternoon wore on. Finally they cleared the fecal river and moved along caked brown earth. H124 shuffled her feet, removing the last of the excrement.

"So gross," Dirk said, scraping the sides of his boots with the knife he'd found during their escape.

"That knife is too disgusting to use for anything. You going to cook with that later?" Astoria chided him.

"It's not so bad. I could sterilize it."

"No amount of sterilization will ever be enough." Astoria gave an involuntary shudder as Dirk wiped the blade off in the dirt, then pocketed it.

The terrain grew a little more hilly, and each time they crested a rise, H124's body cried out for water. The heat was intolerable.

The hills grew steeper, with stands of dead trees stark against the blue sky. A fire had swept through here long ago, leaving only dead trunks. The black soot still showed in many places, while others were white and sun-bleached. A few times they rested in the meager shade of the thin trees. These weren't even big enough to guard their entire bodies, so instead they stuck their heads in the dark, cooler shadows from time to time before pressing on.

Cresting the largest hill, they came to a sudden stop. Fear flooded through H124. At the bottom, just a dozen yards away, stood four Death Riders. They'd parked their jeep by a fire, and were cooking some kind of unidentifiable white meat on a spit.

They looked up, and spotted them instantly.

Whipping their rifles up, the Death Riders trained them on H124 and the others. Two jumped into the jeep and raced away, spraying up dirt. A third talked eagerly into his PRD.

From nearby she heard multiple engines roar to life and accelerate. Rising to the surrounding hilltops, the clamor of machines deafening, the Death Riders streamed toward them.

In minutes they were completely ringed in. Death Riders stood in the beds of trucks, fifty-caliber guns locked and loaded. One climbed down from the cab of the largest truck, and strutted over. He wore the top halves of human skulls as spaulders on his shoulders, and a vicious scar ran down his face. The wound had taken his left eye, leaving a puckered hole.

Her eyes were drawn to an unusual pattern on the side of his jacket, which was made out of a strange leathery material, tanned and stretched. The intricate pattern had been drawn laboriously in ink, featuring some kind of mythical creature with wings and claws, spirals of fire shooting out of its mouth. It looked like something a Badlander would have tattooed on his body. She sucked in a breath, gazing around, realizing what the jacket was made out of. And all of the Death Riders wore that same material.

"Looks like we found this afternoon's entertainment!" the man shouted.

Around them, the Death Riders started pounding on the doors of their cars in unison, a thundering chorus of fists on metal.

"Round 'em up!"

A team of Death Riders emerged from the back of a truck, carrying hefty chains. They surrounded H124 and her friends. Astoria lashed out, grabbing Dirk's knife from his pocket and darting into the throng. Blood splattered as the dirty blade struck home, felling one of the men. The Death Riders poured forth, falling on H124, Byron, and Dirk and bringing them hard to the ground. H124 fought back, but manacles snapped around her hands and ankles, and the weight held her limbs down. Death Riders swarmed over them, the reek of their bodies bringing the sharp odors of sweat and caked blood. She recalled the citizens in the transport, grabbing, kicking, shouting. She felt just as helpless now as she did then.

Then the Death Riders dragged her to her feet, forcing her toward one of the trucks, where they clipped the chain onto the bumper. Next to her, they attached Dirk and Byron, still struggling in their bonds. They seized Astoria's knife, five of them sitting on her while they wrapped her entire body in chains. "Can't wait to see this one fight," one of them growled, and she spat in his face.

He laughed, then slung her up into the bed of a truck.

The lead Death Rider climbed back into his vehicle and gave a sharp whistle. The caravan lurched forward, taking up the slack on H124's chain. She stumbled as it yanked her forward. Pulling against his bonds, Byron tried to free himself, but he, too, lurched forward, marching along behind the trucks.

Dirk gazed wide-eyed at the jeering, bloodthirsty Death Riders.

H124 didn't know where they were taking them, but a cold fear washed over her as she lumbered on, captive once more.

Chapter 15

After half an hour of being dragged behind the caravan, H124's arms and legs ached. Dust from the trucks billowed around her in a thick cloud, making breathing impossible. She coughed and spat out dirt. Her body ached for water. Beside her Byron struggled with his manacles, trying to slip out of them. Dirk only stared out silently; she worried he was in shock.

In the bed of the truck, Astoria rattled her chains, cursing and threatening the Death Riders. They only laughed.

The trucks slowed, and the one she was chained to came to a halt. Then it revved its engine, winding through a series of silver spikes sticking out of the ground. It lunged forward suddenly, and H124 was yanked off her feet. Seeing the spike looming up before her, she tried to roll, but it struck her arm. She heard a sickening snap, and an intense pain shot up her arm. The truck started dragging her, but all she could do was cry out, rolling onto her back to cradle her arm. Still the manacles pulled at her, sending rivulets of agony up her shoulder.

Byron rushed over to her from the neighboring truck, his chains barely allowing him the reach. He reached down and lifted her to her feet. Blood streamed down her arm where the spike had bitten through it, and she could feel the bones grinding together inside. It was broken. She gritted her teeth as Byron helped her keep her balance, tears cascading down her cheeks.

They wound through more spikes, Byron helping her stay upright. Ahead lay a large circular structure, and the trucks pulled up to it. At least a hundred vehicles were parked there already.

Unhooking them from the bumpers, the Death Riders forced H124 and the others to march toward the wall of the huge circle. They opened a door of iron bars, shoving them through. Beyond lay a cement hallway, dark and reeking of the coppery scent of fresh blood. As a rough hand slammed onto her back, she stumbled against the wall, steadying herself with her shoulder. Behind her, two men dragged Astoria in chains. She kicked and writhed on the dirty floor as she slid along.

"Get her out of those chains!" Dirk shouted at them. He bent to help her, trying to lift her, but one of the Death Riders kicked him in the back, spending him toppling on top of his sister.

They drove them forward, paying them no heed. At the end of the tunnel, H124 saw an open steel door that led to a large cage. They passed through the open ingress. The cage looked out over an expansive view of an arena beyond.

The Death Riders shoved them against the bars, then retreated down the hallway, slamming the door shut behind them. They were trapped now. H124 reached out with her mind, searching for a TWR that might be controlling something in the gate. She found nothing, so she reached out farther, again coming up empty. It didn't surprise her. From everything she'd learned since she left New Atlantic, things like theta wave receivers were city-tech. Out here things tended to be analog, slapped together from old parts.

Through a tiny hole in the door, the Death Riders threw down something metal.

Byron grabbed it. "It's a key."

He knelt before Astoria and unchained her, then unlocked all of their manacles. When he got to H124, he moved very gently. She cradled her broken arm, the intensity of the pain unrelenting.

She peered out through the bars at the chaos beyond. The great circle was full of Death Riders, hundreds of them, all standing and chanting from seats that enclosed a central field. She could feel feet stomping in rhythm above her, knowing that even more Death Riders jeered and shouted from the seats directly above their cage as well.

She turned to absorb her surroundings. Others huddled in the cage, taken from other places. They looked at the newcomers with frightened eyes, some trembling in the corners, others wounded and shaking. "What is this place?" she asked.

Astoria stood up, gripping the bars. "It's a fighting arena." She gritted her teeth, rattling the bars.

The circular structure looked ancient. Parts of the opposite wall had fallen and been rebuilt, and the seats there were pulled out. A high wall surrounded the field, and faint traces of old signs were still visible in some places, though some of the letters had worn away: *Edwa— J— nes* and *Pep— Col—*

The crowd roared and cheered. She had no idea there were this many Death Riders. Given the number of people in the cage with them, she got the impression this was a special event, something they'd gathered for.

A man in the corner wept, cradling his small daughter, whose wide eyes stared out in shock. A giant man in one corner met her gaze.

"How long have you been here?" she asked him.

"A week." His body was a patchwork of fresh bruises and cuts.

"What's your name?" Dirk asked him.

"Gil."

"Looks like you've been put through the wringer," Dirk said, and Gil just nodded grimly.

Next to him stood a cement trough full of water. H124 hurried to it, peering into the liquid. Thick, furry green algae clung to the bottom and sides of the container, but she was so thirsty, she didn't care. She bent her mouth to the surface and drank deeply. The others did the same.

In the far wall of the arena, a great metal door rolled open, revealing an equally gigantic hole. A group of Death Riders wheeled out a strange contraption. It was an enormous see-through box, easily fifty feet wide and a hundred feet long. Interior walls had been built inside, a transparent maze winding this way and that.

"The labyrinth!" whimpered the crying man, a huge sob wracking his chest. He ushered his daughter to the very back of the cage, by the steel door.

"What the hell's the *labyrinth?*" asked Astoria, but the man just sniveled and turned his back to them all.

They positioned the maze in the center of the arena. A single hatch stood open on the transparent ceiling, and at the far end a metal square had been mounted on a wall. Some sort of tech.

Two Death Riders marched toward the cage, as the others retreated back into the wall. One held a flat panel.

The other prisoners shrank back, and H124 gripped her wounded arm.

The cage door rattled upward. The captors scanned their prisoners, eyes glimmering with cruel intent. Hunkered back against the walls of the cage, the captives turned their faces away. One of the Death Riders wore a human skullcap on his head. He swept his pointing finger, and settled on Gil toward the back. Though his burly frame towered over the others, Gil's body shook like a feather. "You," the Death Rider said. Gil gazed at the others, pleading with his eyes, but several of his fellow prisoners shoved him forward, turning against him and urging him on.

The next Death Rider stepped up, a necklace of human canines around his neck. His eyes gleamed as he surveyed the huddled prisoners. He saw the man cowering at the back with his daughter. Though the whimpering man had his back turned, he seemed to sense that the Death Rider had locked on him. "No," he whispered fervently. "Please no."

"You!" Canines boomed.

The man looked over his shoulder, tears flowing. "But my daughter!"

"You!" he boomed again.

The other prisoners surged forward, grabbing the man by his arms. They wrenched him away from his daughter, who could only stare ahead vacantly.

"Wait!" Dirk said, but Canines just shoved him back and seized the crying man as he reached the front of the cage. He tossed him out onto the field. When the man tried to run back to his daughter, Canines sent him sprawling backward. He landed in a sagging heap, wailing bitterly.

Skullcap scanned the rest of the prisoners. H124 felt a chill as his gaze settled on her. "And you!"

Byron got to his feet. "No! She's wounded. She can't go out there."

Skullcap didn't even acknowledge him. The prisoners rushed toward her, hands shoving at her back and jostling her arm. She cried out, trying to resist the press of desperate hands at her back. It was everyone for himself in this caged, desperate place.

Byron tore as many of the terrified captives off her as he could, beating them back. But before she knew it, they had shoved her through the open gate, and the bars started lowering behind her. She blinked in the glaring sunlight, heart hammering, arm screaming in pain.

Then suddenly Byron was beside her. He picked her up and threw her back inside the cage just before the bars slammed shut.

She struggled to her feet. "Byron! What are you doing?"

He gripped the bars. "You're wounded. You can't fight right now. It's a death sentence."

"Going out there is always a death sentence," a thin woman said, moving to the back of the cage.

H124 gripped the iron with her good hand, and he closed his fingers around hers. His green eyes met hers, and she felt something pass between them. "Byron," she whispered, scared but determined.

Skullcap seized him by the arm, and dragged him over to the others.

Canines held out the flat panel, and snatched Gil's wrist. The Death Rider slapped Gil's palm against it, and a light flashed on its surface, scanning him. Then he held the panel up to the trembling man's eye, and another light streaked out. He shoved Gil toward the labyrinth.

Next they scanned Byron, who stood there defiantly. Then the Death Riders forced the whimpering man to get to his feet for scanning.

"What is the purpose of this?" asked Astoria.

No one answered her.

"Hey!" she yelled. "What the hell is the goal of this game?"

People averted their eyes, so she stormed through the cage, grabbing the woman who had called it the labyrinth. She wrenched the feeble woman up on her feet, ripping her ragged shirt. "What the hell is he supposed to do out there?"

The woman licked her lips nervously, then said, "It's a maze. Fills up with water. To get out you have to retrieve the hand and eye of one of your opponents and show them to the biometric scanner. There are eyeball extractors and appendage slicers all through the maze. You can't use your own hands or eyes. If you manage to hunt down your opponents before the space fills with water, you can scan their body parts, and a hatch opens on top. If you lose and try to climb out, the executioners will kill you."

H124 saw the nasty jaws of the appendage slicers at intervals throughout the maze, as well as rusted claws designed to tear out eyes. The scanner was on one end of the maze, and the hatch at the start. So even if Byron managed to unlock the hatch, he'd still have to navigate back the entire length of the maze before he drowned.

"And if you win?" Astoria asked.

"You get sent back to the cage. But if you don't win, they kill your companions, too." She shifted nervously. "It's not quick either. On the last day of the festival, they torture people. Set them up on these platforms where people can watch and participate . . ." She sniffed and turned away, wiping an eye.

"They call this fucking thing a *festival?*" Astoria roared. She shoved the woman away. "We're in a fucking kill box. We need to get out of here now." She started checking the perimeter, testing the walls and the steel door.

The feeble woman said, "Don't you think we would have escaped if we could?"

Astoria spun on her, her eyes two smoldering pits. "You shut up."

Dirk moved to the back of the cage, where the little girl stood staring out. He knelt beside her. "You doing okay, kid?"

She made no reply H124 got the sense her mind was far away, that she'd seen horrible things that had closed her off.

Out on the field, Skullcap and Canines were given axes by two Death Riders who disappeared back into the hole. They forced the three men up a steel ladder, shoved them through the top hatch, and slammed it shut.

The glass maze started flooding. The terror-stricken man sped away from the other two.

She watched Byron slosh through ankle-deep water in pursuit, while burly Gil appeared frozen on the spot.

"Why isn't he moving?" Dirk asked.

An old man wearing a tattered sack spoke up, his voice cracked from a dry throat. "He's been picked too many times. I think he's just ready for it to be over."

"You mean he's just going to stand there and die?" H124 asked.

The old man nodded.

The water was streaming around Byron's calves now. He chased the skinny man through twists and turns, hitting dead ends a few times.

Before long Byron was waist-deep in water. He slogged through, struggling to make headway. The little man dove underwater and started swimming. When the water reached his chest, Byron did the same.

H124 held her breath as the water seeped around Byron's neck. He took a deep breath and dove to the bottom, lying in wait. Moments later, the skinny man swam overhead, and Byron shot up from beneath, grabbing him. The man thrashed as Byron dragged him through the water. His mouth opened in a scream, bubbles streaming out as Byron approached one of the appendage slicers. But Byron passed it, instead dragging the thrashing man to the end of the maze, where he pressed the man's face against the scanner, then his palm. The hatch at the beginning clanked open, but he still had to make it all the way back.

The last bit of air disappeared inside the maze. The little man thrashed and panicked, so Byron grabbed his arm, dragging him back to the start. Halfway there, the man convulsed and went limp.

The hulking man still floated by the hatch, making no attempt to climb out. The executioners waited with eager faces, fingers flexing on their axes. H124 could see Byron struggling, panicking the last of his breath away. He swam up to the top in case any air remained, but found nothing, so he pushed off the corners of the maze to propel himself forward.

At last he reached the hatch. His head burst through, gasping for air. H124 took a breath no less relieving. Then, to her astonishment, he dove back down, grabbing the little man and tossing him out through the hatch. He grabbed Gil next, jerking him toward his salvation. The man resisted, sinking back into the tank. Byron pointed at the hatchway, but the man shook his head.

Byron's head breached the surface for a second time. The thin man lay on its roof, coughing violently. Byron heaved himself up through the opening, and stood on top of the cage.

Launching himself off the tank, Byron handed hard on Skullcap, sending him sprawling back into the dust. Byron landed a solid punch to the Death Rider's throat. The executioner sputtered and coughed, wriggling away from Byron on his back. Still gripping the axe with one hand, Skullcap grabbed his throat with the other, wheezing. Byron stomped down on his wrist, trapping it, then wrenched the axe free.

Canines ran around the side of the tank, closing in on Byron. The Badlander lifted the axe high and struck deep into Skullcap's throat. As Canines reached him, Byron spun, swinging the axe around. Their blades clashed and clanged. Canines shoved Byron back, and the latter's boots slid through the dirt.

Treading water inside the tank, Gil stuck his head out of the hatch. He pulled himself up, water streaming off his hulking frame.

As Byron struggled to gain some distance for another swing, Gil leapt off the tank and landed hard on Canine's back. Pressing him down with his boot, the giant grabbed the executioner's head and twisted it until his neck snapped.

The crowd roared to life. Everyone was standing, everyone chanting.

H124 thought they would have been furious watching their own get killed, but apparently they didn't care who died. As long as someone did.

Gil walked over to the whimpering man, both still dripping the water that would have been their death. Grabbing the coughing man under his arm, he helped him to his feet. The smaller man bent over, hands on his knees, retching water.

Three Death Riders emerged from the hole. Quickly Byron and Gil stood back to back, each gripping an axe. The Death Riders approached, grinning, drawing their flash bursters. They fired from a distance, hitting both men. Byron toppled over, teeth bared, body jittering. After tearing the axes out of their prone hands, they dragged Byron and Gil back to the cage. The shivering father needed no such coercion. He ran ahead of them, ready to enter as soon as the bars lifted.

He was the first through the gate, and made straight for his daughter. He hugged and kissed her, but all she had to greet him with was a blank, lifeless stare.

After tossing Byron and Gil on the ground, the Death Riders slammed the gate shut and stormed off. Byron struggled to roll over as the skinny man knelt beside him. "Thank you!" He grabbed Byron's hand. Uncomfortable, Byron pulled it away.

"Yes," Gil said, getting to his feet. "Thank you. You've consigned us to another day of hell."

"Were you really just going to stand there and die?" H124 asked him.

"After a while here, that would be a blessing." He stumbled to the back of the cage, body shaking from the flash burster, and slumped down on the ground.

"Then why did you help?" Byron asked.

"Because it felt good to kill one of those fuckers."

Another group of Death Riders appeared from a hole in the wall. They dragged off the executioners' facedown bodies, treating the corpses like shanks of dead meat. Near the far wall, they heaved them into a makeshift pile. Then they hit a release on the tank, and water flooded onto the field, draining in a hissing outpour.

Soon they dragged away the labyrinth, and the hole sealed shut again. Moments later it reopened, and three Death Riders stomped out, beelining for the cage. One, a tall woman with blonde dreadlocks and black triangle tattoos on her ivory face, wore a breastplate of human ribs, still crusted with dried meat. The other two were men, one boasting a shaved head and a mahogany face tattooed in the form of a skull, and the other gangly and manic, his greasy brown hair hanging halfway down his back, his tanned face riddled with scars, one of them having split his lip just under his nose to reveal his gums.

They threw their fists in the air as the crowd cheered and roared. Then they vanished back into the hole, only to emerge moments later driving massive trucks. They rumbled over the field with tires so huge they had mounted ladders on the vehicles to reach the driver's seats. Gleaming nozzles were mounted on the grills, with hoses winding back into the trucks. They swung the giant nozzles back and forth as the crowd raved.

"Oh, god, no," a man whispered, moving to the back of the cage.

After driving in chaotic patterns around the field, the three Death Riders dismounted and marched toward the cage.

Breastplate took first pick as the bars swung open. Eyeing them all with cruel, beady eyes, she spotted Astoria. "You."

"The hell I will!" shouted Astoria, only to have the panicked prisoners push her out. H124 grabbed Astoria's arm, shoving the desperate people away.

"Astoria!" Dirk yelled, punching one of the attackers in the face. The man crumpled to the ground. Another kicked Dirk in the stomach, sending him crashing back against the wall.

"Leave her alone, you selfish bastards!" H124 shouted, striking a woman under her chin. But there were too many. They shoved Astoria out the cage door, sending her tumbling onto the field.

Next Skull Face and Greasy Mop chose two men and a woman who had been huddled near the back, quiet and unassuming until now.

"No!" the woman wailed, as her fellow prisoners seized her with rough hands and shoved her through the door. "Please, no! I have two children!"

One of the prisoners repelled her as she tried to reenter the cage. "I don't care if you gave birth to a whole litter. Better you than me." He kicked her in the gut.

Bucking their feet, the two chosen men fought as they were dragged after her and thrown down on the field. The cage slammed shut.

"What should we do?" Dirk cried. "Byron! Get the hell up!"

Byron groaned on the ground, still suffering from the flash burster. He labored to sit up.

Dirk turned to the feeble woman. "What are they going to make her do?" he demanded, grabbing her roughly by the shoulder. She merely stared through the bars as they herded the others toward the center of the field.

"It's the Flesh Eater trial. Your friend won't make it."

"She's my sister!" he growled, sounding more like Astoria than H124 had ever heard him.

"Well, your sister's toast," the woman spat back. She shrugged him off and pressed herself into the corner, where she proceeded to rock back and forth.

Dirk ran up to the bars and rattled them. "This is bullshit, you fucking cowards! Caging us like this!"

The three Death Riders climbed back into their vehicles, and as the motors roared to life, everyone but Astoria took off for the far sides of the arena. She alone stood her ground, watching as the vehicles resumed their frenzied maneuvers, crisscrossing paths, engines revving.

The woman's truck raced dangerously close to Astoria, but she didn't even flinch.

"What is she doing?" Dirk asked. "Run!" he shouted at her.

Greasy Mop bore down on one of the men, but he darted aside at the last minute, narrowly avoiding being crushed against one of the walls. He made a break for it, pumping his legs, his face a silent scream. Just as H124 thought he was going to outmaneuver Greasy Mop, the Death Rider aimed one of the nozzles at the man. Liquid shot out, spraying the ground behind him. He screamed, trying to push himself faster. Then another stream shot out, bathing his back. The man shrieked and fell, the liquid eating through his clothes. H124 watched in horror as his skin started to bubble and burn. As his flesh dissolved, the man picked himself up and kept running, but Breastplate moved to intercept him, the giant tires of her truck spraying up dirt behind her.

She and Greasy Mop cornered him against the wall, and she aimed two of her nozzles at him. He tried to dart away, but an arc of fire shot out of her truck, instantly setting his clothes and hair aflame.

H124 watched helplessly as he dropped into the dirt, screaming and rolling, trying to put out the flames. Breastplate cut the flamethrower, and the man managed to extinguish the fire. He got up again, moving weakly now, but rather than finish him off, they grinned and turned away.

They want to make his suffering last, H124 realized, horrified. Who were these people, and how had their culture evolved? Why were they so evil? What was the point of it all?

At the far end of the arena, the other man and woman raced to the edge of the wall. He cupped his hands so she could step onto them, and she leapt for the top of the retaining wall. But even with his help, she was still coming at least fifteen feet short. They tried again and again, even as Skull Face bore down on them with his truck. A spray of acid blasted out of one of his guns, but they leapt aside just in time, and headed in opposite directions. All the while Astoria stood her ground in the center of the arena, refusing to run. H124 could feel the hatred wafting off her. Greasy Mop wheeled his truck around, heading straight for the stubborn gladiator.

Just as his bumper was about to touch her, Astoria dove to the side, rolling out of the way. He passed her and made a sharp U-turn, shooting up clumps of dirt behind him. He opened up the flamethrower nozzle on his truck and sprayed the area with fire. Astoria rolled again, keeping out of reach.

The injured man across the arena struggled toward the cage. He reached it and shook the bars. H124 reached out and touched his hand. "Help me," he begged. His skin bubbled and burned, a raw mess of blisters and burned flesh. "I'm sorry," she whispered. He kept rattling the bars, moving along the length of the door.

"Someone help me," he begged. "Please!"

Spotting him, Skull Face revved his engine and raced toward him. The wounded man sensed the danger and limped feebly away, but he was moving too slowly. Skull Face released another stream of acid, hitting the man full on his back and legs. The man screamed, tearing at what was left of his clothes, his skin simmering and bubbling. Skull Face still didn't finish the job. He only jumped up and down in the driver's seat, laughing in pure glee.

She'd seen the indifferent, mirthless expression of the Repurposers, seen the cold pleasure of the one in New Atlantic who had threatened to wipe her. But this was something different. She didn't know which was worse.

Skull Face wheeled his truck around, momentarily blocking their view of Astoria. He picked up speed, kicking back dirt in huge clods behind his tires. He tore up the field, bearing down on her. Astoria darted to the side, so he overshot her, then spun around and turned on his flamethrower. The fire missed her by inches.

"Oh, god," Dirk whispered next to H124, his hands clenched around the bars. She gripped his arm. He looked sick, trembling, a frightened animal.

Greasy Mop spun his vehicle around, and both Death Riders now homed in on Astoria. She stood motionless, feet planted firmly, watching them approach from either side. They careened toward her, both picking up speed, and for a second H124 thought they were going to hit one another, smashing Astoria between their grills. But at the last second, Greasy Mop weaved to the side, and Skull Face drove right over Astoria, who flung herself to the ground. After Skull Face roared over her, her body was gone.

H124's eyes swept the field, but she didn't see her.

Breastplate zeroed in on the man and woman, jetting out an arc of acid that splashed against the wall. Some of it bounced onto the woman, and the man tried to wipe it off with his ragged shirt as she screamed.

Then H124 spotted Astoria, crawling up the rear bumper of Skull Face's truck. She'd grabbed the underside as he passed over her. Pulling herself up the back of the vehicle, she gripped the roof rack, using the hoses strung along the acid and flamethrower tanks to steady herself. Skull Face spun the truck, heading for the man and woman, oblivious to his new passenger. He turned with such force that for a second Astoria's legs went flying, but she held fast. Then she was crawling forward again, toward the cab.

As Skull Face let loose a stream of flame at the helpless pair, Astoria reached the front of the vehicle. She gripped the top and swung her legs in through the open window, connecting with Skull Face's head. The truck veered wildly out of control, slowing, and for a moment H124 couldn't see Astoria. Then the passenger door opened, and Skull Face came tumbling out, lying still in the dirt.

Astoria backed up the truck, bumping over him, then drove forward and back again, grinding his body into a bloody mess on the field. When she was done she wheeled the vehicle around and raced toward Greasy Mop, who had just unleashed another wave of flame at the man and woman. The man's shirt caught fire, but he rolled in the dirt, managing to put it out. His friend grabbed his arms, yanked him to his feet, and together they ran.

Astoria pulled up on Greasy Mop's tail and let out a huge blast of fire. He tried to swerve away, but all he did was expose his open driver's window to the flame. He screamed, leaping from the truck's cab. He tried to roll on the ground, but she laid a continuous stream of fire on him. He became a running ball of flame, shrieking in agony. Then he fell over, and moved no more.

Breastplate swung her truck to face her target. Astoria accelerated, issuing another fire jet. Breastplate balked, trying to veer away at the last instant, and Astoria rammed her truck. The clash of colliding metal rang out over the field. Astoria aimed the acid nozzle at Breastplate's window. The woman cried out as Astoria released a voluminous stream, splashing over the truck and into the cab. Breastplate shrieked, trying to back away, but the acid ate through the windshield. H124 clenched her teeth as Breastplate readied her flamethrower. Astoria threw her truck into reverse, tearing away from the wreckage, bumpers grinding as they separated. But the flamethrower streaked along the side of Astoria's vehicle, followed by a blast of acid. It started eating through the passenger window.

Inside her truck, Breastplate cried out, ripping off her acid-covered clothes. She was too distracted to notice Astoria leaping from her driver's seat and running to Breastplate's door. She wrenched it open, grabbing Breastplate and dragging her from the truck. The woman landed in the dirt with an *oomph*. Astoria stomped down on the woman's throat with all her weight, and Breastplate went limp.

The hole in the wall opened, and two Death Riders emerged with machine guns. Spotting them, Astoria ran back to her truck. She opened up the flamethrowers on the pair, and they shrank back out of range. Her truck lurched forward as she bore down on them, but then a third Death Rider appeared, heaving a gun with a long barrel. He shot something at her through the window, and the truck slowed to a stop. Astoria slumped forward on the wheel.

Dirk gripped the bars. "No!"

The two Death Riders with machine guns jogged to the truck and pulled her out. They dragged her limp body over to the cage. Everyone backed up as the bars swung upward. H124 saw a strange dart sticking out of Astoria's arm. As they threw her inside, H124 realized Byron was standing next to her. "They tranqed her."

The Death Riders threw her down in a heap, then grabbed the man and woman off the field and threw them back inside along with the gravely burned and acid-scalded man. He didn't look like he'd live for much longer. The dead were dragged away and stacked unceremoniously on the pile by the hole.

H124 bent down next to Astoria, joined by the others. Her arm throbbed. How long would this go on? Until they were all dead? "How long does this 'festival' last?" she asked the feeble woman.

She met H124's gaze with dead eyes. "Until we're all dead."

They needed a plan. The only time they were out of the cage was on the battlefield, so that's when they had to make their move. But they were never out there all at once. She moved to the steel door, checking again for weaknesses, but found none. Then she moved to the cage bars, studying its mechanics.

As the vehicles were removed from the field, the crowd grew restless. Chanting filled the arena, as did the cacophony of hundreds of people stomping their boots. The whole place shook. H124 returned to her friends. Astoria was still out cold, but Byron was starting to feel better.

"We need to overpower the guards the next time they come to the cage," H124 whispered to her friends.

"What are you thinking?"

H124's thoughts were interrupted as the crowd grew louder. Something was stirring them up, and a thousand gleeful voices filled the air, as if the main event had just arrived.

Three new Death Riders emerged from the hole, stomping over to the holding cage. One held a long staff.

"Let's subdue them now," H124 whispered.

The bars lifted, and H124 rushed forward. Byron landed a solid punch to one of the Death Rider's guts, and H124 kneed him in the face as he bent over. The second Death Rider grabbed her, painfully wrenching her arm, and she cried out. Dirk rushed forward and body slammed him to the ground. As all three friends emerged onto the field, Dirk grabbed the staff, shoving it under the cage bars to keep it from lowering again. H124 heard the gears groaning as the gate controller tried to shut it. She glanced around for a way out of the arena, searching for a lower place in the wall, another door, anything. "We have to make it to the hole!" she shouted, pointing to the spot where the Death Riders had emerged.

But just as she said it, ten more poured out of the darkness there, each wielding a flash burster. As they closed in, sweeps of blue lightning shot out all around them. She felt one hit her just as she tried to dart away. She went down hard in the dirt, jittering. Her teeth clacked shut, and she bit her tongue.

Then rough hands dragged her away. Her body convulsed as she heard the bars slam shut again.

When she stopped shaking, she looked up to see that she was on the outside of the cage, lying next to Dirk.

"H!" Byron shouted. She propped herself up on her good elbow, trying to clear her head. Byron knelt on the other side of the bars, inside the cage.

Next to her stood a three-sided glass cage with interior handles. It was open in the back, about six feet tall and almost three wide. A silver ring was mounted in the top. It looked like she could stand inside the cage, using the handles to resituate it, a movable body shield of sorts.

She shook her head, and rose to her feet. She approached a groaning Dirk. Another moveable shield stood beside him. She helped him up, and scanned the arena. What were the shields for? They were alone on the field. The Death Riders had retreated back into the hole. Then the metal door rolled to the side, and she saw something stirring in the darkness beyond.

"Oh, no," Dirk said, staring into the shadows. Something crawled into view on all fours, a mottled grey-and-black thing with a tapered skull and long, muscular forelimbs that ended in curved claws. Green, beady eyes blinked in the sunlight. It hissed through its jagged teeth, and looked around with narrowed eyes. She'd never seen one before in the light, but already she knew what it was. A night stalker.

She marveled as it crawled out, its hind feet flexible and articulate, practically a second set of hands. It slunk forward in long, lanky strides, keeping low to the ground, rear legs bent back, eyes continuously sweeping the terrain.

"No one's lived through this," the feeble woman whispered through the bars.

H124 rocked back on her heels, as more movement in the hole caught her eye. Another night stalker emerged, hissing at the bright light as it moved alongside its companion. Then a third leapt into sight, padding out of the hole much more quickly, racing toward the far end of the arena only to find the wall there. It ran along the perimeter, clawing and leaping, looking for a way out. Its speed and nimbleness staggered her every time it leapt up at the wall, muscles rippling. Though the wall was more than twenty-five feet high, it almost made it to the top a few times, its claws falling just shy of the upper edge.

H124 darted inside her shield and lifted it up, moving it clumsily with one arm. The thing weighed a ton. She barely managed to half-lift, half-drag it over to the wall. She braced her back there, and pulled the shield in tight. The panicked night stalker raced right by, still leaping and testing the walls.

To her left, Dirk tucked into his shield and carried it over to the wall, following her lead. But she knew that if the night stalkers wanted to, they could pry their claws in along the edges, and tear the shields loose.

The creatures stalked around the field, studying Dirk and H124. He lifted his shield and slid along the wall until he came up flush with her.

Slowly the night stalkers approached them, their movements sinuous. She noticed that their ribs stood out prominently, their thin black, mottled skin stretching over the bones. They'd been starved.

The nearest pair leapt with sudden ferocity, slamming into the glass. The impact hurt her eardrums. Claws scrabbled against the cage surface, then searched for the seam where the shield met the wall.

The creatures ripped at the shield. One got its claws in under the edge while the other tried to dig under the bottom edge. H124's fingers found a button along the underside of one of the handles. She pressed it. A metal skirt extended from the base of the shield, punching into the ground. It struck the digging night stalker in the head. The creature jerked away, shaking its skull.

But the stall wouldn't last long. The shields were meant to delay the carnage, not prevent it.

As the night stalker began to pry the shield away from the wall, H124 noticed a button on the other handle. She pressed it, hearing a solid click as the shield suddenly moved backward, adhering to the wall. The night stalker howled as its fingers got pinched, and pulled free, growling. The metal wall cold at her back, she pressed the button again, and the shield released. Then she hit it again, and it stuck fast to the wall. The rim of the shield was filled with powerful electromagnets.

She looked over to Dirk, noting that he'd found the same buttons.

"What do we do now?" he shouted through the glass. She could barely hear him. The night stalkers paced before them. The panicked one gave up its perimeter check and joined its pack. It lunged forward, scrabbling at the edge of her shield, but the cage remained locked fast to the wall. Just when it seemed they were at an impasse, the arena door rolled to the side again, revealing the hole.

H124 braced herself, expecting to see more night stalkers burst out. But instead she saw a gleam in the shadows. The spiked leg of a machine stepped out, flashing in the sun; then another leg, and another. She counted six legs in total as it strode into view like some giant insect. Unlike the vehicles, this one was not driven by a Death Rider. It had no cab or cockpit.

Two shorter appendages were mounted at the fore, each sporting a vicious pincer. It motored forward, gears humming, easily twenty feet tall, its robotic eyes fixed on them.

"I don't think the night stalkers can tear us free," Dirk shouted. "But I'll bet that thing can."

The big insect trundled toward them, its every leg piercing the ground as it went. The night stalkers scuttled toward it, leaping up eagerly, winding about its feet. They didn't try to attack it; they merely cavorted around its legs, jaws open, teeth bared. They knew it had fed them before.

The monstrous insect homed in on H124. One of its pincers lowered onto her cage, gripping the silver ring. She felt the magnetic hold weaken. The protective cage flew out of her hands, landing in the dirt ten feet away.

The night stalkers let out an eerie, keening wail as they sped toward her. She leapt to the side, grabbing the cage with her good arm and rolling it over on top of herself. But it was open at her feet, and she screamed as a pair of jaws closed down on her boot and started to drag her out.

She craned her neck, trying to catch a glimpse, kicking her foot at the beast. She connected with its face, but it quickly clamped back down on her boot.

Dirk pulled away from the wall, and ran toward them with a battle cry. Diving through the air inside his cage, he landed hard on the night stalker who had her foot. It snarled and took off.

Now they both lay under their shields. The night stalkers would soon pounce again. H124 and Dirk struggled to their feet and ran back to the wall. They reengaged the electromagnets, and dug into the ground.

This time the machine closed in on Dirk, gears whirring. The pincer came down, locking onto his cage and wrenching it away from the wall.

It landed a few feet away, sending a plume of dirt billowing upward. Dirk dove for it as all three night stalkers came after him. He managed to right it and get inside, but his back was exposed. As they started to circle him he pivoted, keeping his back safe, but H124 knew he didn't have much time.

One of them leapt, landing on top of the shield. Dirk staggered under the weight, and the shield toppled, trapping him beneath. They prowled around his exposed feet, so he kicked at them. Managing to stand once more, he kept pivoting, moving closer to the lumbering mechanical insect.

He edged backward, keeping the shield between him and the night stalkers and his back to the machine. When he got within a couple feet of one of the legs, he pressed the button that extended the shield into the ground.

Then he spun inside the shield, and jumped onto the robot's leg. He climbed it, using toe and finger holds in the framework.

The machine spun, trying to throw him off, batting the shield to the ground. But Dirk continued to climb. The night stalkers howled and leaped, trying to reach him. One of them started to climb up, but Dirk kicked it in the head. He kept climbing, reaching the top of the insect.

H124 watched him tear into a control panel, removing a mess of wires, circuits, and control crystals. The insect thrashed and started to run, trying to buck him off, but Dirk planted his boots inside the framework and held tight, his fingers twisting wires and adjusting the crystals.

The night stalkers ran along the base of the robot, trying to jump onto it. It spun in circles, and for a moment all Dirk could do was hang on.

H124 remained pinned against the wall. The machine ran toward her now, as Dirk's fingers went back to work. It stretched out a pincer to grab her shield, but the claw stopped in midair. She heard it power down, and the whirring gears slow. Then it stopped altogether.

The night stalkers howled and leapt around its feet. Two of them grabbed on to its legs and started climbing again, eager to reach Dirk. Then the machine powered up once more. Dirk held a number of wires, and made them touch. The pincers swung around, plucking up the night stalkers and flinging them off.

"Ha!" Dirk yelled triumphantly. The third stalker darted away warily. Dirk wheeled the machine around, grabbing a predator in each pincer. He flung them high into the stands, and H124 heard Death Riders screaming as the creatures landed among them. He picked up the third and sent it sailing into the crowd as well. She watched it fall on a fleeing group, blood spraying up from its claws as it landed.

H124 disengaged the magnets and let the shield drop. She raced over to the cage as Dirk lowered the pincers to grip the bars. He tore the gate away. As prisoners streamed onto the field, Byron ran up to H124, wrapping his arms around her. "Are you okay?"

She grinned. "Let's get the hell out of here!"

They ran back in the cage and picked up Astoria, who was just coming to. "You should have seen your brother!" Byron told her. "What a badass!"

"Dirk? What, they hit you with a hallucinogen or something?" she mumbled.

They quickly made for the mechanical insect, and Byron helped H124 climb onto its back. Astoria soon joined them.

Dirk spun it around, making it face the wall. It climbed over the barricade, moving up through the stands. Death Riders scattered beneath its sharp, spiked legs.

The stands went up and up, but at last they crested them, climbing into the open. The open desert awaited them below. Dirk motored the creature over the edge. The drop-off was steep, so he gripped the edge of the arena, lowering the insect as far as he could down the wall. "Hold on!" He released the back legs, and they plunged downward, coming to a jarring landing below. H124 almost lost her grip, but Byron held on to her.

Behind her, she could still hear the screams of the Death Riders as the night stalkers tore through them. Again Byron pointed the way toward the weather shelter, and Dirk wasted no time crossing the terrain, speeding away from the arena. To her rear, she saw the sprawl of the Death Rider camp, banners flapping, more spiked skulls mounted along the perimeter.

They crested a dusty hill and passed down the other side, and the Death Rider camp fell out of view. As the wind streamed through her hair, H124 let out a nervous laugh. It was just her and her friends again, back on their mission.

Chapter 16

The heat was intolerable as it rose up from the brown, caked ground. Waves shimmered off the flat expanse of earth, miles of dead terrain stretching out in every direction. H124's legs were sore from her cramped spot atop the metal insect, and everyone had fallen into their own silent world.

They'd traveled through the night, not once daring to stop. Now the heat had returned with the sun.

Sometimes they passed through the remains of long dead settlements. She saw the ubiquitous red-winged horse buildings that seemed to be in so many of these old towns. They passed the remnants of endless multi-doored structures, some with signs that still faintly read *M-O-T-E-L*, but most had fallen symbols that had weathered away.

Her arm had swollen up, but they had nothing to treat it with. Nothing to even clean the wound. She tried to block out the pain. She had never been so thirsty. Her head was pounding, and her tongue felt too big for her mouth. Her mind drifted to Delta City and her meeting with Olivia. Was it all true?

"Hey Halo," Byron said, cutting into her thoughts. "You in a trance?"

She looked over at him, wondering how much she should say. She adjusted her position so that she could face him. "Back in Delta City, the PPC exec they took me to said some really intense things."

"Like what?"

H124 brought a hand to her forehead. She wasn't sure where to start.

"Was it that bad?"

She ran her hand down her face. "She told me she was my grandmother, and that Willoughby was my father."

"Willoughby? The PPC guy who helped us out?"

She nodded. "But she also said Willoughby killed my mother."

Byron started. "Wait—I thought you were a worker in New Atlantic. Did you even know your parents?"

She shook her head, bewildered. "No. The whole thing's crazy."

"Do you believe her?"

H124 looked off into the distance. Her gut didn't feel right about the woman. "No," she said at last. "I don't think I do."

"What are you going to do?"

"Talk to Willoughby when I get my head together, I guess."

As the power cells on the mechanical insect started to deplete, Astoria and her brother spoke quietly to one another, talking of the weather shelter. Byron and H124, meanwhile, watched the scenery roll by, speculating about the history behind the structures these long dead people had built.

They rode past a monstrous concrete sculpture depicting a four-legged animal she didn't recognize. Its once black-and-white coat was weathered off in most places, revealing a wire understructure. Horns sprouted from its head, a small tail from its back. It stared off toward the distant hills in the west.

"What in the world is that?" Byron mused.

She'd seen a lot of animals with horns in the field guides, but couldn't remember them all. Maybe the weather shelter would have more books on animals. She found herself excited at the thought of learning more. The world out here, though harsh and unforgiving, was also endlessly fascinating. She tried to picture what it must have been like for these people, living their lives out here, the land around them green and fertile, long before the intolerable heat, drought, and storms that could kill anyone who was exposed.

"Do you think they worshipped it?" Byron mused. "Is that why they built sculptures of it?" He cocked his head in thought.

The next town over, they passed another sculpture of the horned creature, this one even larger. It stood above a one-story building with huge fork and knife effigies standing sentinel before this forgotten place.

"Do you think it was a sacred eating place? A communal spot of some kind?" Byron's gaze lingered on the giant horned statue. "Maybe they gathered here to revere them."

"Any of this look familiar?" Dirk asked Byron. "We getting close to the shelter?"

Byron scanned the small, dilapidated town. "Think so. It's been a few years."

The heat had grown insufferable, the air barely breathable, and H124 found herself missing the bulky heat suits they'd used when they ventured to the radar facility. Byron pointed to a toppled structure on the western side of town. "See that? That building with the old marquee?"

H124 shielded her eyes from the sun, spotting a partially intact building ahead. It had a curved, elegant overhang out front. She could tell that it had once been a sign. Now only one letter still clung, a sideways J, held there by decades of windblown dirt.

"I remember that place. It's under that building."

Dirk steered them toward it, where they dismounted. They began searching through the rubble at once.

"Was it this rundown when you were here?" Astoria asked Byron.

"I don't think so."

Dirk lifted a piece of fallen metal. "When were you here?"

Byron rubbed the back of his neck. "It's been a while."

Astoria stopped digging through a pile of stones. She put her hands on her hips, and squinted in the heat. "How long ago?" she demanded.

Byron hesitated. "I may have been about seven at the time."

She threw her hands up into the air. "Oh, great! So it was here, give or take *twenty years ago!*"

H124 moved aside a flat, rusted piece of metal, revealing cement stairs. She spotted the familiar weather shelter icon, a blue emblem with a tornado and a figure running through a door to safety. "This is it!"

Together they cleared the debris on the staircase until there was enough room to descend. "I don't think anyone's been to this shelter in a while," Astoria said.

H124 had to agree. The ones she'd stayed in before, when she was seeking the Rovers, had been relatively clear to access. Given the amount of moss growing in the damp, shaded space of the stairwell, this building had toppled years ago.

At the bottom of the stairs, Byron entered a code, and the door slid open. They stepped into the confines of the shelter, and were instantly greeted by the smell of mildew. It was stiflingly hot inside, and the air hung heavy. Dirk switched on the climate control, and moments later a cool breeze blew in from the vents.

Instead of the usual stocked shelves, only a handful of MREs greeted them. The bookcase was completely empty, and the cots in the sleeping quarters had no blankets or pillows.

"They stopped maintaining this one," Dirk said, speaking of the Rovers.

"Probably because it's too close to that Death Rider camp," Astoria reasoned. She moved to the food shelf and pulled down a few remaining MREs. After sitting down at the dining table, she put her feet up on one of the chairs. Tearing open an MRE, she chewed it thoughtfully.

On the bottom shelf of the bookcase, H124 spied a lock box. It was the same kind in which she'd found the old PRDs that Raven had recorded his videos on. She pulled the box out, and found two older model PRDs inside. Neither held a charge.

She gathered them up and went outside to charge them in the sun. The heat socked her in the face.

She set the two PRDs down on the ground and sat beside them, wilting under the brutal sun. The devices were identical to the ones she'd first found. She remembered listening to Raven talk in the videos, her nights spent hiding in shelters and driving west, trying to find the elusive Rovers, unsure if they still existed. Raven's talks had become a comfort to her, and now she hoped with a feverish heart that he had made it away safely from Delta City with the piece of the spacecraft.

She then heard someone come up the stairs behind her. It was Byron. He knelt beside her. "How dead are those things?"

She looked at their power indicator lights. They weren't even glowing yet. "Pretty dead."

He touched her back lightly. "And your arm?"

She tucked a strand of hair behind her ear, and lifted up her arm. She was dreading it, but she'd have to set the bone and dress it. "Hurts pretty bad, to be honest."

"Well, you're in luck."

She looked up at him. "How so?"

"This old shelter has a medpod. It's a basic one, can't do heart surgery or anything like that, but it can definitely fix your arm."

She perked up, and sprang to her feet. "Take me to it!"

They returned to the shelter. Dirk and Astoria sat at the table, eating and talking. The medpod was in a corner of the sleeping area, sealed inside a closet flush with the wall. A small white cross on a red background was the only indication of its location.

Byron pressed the symbol, and the door slid open. The medpod emerged, a tall cylinder with a glass anterior. It eased out into the room, lowering flat. It was definitely older than the ones the Rovers used now, but it looked pristine all the same.

She lay down inside it, and the glass sealed over her. Closing her eyes as the scanner hummed over her body, she finally let her body relax. She'd been tensing every muscle for what felt like days, ready to fight at every turn.

Now she was safe, here with her friends, the medpod quietly humming around her. It zeroed in on her arm, and she felt the brief sting of a numbing agent pricking her vein.

Byron stood above her, watching with a warm smile.

She felt a jerk as the clamps straightened her bone. Then came a comforting heat, seeping into her upper arm as the bone was repaired.

She knew it would ache for a while as the final phase of convalescence took its course, but she was grateful for the speed of this method. When the medpod finished, the glass hissed open. Byron helped her out, then pressed the button so the pod could return to its cubby. She flexed her fingers. Only a thin red line where the spike had penetrated her arm marked the former wound.

She longed to sleep, but couldn't decide if it was food or sleep she desired more. Finally she ate an MRE, something that simulated a "broccoli and cheese pot pie." Then she used the dry disinfectant chamber. They drank what little water was still in the shower reservoir, not wanting to waste any on bathing. It looked like this place had been in a megadrought since time immemorial. Afterward, she lay her aching body down in the sleeping room. After the others had cleaned up, they too laid down, and turned off the lights.

She lay looking up at the ceiling in the darkened room, hearing the soft breathing of her friends in the neighboring bunks, punctuated by the occasional snort from Dirk.

She could feel Byron's presence in the adjacent bed, as if he were also awake. She remembered their first night together when she'd been captured by the Badlanders.

Turning her head, she tried to see if he was asleep, but the room was too dark, and all she could discern was his quiet breathing. They'd been through hell together. He'd taken her place in the arena. At first she'd thought him a brute, a danger, but she was coming to see him as something more.

She closed her eyes, and at last sleep found her.

* * * *

H124 awoke to soft voices coming from the other room. The sleeping room still lay in darkness. Stretching, she could hear that someone else still dozed in the room with her. She found her boots in the dark, and tiptoed to the door. When she opened it, light spilled in through the crack, and she turned to see Byron was sleeping on his side, hair spilling over the pillow.

She slipped out, quietly clicking the door closed. At the table sat Dirk and Astoria, moving thin paper objects around on the table.

She walked up to them, peering over Dirk's shoulder. The pieces of paper had symbols and numbers on them, and both twins held some in their hands, while the rest were spread on the table. "Do you have any sevens?" asked Dirk.

"Go fish," his sister told him.

"What's this?" H124 asked.

"Go Fish," Astoria said, as if it were obvious.

"I haven't asked you for another card yet," her brother said.

Astoria smirked. "I'm telling her what the game is."

"I mean," H124 said, reaching out to pick up one of the flat papers in the center of the table. It was firmer than she thought. "What are these?"

Astoria leaned back in her chair. "Oh, wow," she said, as if H124 were truly and woefully ignorant. "They're cards."

H124 turned it over in her hand. It was very thin yet sturdy, made from some kind of durable plastic-coated material. The back had an elaborate green and purple design. "They're beautiful."

Astoria rolled her eyes. "Oh, jeez. They're just cards."

"And you fish with them?" H124 asked, at which Dirk burst out laughing.

"Yup," he said, "just like my sister is about to do."

"You got any fives?"

"Nope. Go fish," he told her.

"Let me fish!" H124 said, and pulled a card out of the center pile without looking at it. She handed it to Astoria. "Is it a good one?"

Astoria tucked it into her hand. "What do you know. She fished my wish." Astoria laid down the rest of her cards. Dirk threw his remaining ones into the center pile. "You always win."

H124 moved to the disinfectant chamber, and cleaned her teeth.

Feeling refreshed, she went upstairs to the outside, instantly staggering in the heat wave. The two PRDs had charged in the morning sun; their power indicator lights now glowed green. She turned one on. On the videos section of the floating display, she saw copies of the talks Raven had made and distributed through the other weather shelters. Using the code that the Badlanders had developed, she used a scrambled channel to contact him.

He answered. "H!" he said, breathing a sigh of relief. "Are you out of Delta City?"

"Yes. We made it out."

"I've been worried. I expected to hear from you before now. Chadwick and I waited for hours, but a PPC airship started patrolling the area, and we had to get out of there. Are you all okay?"

"Yes. We had a bit of trouble on our way out."

"Where are you now?"

"At a weather shelter." She sent him the coordinates off the PRD. "What about you? Did you make it out with the spacecraft section?"

"I did, and I returned it to Sanctuary City. Rivet is starting to piece the sections together. It's a steep learning curve, and from what she's told me, we need a whole other separate craft and nuclear device to make this thing work."

"What do you mean?"

"We have to arm it with a nuclear payload, then find a way to launch it into space. The spacecraft itself is something that isn't capable of that. From the data disks we've been studying, they used these massive rockets to carry things like it into space."

"Do these rockets still exist?"

"We don't know. Onyx is still poring over the data you brought from the university in New Atlantic. A lot of it is corrupted, and we're still piecing things together as she repairs each new disk." He looked over her shoulder at the ruined cityscape. "How are the others?"

"A bit worse for wear, but in pretty good spirits."

"I can't tell you how relieved I am you're all okay. I felt terrible leaving you like that." He talked to someone offscreen, then returned to her. "Let me go talk to Gordon and get an ETA for when we can retrieve you."

She smiled. "Thanks."

The comm window flashed off.

She sat, watching how the heat waves distorted the buildings around her. Above, the sky was pale blue, not a single cloud in sight. Sweat beaded on her brow, but the heat felt good on her aching arm. She rubbed it, and flexed her elbow.

She wondered how Rowan was faring setting up the new Badlander camp. She felt distant from him after everything she'd just been through in Delta City and the Death Rider camp.

The image of Olivia's face flashed in her mind. Once again Willoughby had come through for her. She wanted to call him, to confront him with what Olivia had told her. Her whole life she'd thought she was raised solely in the child-rearing ward by caregivers, wondering who her parents were. Since she was a worker and not a citizen, that meant she'd never know.

At least citizens could see their parents' avatars and interact with them over the media streams. But workers had no such luxury. They weren't connected to the network, and their lives were structured solely around the tasks they were required to perform.

Part of her ached to think she had parents who cared about her. But to find out that she had a mother only to learn she'd died in a horrible way made her heart pang with a crushing loneliness. She lifted the PRD to call Willoughby, but hesitated.

Finally, she opened the comm window.

He answered with an affable grin. "You made it." The relief in his voice was thick.

"Thanks to you." She looked behind him. He was in his new office in Delta City, she guessed, replete with an elaborately painted vase on a shelf to his rear. "Are they on to you?"

"I don't think so. I replaced the media feeds I cut into with transmissions from BEC City. We've been receiving more and more of their broadcasts, so I think it went unnoticed."

She wrinkled her brow, unsure how to begin.

"What is it?"

She decided to just plunge in. "While I was in that exec's office, she told me some things."

Willoughby went pale. "What did she say?"

H124 swallowed. She had a racing heart, and a sudden lump in her throat. She longed to have a family, but if what that woman said was true, that Willoughby had murdered her mother, everything was about to change, and in a bad way. She decided to start with the easiest part. "That she was my grandmother."

He looked away, biting his lip. "I see."

"And that you . . . you are my father."

He let out a guttural sound, an outburst of air, and brought his hand to his face.

"Is it true?"

He remained still, hand pressed to his face, until he finally lowered it. "Yes. I should have told you sooner. But . . . I was worried what would happen if word got out . . . if Olivia knew you had survived. I wanted to tell you, just *you,* secretly, but by then it felt like I should have told you sooner, and . . ." He trailed off.

She swallowed again, ready to drop the bomb. "She said you killed my mother."

Willoughby gawked at her, mouth agape. "No! Absolutely not! I loved your mother. I helped her get out of here." He shook his head and took a deep breath. "Let me tell you what happened."

H124 looked over her shoulder at the weather shelter. Everyone was still inside, but she wanted privacy. Walking a block away, she sat down in the shade of a collapsed building and leaned back against the warm concrete. "Okay."

"I met your mother in Delta City. I was a junior exec there, just starting to make shows. Your mother, Juliet, was very high up in the PPC because of Olivia's status. We grew close." He met her gaze. "And we had you."

Unwelcome tears came to her eyes.

"But Olivia was cruel and controlling. She didn't want Juliet to be with me. As my shows grew more successful, New Atlantic started to woo me. They wanted me to move there. We saw it as the perfect chance to get away from Olivia. Juliet was a news gatherer, normally relegated to digging up gossip for the media streams. But she was onto a story. It was big, and involved the PPC.

"One night, she was supposed to meet with an informant. Juliet had forgotten her PRD at Olivia's office, so I went there after hours to retrieve it. I had you with me. Olivia's desk was locked, but I hacked it. And I found more than just Juliet's PRD. Inside a drawer was a handwritten obituary for Juliet, saying she'd died tragically in an autotransport crash, and that Olivia was taking consolation in raising you as her own after I had moved on to New Atlantic.

"I immediately called Juliet. She was waiting for the autotransport to arrive. I told her not to get inside, begged her to wait until we got there." Here he paused, blinking more rapidly. averting his watery eyes.

H124 waited as he gathered his thoughts.

"Back then the autotransports were known for being faulty, often delivering people to the wrong address. While they weren't known to malfunction and crash, I knew no one would think it was too odd if one did. Olivia's plan was a good one. I'm not proud of this, but I didn't know what else to do. I got two dead bodies from an alley, a woman and a baby. I met up with Juliet, and we stowed the bodies inside the transport. It wasn't a block away when it exploded, burning the bodies beyond recognition. I helped Juliet to the wall and got her out of Delta City using an outside contact we had. It was going to be a dangerous journey, so we decided that you should stay with me. I hid you. The next day, I was told of the terrible accident which claimed you and your mother. I played the bereaved husband, then left for New Atlantic as soon as I could, taking you with me.

"The story your mom was working on had something to do with Olivia arranging the street purges where people were rounded up and taken to the food processing centers. But she wasn't able to get the proof she needed before she left.

"In New Atlantic, I entered you into the worker program. It was the most anonymous thing I could do with you. I didn't want you to be a citizen, to be installed with a head jack, like a mindless sheep. But I couldn't keep you with me because Olivia would realize what we knew, and would come after both of us.

"People disappear all the time, after all . . . Repurposers come and . . ." He sighed. "I don't know if what I did was right by you. I kept an eye on you all these years. Wanted to make contact with you. When I saw it was you in the PPC tower lobby that night, I came down immediately."

H124 let his story sink in. "What about my mother?"

He exhaled. "I wish I knew. Our contact was supposed to keep her safe. But when I left for New Atlantic and stopped by his place . . ." His voice trailed off.

H124 waited.

Willoughby pressed on. "He'd been murdered. She wasn't there. May have been Death Riders passing through. He'd been burned alive."

"And you didn't find her?"

His weary gaze settled on his daughter. "No. I never did."

She exhaled. "So she could still be out there? Alive?"

He pressed his lips together grimly. "I don't think so, kid." He fell silent. "I'm sorry," he added at last.

She shook her head, trying to absorb it all. "Me too."

They sat quietly for a while, collecting their thoughts.

Finally he cleared his throat. "So what's the status of the quest?"

She took a deep breath, and wiped her eyes. "We have two pieces now. One more to go."

"That's great!"

"Do you think you'll be safe there now?"

He glanced over his shoulder at his office door. "I think so. For now."

"Thank you for telling me what happened. I'm . . ." She wanted to say that she was glad to know him, but she was overwhelmed at the thought of actually knowing her father, and words wouldn't come.

"Me too," he finished for her.

They said their goodbyes, and she shut down the comm window. She then trudged back through the heat to the weather shelter, where she took a seat at the top of the stairs. She wasn't ready to go back in there with the others.

Moments later the door opened, and Byron climbed up. He sat down next to her, observing her somber demeanor. "Did you talk to Willoughby?"

She nodded.

"What did he say?"

"It's true. Part of it, anyway. He's my father."

Byron raised his eyebrows. "Damn."

She laid her elbows on her knees, and her cheeks in her palms. "It doesn't feel real. I didn't think I'd ever know who my parents were."

"And the rest?"

"He said it was Olivia who arranged for my mother's murder. Her own daughter. Willoughby helped her escape, but he lost touch with her after."

"So she could still be out there somewhere?"

H124 looked at him. "Willoughby doesn't think so. He thinks she might have been killed." She saw Byron gazing out over the ruined city, eyes squinting in the glare. "What about your parents?" she asked. "Do you know them?"

The question caught him off guard. "Oh, uh . . . yeah. I knew them."

She noticed the past tense. "What were they like?"

A smile flickered on his face. "My mom was a total badass. Best fighter I've ever seen. I learned a lot from her." He gave a small chuckle. "My dad couldn't have been more different. He liked to illustrate stories. He had this crazy idea that he could depict the entire history of the Badlanders in a series of murals. They're still up there, in the north country. I saw them just a couple years ago. He'd just finished them when . . ." Byron went quiet.

"When?" she asked.

He looked away, elbows resting on his knees, fingers laced. She watched his nails turn white as he pressed his hands together. "A PPC attack. My dad tried to lead them away from me and my mom. He was killed outright." Byron looked down, kicking at a little pebble on the stair.

"And your mom?"

"She was hurt. Bad. We knew there was a satellite PPC location, a place where troops could restock supplies and weapons. I thought if I could just get her to the medpod there I could heal her.

"Another Badlander helped me load her into his car, and we raced over there. The troopers were gone, deployed somewhere. We thought the outpost was empty, and started hacking the lock. But then a voice spoke to us. It was some visiting media exec. They used to go out there to assess areas for possible transmitter sites. Every time we hacked the door code, he changed it from the other side. I begged him to let us in, to save my mom. Promised him we wouldn't hurt him. But he . . . he laughed. He said that vermin like us deserved to die. I pounded on the door, begging him. Then the Badlander called me over to his jeep. She had passed away." He turned his face away, bouncing his leg under his elbows. His wiped his eyes roughly with one sleeve, and faced her. "We could have saved her. If that asshole had let us in, she'd still be alive."

H124 placed a hand on his shoulder. "I'm so sorry." He reached up, laying his hand upon hers. He wiped his eyes again on his shirt. "Thanks. Hey," he said, changing the subject. "I got a hold of Marlowe. She's not that far away. She says she can come get us. Drop us off at that hyperloop you were telling us about."

H124 remembered Marlowe, the incredible helicopter pilot who'd risked her life to retrieve her and Gordon off the mountain. It would be good to see her again.

"You get a hold of Raven?" he asked.

She nodded. "He made it back to Sanctuary City with the spacecraft section." She told Byron about the additional tasks ahead of them, such as finding the nuclear device and launch vehicle.

He put his head in his hands. "Just when I think we're winning."

Her PRD beeped. She opened the comm window. "Gordon says he can leave within the hour," Raven said. "So sit tight."

"Actually, I think we have a different way home. Marlowe can take us to the hyperloop. Can you send me co-ords to the one that leads to Sanctuary City?"

"Of course." Seconds later, the coordinates arrived on her PRD. "I guess I'll see you all soon. We'll have a big meal waiting for you when you get back. Good luck." Raven signed off.

They spent the rest of the day lounging around the weather shelter in the cool air, playing cards and talking. Toward evening, the sound of Marlowe's helicopter filtered into the shelter. They gathered their belongings and moved outside.

Marlowe touched down out front, and climbed down from the cockpit. She walked over to them, her tall, lanky frame a welcome sight. They all hugged her like an old friend, and H124 thanked her again for her daring mountain rescue.

Marlowe looked a little shy, then smiled, her white teeth brilliant against her mahogany skin. "No problem."

They piled into the helicopter, and she took off, banking to the west. They arrived at the hyperloop entrance an hour later, and thanked Marlowe once more as she departed back to her nearby Badlander camp.

Once inside the hyperloop, H124 slept most of the way back to Sanctuary City. She woke a few times, gazing sleepily around the hyperloop pod, seeing Astoria and Dirk playing cards at one point, and Byron sleeping a few rows over, sprawled across the empty seats.

When they reached the end of the line in Sanctuary City, the door opened to reveal a familiar face.

"Rowan!" she said, hurrying toward him. His face lit up, blue eyes glittering beneath his crop of spiky blond hair. When he embraced her she breathed in his welcome scent.

"Thought you could use a little help up here."

Dirk and Byron clasped his hand warmly. "Firehawk," Byron said. "You get everyone settled into their new digs?"

Rowan nodded, grinning. "The new place is secure. It's looking real good down there. You're all welcome anytime you need a place to stay."

Astoria actually smiled and hugged him. "Thanks," she said. H124 wondered how long they'd known each other, and if Astoria might even treat her to a smile at some point.

In the heart of the underground tunnels everything was just as she remembered it, a comforting sight. People bustled about the de-extinction lab, the forests above, and the food preparation area below. She passed labs with signs that read Chemistry, Biology, Med Lab, Oceanography, Meteorology. At the last one, she poked her head in the door and introduced herself to the meteorologist, Nimbus, who was busy studying some weather patterns off the eastern Pacific. "Thanks for the hurricane data," she told the scientist. "Really came in handy."

The woman rose from her seat, her wavy black hair cascading down her back. A smile lit up her bronze face. "So you're H124?"

They shook hands.

"How's it going?" H124 asked her, gesturing at the display she'd been working at.

Nimbus sat back down in her chair. "Good. Interesting. Well, not good. Bad. Bad news, as usual. But interesting. Eastern Pacific is really warming up. Looks like we might get some hurricane activity down by Baja. Worse this time around, and the last few were absolute decimators."

H124 could feel the hive mind buzzing around her, everyone doing research and trying to improve things in a collective for good. For knowledge. The stark contrast between this place and the megacities was staggering.

"Where are you off to?" Nimbus asked.

"To find Raven. See how they're progressing with piecing the spacecraft together."

Nimbus nodded. "Enjoy! *Hasta luego.*"

H124 continued down the hall. She found Raven, Rowan, and Dirk in Orion's office. As she entered, Raven turned and beamed. "We've got some amazing news, H."

Just then Astoria peeked her head in. "I've just come from the engineering lab. Your engineer is named Rivet. Your meteorologist is Nimbus." She stifled a laugh. "What is your chef called? Fork? Saucepan?" She looked at Orion. "You're the astronomer, right? What's your name? Planet?"

"Orion," he said, looking nonplussed.

"We choose our own names," Raven said.

"So I noticed. You got a Dr. Rusty Scalpel?" She ducked out of the room, sniggering. They could hear her laugh echoing down the corridor.

Orion and Dirk sat at a display table together, calculations spread out before them. Dirk pored over them, moving numbers and adjusting equations.

"So what's this amazing news?" H124 asked.

Raven turned to Orion. "You tell her."

The astronomer looked up. "Those drives you brought back from Lockhardt Aeronautics had an incredible wealth of information. Before they started to build this bigger craft to deliver the nuclear payload to the main asteroid, they built a much smaller one, with a smaller payload, to try their method out on the biggest fragment."

"So it's already been blown off course?" H124 asked.

Orion shook his head. "No, unfortunately. It looks like it rendezvoused with the fragment, and then there was a political storm over the use of nuclear detonation. They argued to find a different way, something called the kinetic impactor technique."

"What was that?" she asked.

"It uses a spacecraft to ram the asteroid, nudging it off course. The initial push wouldn't be much. But over many years, the change in trajectory would start to add up, so that by the time it was due to impact Earth, it would have been well off course."

"Did they try it?" Rowan asked.

"No. Right after that, the project lost funding. Everyone was sent packing. The impactor craft was never built. Looks like they just landed the smaller craft on the fragment and waited to see what was decided. They wanted to conserve its fuel. They never detonated the craft."

H124's mouth hung open. "You're saying it's still up there?"

Orion beamed. "It is. And I've been able to establish contact with it."

"This is amazing!"

"Check this out." Orion brought up a large floating display. "I worked up this model with Dirk's help." The display showed the two remaining fragments as well as the main asteroid. He pointed to the biggest fragment, the one due to hit next. "This is the one that's going to hit BEC City. Not only is it larger than the first, but a continental strike will mean far more destruction." He moved on to the next fragment. "This one will land in the Pacific Ocean, creating a ring of tsunamis." He saved the worst for last. "This monster is going to be a land strike, too. An extinction-level impact." He moved back to the first fragment. "The blast deflection craft is on this fragment. Its fuel is nearly depleted. It's been using the heat from the radioactive decay of plutonium-238 to generate electricity. It wouldn't have enough fuel to rendezvous with the larger asteroid. It's probably got just enough to take off from this fragment and detonate its nuclear payload.

"But if we *could* deflect this larger fragment away from the Earth, avoiding that land strike on BEC City, it would be huge. And we could use that data to inform our mission to deflect the main asteroid. The blast deflection technique is the fastest-acting method of all the ones I've read about on these drives. If we can get all the parts to build the deployment craft, and locate a large enough nuclear payload to divert the asteroid, we're in business. But we have to work fast. Getting that final piece of the craft is vital. The sooner we can change the trajectories of these pieces, the safer we'll be."

Raven walked around the display, studying the images. "When can we try to deflect the larger fragment?"

Orion opened his arms wide. "Right now. We're going over calculations, and we'll be running some simulations in no time." He paused. "Are we all in agreement that's our best course of action? To test out the existing craft on the big fragment, while building the one that'll deflect the main asteroid?"

"Sounds good to me," Raven said.

H124 and Rowan nodded.

Orion moved closer to the display and had it reveal their calculations. "Okay." Dirk studied them, and they conferred on the best angle to set off the detonation. It had to be very precise, or the blast could send the asteroid fragment hurtling toward them at an even greater velocity or more dangerous angle of impact.

She and Raven clustered around the display, the tension heavy in the room. Speaking in hushed tones, Orion and Dirk compared their calculations, then tried a series of simulations on the model Orion had built. They'd just finished the third simulation when suddenly Dirk stood up, rigid. His eyes fluttered, and he let out a strangled cry. He crumpled to the floor, convulsing. H124 rushed over.

"Has this happened to him before?" Raven asked.

"Not that I know of," Rowan told him.

H124 ran to the door. "Where's Astoria?" She took off down the hall. She heard Raven calling for the Rovers' doctor.

She raced through the corridors of Sanctuary City, finding Astoria sharing a drink with two freighter pilots in the common room. When she saw H124's expression, she immediately stood up. "What is it?"

"Dirk, he's having a seizure."

Astoria tossed her drink aside and ran with her back to Orion's office, their boots clomping down the corridor. "What happened?" Astoria asked as they ran.

"He was just standing there, doing calculations with Orion, and all of a sudden he collapsed."

"Damn it!"

They passed Byron in the hall and he joined them, sprinting in through the doorway. The Rover doctor, Felix, stood over Dirk, who lay immobile on the floor.

Astoria raced to her brother's side. "Is he . . . ?"

"Unconscious," Felix told her. "Does he have a history of seizures?"

She shook her head wildly. "No! Never!"

"We need to get him to a medpod."

They loaded him onto a stretcher and hurried him to the med facility. Astoria clutched his hand the whole way, though he continued to convulse, oblivious to the world. Once in the doctor's office, they lowered him into a medpod, which scanned him at once. Felix stared at the display, narrowing in on the cerebral section. "What's this?" he asked Astoria, pointing to a small sphere inside Dirk's brain.

"I have no idea!"

The doctor zoomed in on it, rotating the image. "It's not natural. Seems to be made of surgical steel." He read the data streaming in on a corner of the display. "It's a transmitter, giving off signals to his brain. It told him to shut down."

Astoria was incredulous. "What?" She looked back at her brother, pressing her hand against the medpod's glass.

"Do you know where he could have gotten this?"

Astoria turned to meet H124's eyes, a piercing glance that almost made H124 look away. "Murder City. Dirk and I were separated for most of the time. They could have done anything to him."

H124 felt terrible. If they hadn't tried to save those citizens, the PPC wouldn't have captured Dirk. Astoria was in H124's face before she had time to step away. "You did this. You made this happen!" she snapped, raining spittle on H124's face. H124 held up a placating hand. "I'm so sorry."

"If you didn't have such a damned bleeding heart, my brother wouldn't be lying here fighting for his life!"

Byron put a hand between them, trying to calm Astoria. "Dirk has just as much of a bleeding heart. He would have helped those people even if H124 hadn't suggested it."

Astoria locked Byron in with a hateful glare. Then her chin trembled, and she melted into sorrow. She turned toward Felix. "Can you take it out?"

"I'm damn well going to try," he told her. He gazed at each of them in turn, then pulled out a handheld scanner. "I think I'd better make sure the rest of you don't have one of these." He moved it around each of their heads, watching the readout on his PRD. When he finished, he lowered it. "You're all clear."

Giving him space to work, they left the room, watching his progress on a large floating display through the window. He instructed the medpod to enter Dirk's skull, using its extractor tool. Dirk began to convulse more violently, his body slamming against the walls of his medpod.

They heard Felix curse, and watched him try again, but each time Dirk's body fought against the extraction. Astoria kept her hands flat against the glass, as Raven comforted her with a hand on her shoulder.

"I'm going to try a controlled EMP," he told them. He adjusted the settings on the medpod and set off the electromagnetic pulse, only to have the medpod's control report that the EMP had failed to shut down the sphere. It was shielded.

Again and again Felix tried to extract it, but the sphere sent a seizure-inducing signal to Dirk's brain every time, and his heartrate jittered so fast he risked cardiac arrest.

Finally Felix stopped trying and Dirk went still, his heart rate returning to normal. The doctor turned to them through the window. "I can't get it out," he told them. "And I'm afraid it seems to be sending out a countdown signal."

Astoria's face contorted in anguish. "Counting down to what?"

"My guess is an electrical surge that will kill him."

She punched the glass, sending a ripple through the window. Rowan tried to reach out to her, but she shoved away his hand and stormed off down the hall, striking several other windows along the way.

"What do we do?" H124 asked Felix.

"I'll keep searching for ways to stop it. Look through some records. Maybe there's a record of this PPC device being used in the past."

Orion, who'd been watching in silence, turned sadly away from the glass. "He was amazing. Never seen someone who could run calculations that fast."

"He's not gone yet," H124 told him. "He's not going to go down without a fight. We'll figure this out."

"Can you continue with the calculations in the meantime?" Raven asked him.

Orion nodded. "It'll just take longer."

Raven clapped an encouraging hand on the astronomer's shoulder, and Orion slumped off in a daze.

Raven turned to the doctor. "Keep us posted, okay?"

Felix nodded, then turned back, flipping through records on his PRD.

H124 left to find Astoria. She searched the common rooms, the de-extinction lab, her quarters, and a host of other rooms, all to no avail. Finally she went topside to the stratified forest. There she found Astoria sitting beneath a tree. The mohawked warrior stared off at a pale blue sky, tracks of tears staining her face.

"Astoria?" H124 asked quietly.

She didn't answer.

H124 drew closer. "Astoria? The doctor said he's going to do some research until he finds a solution."

Astoria merely stared off into the distance. H124 crouched down next to her, but Astoria made no indication that H124 was even there. She wasn't sure what to do for her, so she reached out a hand, touching Astoria's fingers. "Can I do anything for you?"

Astoria yanked away her hand, refusing to even look at H124.

Taking the hint, H124 withdrew, returning to the lift and traveling down. She stepped out to a quiet area in a side hallway. Maybe Willoughby would know what to do. She pulled up a comm window and called him.

He answered right way. "H," he said, smiling. "You safe?"

She nodded. "I'm back at the Rover city. How are things on your end?"

He glanced around his office. "So far so good."

"Something's happened to Dirk."

Willoughby frowned.

"The doctor thinks it's some kind of PPC device that's been planted in his brain. It's sending out an electrical signal, which the doctor thinks will kill him."

Willoughby cursed under his breath. "I think I know the device you're talking about. It was only recently developed. It's what Olivia calls a 'coercion tool.' You use it to threaten people to get what you want."

"The PPC tried to get Astoria and Dirk to reveal the location of Sanctuary City."

"And did they?"

"They didn't know where it was at the time."

"Once that device is implanted, it's only a matter of time before the person dies."

"How do we get it out?"

"I'm not sure. Let me do some digging and get back to you."

"Thank you. So you're okay there?"

"It's getting more dangerous here by the minute. I'm not sure how much longer I'll last before the Repurposers pay me a visit."

H124 shuddered just thinking of the black-clad men. "Watch your back. Let me know you're okay." She shut down the comm window and entered the main hall.

Raven ran by. "There's a problem," he said when he saw her.

"With what?" She fell in alongside him, jogging down the hall toward Orion's office.

"With the blast deflection craft."

They entered the astronomer's office, finding his hands flying over the floating display, flipping through windows and entering commands. Onyx stood next to him, inputting commands in her own PRD console. She looked up at Raven.

"What's happening?"

"We've been locked out," Orion told him, staring wide-eyed through the display. "I don't know how, but Delta City PPC hacked us. They're now in control of the craft."

"What the hell?" Raven walked over to Onyx. "Can you return control to us?"

She shook her head, dazed. "I'm trying, but whoever is on the other end is good. *Really good.*"

"And what is the PPC doing with the craft?" H124 asked.

Orion met her gaze. "We don't know yet. So far they just wrested control. The craft's just sitting there on the fragment, where it's always been."

Onyx entered more commands. "Damn it! I can't get control back."

Orion threw his hands up. "What can they be planning? What's the point of taking this thing over? Don't they know we're trying to stop it from hitting?"

H124 approached him. "Wait a minute . . . can they see your simulations of where it will hit?"

He waved at his display with disgust. "Right now they can see everything."

"So they know it's going to hit BEC City?"

Raven looked up, meeting her eyes in simultaneous understanding.

"They want it to hit," he whispered.

"It'll get rid of their worst competition," she added.

Onyx stared at them in disbelief. "But the fallout, the side effects. It's not just going to damage BEC City. The whole world will be affected."

Raven turned to her. "We know that, but they don't. They lost all knowledge of science like this. They probably think it'll just destroy the city. The smaller fragments that hit New Atlantic haven't affected them too much in Delta City. They would have suffered an initial earthquake, some fine debris dusting the city, but other than that, the sky is redder, the temperature's a little cooler . . ."

H124 couldn't believe it. She felt frozen. "We have to get control back," she said.

Onyx started entering commands again.

Orion stepped through his display so he could face H124 and Raven. "It's more important than ever that you get that final piece of the craft. If this thing makes impact, the global implications are going to be catastrophic. And if that monster asteroid hits, well . . . we're dead."

Chapter 17

Byron and Rowan met up with H124 in Raven's office. "We need a plan," she told them.

She opened up the binder, showing the location of the last piece. "It was built in an underground facility by a company called Bering Aeronautics. Later on, Basin City was built on top of it."

"I'm sorry. *Where* did you just say it was?" Byron asked, his jaw going slack. "Because I thought you just said *Basin City.*"

Raven gave a mirthless smile.

"You know that place is lethal, right?" Byron pressed. "Even Death Riders don't go there."

H124 had never heard of it.

"We don't have a choice," Raven told him. "We need that last piece."

"Can't we just build it somehow?" Byron asked.

"It's specialty equipment, something that took them years to build. We don't have that kind of time or," he added ruefully, "the know-how."

H124 turned to Byron. "So what are we up against?"

Rowan came forward, a grim look on his face. He brought up the display on his PRD, expanding the view so they could all see it. He entered a few search commands, and a rudimentary map flashed up on the display. "This is all the terrain we've ever been able to map in Basin City." It showed just a handful of streets on the outer perimeter. Large red X's marked the ends of each street. It didn't even extend a quarter mile into the city. "No one has lived beyond these points."

"What's wrong with this place?" she asked.

Raven brought up a series of history files on his PRD. "Years ago, this area of the country was a hotbed of coal and natural gas extraction. They got careless in their extraction methods, and an accident led to a series of underground coal seams igniting. They thought they could extinguish it, and just kept building the city out. Decades later, the fire still burned. They couldn't access the coal, so they tried fracking for natural gas, but that opened up even more fractures, allowing the fire to spread even more. This whole city is a warren of unstable ground and clouds of poisonous gases— carbon monoxide, hydrogen sulfide, not to mention arsenic, selenium, and fluorine. The fire is really close to the surface in some places. If you fall through one of those cracks . . ." He thought a moment. "We're going to need pyrometers."

"What are those?" H124 asked.

"Instruments that can measure surface temperature from a distance. We aim an infrared beam at the ground, and the device tells us if we can walk safely over that section."

His display showed historical video of underground coal fires, fissures with billowing gas, and barren ground.

Raven turned off his display.

"But it's much worse than just fires," Byron said. "Night stalkers are all over that place. We don't know why there are so many. Maybe it's the warmth, or all the smoke that dims the sun. But this place is night stalker central. No way we get in and out of there."

"I have an idea about that," Raven said. He brought up an image of a small furred animal with wings. "This is a bat. There used to be millions of these important pollinators. But pesticides and a fungal disease known as white-nose syndrome wiped them all out. They were some of the first creatures I brought back in the de-extinction lab, and now there's a growing population of them in the forests above. They use echolocation to find their insect prey. I think night stalkers hunt in the same way. In the bat population, I've noticed that they'll sometimes use their echolocation to jam the radar of another bat, essentially messing with its ability to zero in on an insect. Then the second bat zooms in on the moth itself. We use a similar jamming system to keep the bats away from our wind turbines. If we could build a small device that uses similar technology—"

Rowan's face lit up. "We could essentially jam the night stalkers' radar. But couldn't they just see us if we do that? With their regular vision?"

"We think night stalkers have very limited eyesight," Raven told him. "They abhor bright light and hunt mainly in the darkest part of the night. From the few close observations we've made, they seem to suffer from some kind of genetic deformation that has hindered their sight."

H124 watched Rowan already turning over possibilities. "What frequency do they echolocate at?"

"The ones we've recorded on ultrasonic mics pulsed at 1 kHz to 72 kHz."

"So we'd need an emitter in that range." Rowan brought a hand to his chin. "I think I can build one."

"You might be able to adjust our existing bat jammer design to make it more mobile. Something we could wear."

"Can you build four of them?" Byron asked. "I'm going." He glanced around at them. "I don't think we can expect Astoria to come with us. There's no way she's going to leave Dirk in his condition."

H124 agreed. "No way."

"We'll need weapons," Byron added. "What do you have?"

Raven gestured down the hall. "You're welcome to take a look at our armory."

"I will." He left the room.

Rowan turned to Raven. "Where can I get to work?"

"I'll walk you over to the engineering lab," Raven offered. "Rivet should be able to fix you up with space and materials."

"I'll go find Gordon," H124 told them. As they left, her stomach knotted. She had a bad feeling about this.

She found Gordon out on the airfield, tinkering with the Flying Flapjack.

"H! You're back!" He hugged her. "How did it go?"

"The hurricane was easier."

"Ouch. That's saying a lot."

"How's it coming on the plane?"

He stepped back, looking the craft over. "I hope to get it up in the air in a week or so." He smiled. "This place . . . the Rovers . . . if I'd known they were up here, I'd have come a long time ago." He chuckled, pulling a rag out of his back pocket and wiping off his hands. "I admit I was starting to feel pretty dusty and old before you found me. Now I feel like I've started a whole new life."

She smiled. "I feel that way too, Gordon."

"I'll bet you do, kid. Your lot in life wasn't a pretty one before this."

She thought back to New Atlantic, dragging the bodies of the deceased to the incinerators, catching glimpses of the citizen lifestyle she'd never have. It was all gone now—the entire city vaporized.

He clapped his hands together. "Tell me we're off on another adventure."

She couldn't help but crack a smile. "We are. This time to a place called Basin City. Have you heard of it?"

He cringed. "I have."

"From what Rowan and Byron told us, it's not going to be an easy trip."

"I'll say. No one goes there anymore. Not even Death Riders. And . . ." He cleared his throat. "They say it's haunted."

"Haunted?"

"Things moving in the dark. The ghosts of everyone who's died there."

"Great! What can possibly go wrong?"

He puckered his lips and blew out. "With our luck? Everything."

Chapter 18

Rowan worked late into the night. H124 checked on him a few times, helping him build the emitters. In the wee hours, she finally turned in, leaving him to the finishing touches. She slept poorly, constantly worrying about Dirk and infiltrating Basin City. Finally she got up before it was light, and got dressed.

She went down to the med lab, and stared through the window. Dirk still lay unconscious in the medpod, and Felix had fallen asleep at his work station. Astoria sat next to Dirk, asleep in her chair. H124 looked at Dirk's vitals on the display. No change from the day before. Felix stirred as she turned away.

"There's no change," he whispered, not wanting to wake Astoria. "But that thing is still counting down."

H124 brought a hand to her forehead, and felt her temples starting to pound. "This is terrible. I've contacted my friend in Delta City. I'm waiting to hear what he can find out."

"Thank you."

H124 crept away, letting Astoria sleep, and walked to the armory to meet Raven and the others. "There's no change with Dirk," she told them as she entered.

They all exchanged looks. Everyone was on edge.

Raven spoke up, gesturing to four red suits hanging from wall hooks. "These heat suits have been modified. They're much more lightweight than what we wore to the radar facility. They also have built-in gas detectors, so if we come to sections with toxic emissions, we'll be protected."

Rowan moved to a table in the center of the room. "I've built emitters for each of us." He held up small round disks with red lights on them.

"They clip on to our heat suits. We can't hear their ultrasonic signals, so if they're working, they're blinking. Keep an eye on them at all times."

Raven joined him at the table, where four black handheld devices lay. They almost looked like pistols. "These are the pyrometers. Point one at the ground, pull the trigger, and an infrared beam measures the temp there. Don't step anywhere without first using one of these."

"And we'll all need weapons," Byron said. He'd made a cursory visit to the armory the night before, but now it was time to choose.

Raven gestured at the far wall, which held a rack with a number of guns. Byron paced alongside it. H124 joined him, selecting an energy rifle that could both stun and kill. Rowan took an energy rifle and a sonic weapon, and Raven chose a handheld flash burster.

"I'm not taking any chances," Byron said, rejecting those choices. He stopped at the edge of the rack. "I'll be," he said, taking down a rifle with a wood and metal stock. "Is this a Henry repeating rifle?"

Raven nodded.

"You got ammo for this thing?"

Raven pulled down several boxes from a nearby cabinet. "Here you go."

Byron loaded up a satchel with the boxes. "Excellent."

They all gathered their gear, then took one last look at the armory. Byron grabbed a pocket torch. "In case we need to cut through any doors. We won't have Dirk with us this time."

"Okay. Let's go hitch a ride," Raven said, turning the lights off.

* * * *

Out on the airfield, they met up with Gordon, climbing into the Lockheed Vega and stowing their gear. In moments they were off, flying south, leaving the wondrous green land behind them.

H124 dozed on and off as they flew, the turbulence waking her up now and then. The others did the same. She checked for a message from Willoughby, but there was none. At last they neared their destination.

The broken sprawl of the megacity was staggering from the air. H124 could see the curve of the shield wall, eerily naked with no shield glowing above it. The streets themselves were dim and hazy, obscured by a layer of smoke that hung in the air above the city. Black fissures snaked through the streets, as heat waves lingered above them.

There were no open spaces for Gordon to land the Vega inside the city, and due to the tectonic instability, he decided it would be safest to land just outside the western wall, at a location closest to the aerospace facility, Bering Aeronautics. He banked, and she saw Basin City's PPC Tower in the distance, its grand spire and massive antenna broken off and lying twisted below. It had taken out several city blocks when it toppled.

As they descended, she peered out of the window until the gigantic retaining wall blocked her view and the plane's wheels touched down on a flat, dry section of land. The plane bounced a few times, slowing to a stop. Gordon turned in his seat. "I'm going to find a place to refuel. Call me when you're ready to be picked up."

They each grabbed their pack, Raven checking over the maglev sled before he zipped his up. As she passed the cockpit, Gordon reached for her hand. "This place . . . I don't like it. If those emitters don't work, you get the hell out. Spacecraft be damned. You hear me?"

She nodded, even though they both knew that the spacecraft was of utmost importance, more so than any of their lives. She leaned down and hugged him, feeling the rough of his white whiskers against her face. "I'll be careful."

"I'll be waiting on your call," he said, pointing at his PRD.

Outside the plane they suited up in their lightweight heat suits. The built-in oxygen tanks contained CO_2 scrubbers to recirculate their air. Each of them checked their pyrometers, and Rowan attached the ultrasonic emitters to the fronts of their suits. The emitters started blinking, letting them know they were operational.

They set off, H124 checking her O_2 supply and blinking light.

It wasn't hard to find a break in the retaining wall. Most of it had crumbled or collapsed into fissures in the steaming ground. Raven led the way, holding out his pyrometer. She could see the ultrasonic emitter pulsing on his chest, its red light flashing against his sleeve.

"Don't step anywhere without first testing the ground temp," he reminded them.

H124 adjusted her oxygen levels as they stepped through a wide opening in the wall. Fissures split the ground everywhere as smoke billowed up, the ground white and chalky in places.

Whole blocks of buildings had collapsed into gaping holes. She checked her pyrometer, aiming its infrared beam ahead. About fifty feet in front of them, the ground temp measured 217°F. They skirted around the section, then angled back in the direction of the aerospace facility.

In a few places buildings still stood, their windows shattered. On a few streets, crashed autotransports blocked the road and they had to weave between them. Byron and Rowan were right—in any other place, these transports would have been stolen or stripped clean. But these still had all their tech.

She could move much more freely in the lighter heat suit, and the fire boots felt solid on her feet. Slowly they made their way across the western part of the city, having to take long detours as they went. Her PRD read high amounts of hydrogen sulfide and carbon monoxide in the air, hovering in pockets over deep black cracks of hissing smoke.

They reached a more stable section of the city. Most of the buildings here still stood, and her PRD read only trace amounts of sulfur dioxide. She aimed her pyrometer at the ground, and it came back as 90°F, not that different from the normally blistering temperatures in this area.

In a few places, rooftop gardens had grown out of control, crawling down the sides of buildings. In other places the toxic air had killed them, leaving only brown shriveled vines. They moved through this clearer area more quickly, making good progress.

A low rumbling sounded from the ground, and moments later the earth shook. H124 went down on one knee, bracing herself on the ground. Rowan went off balance, but Raven caught his arm before he fell. The tremblor passed, and they forged on.

A blinking arrow on her PRD's map showed they were close to Bering Aeronautics, which long ago had stood a half mile from their location. H124's heart sank as she saw the ground ahead crisscrossed with smoking fissures. The sulfur dioxide and carbon monoxide levels here were lethal. Another quake shook the ground, the broken pavement under her feet undulating and throwing her off balance. She caught herself on an old metal pole. The shaking passed, but they had only gone a few more feet when it returned violently, and the ground thrust up under her feet. She went over on her back as a belching crack split open next to her; the ground was tearing itself apart.

Rowan stood a few feet away, back turned to the gaping fissure. "Rowan!" she shouted. He spun, his eyes going wide as he saw the yawning black maw cleaving toward him. He dove to one side, but the crack opened wider, its sides sloping down beneath his feet. He grabbed desperately for a handhold as the ground dipped away beneath him. He slid down the broken pavement toward the smoking fissure. She stood up and ran to him, the ground trembling so powerfully beneath her that she stumbled and fell repeatedly.

As his feet plunged over the edge into the darkness, Rowan managed to dig his fingers into a thin crack in the pavement, stopping his fall. She reached him, lying flat on the ground and extending her hand to him. He grippcd it, and she pulled him up. His feet found purchase on the broken cement, and he managed to scramble back up to the others. Raven and Byron grabbed his body and hefted him the rest of the way.

Rolling onto his back, Rowan closed his eyes. "I think my heart's trying to pound right out of my chest."

"We need to get out of this area," Raven said. "Too unstable. Let's see if there's a safer way around." He scouted out, taking readings on his pyrometer. She could see the blinking red on his emitter when he vanished into a cloud of sulfur dioxide gas. He returned and scouted in another direction. "This way!" he called to them.

They helped Rowan to his feet and followed Raven, taking a wide circuit around a section of white chalk earth. She could hear the crackling of the coal seam fire beneath their feet, and had to fight off images of plunging suddenly through the crust and burning alive.

At last they reached the location of Bering Aeronautics. To H124's relief, the block of buildings there was largely undamaged. The building directly above the spot where the facility had been was now a residential structure. Since the city had no power, getting inside was a matter of brute force, as the TWRs were inoperable.

They slid open the metal doors and filed into the hallway. This residential building looked identical to the ones she'd worked at in New Atlantic.

She walked with them down to the subbasement, where pod cleaners had once delivered dirty linens to be washed, and where corpse cleaners like her had sent incinerated human remains to special holding tanks. As she moved into the lead and couldn't see the others behind her, her mind tried to play tricks on her. This building was so identical to the countless others she'd worked at in New Atlantic, that as she passed the human remains holding tank and saw that the gauge on it was almost full, she thought she was back working in New Atlantic, that her escape, her journey, had all been a dream, and she was back to her dreary existence.

"See any way down?" Byron asked.

She turned, took a deep breath, and saw the others exploring the room.

"There's usually a drain in each living pod building," she told them, "holdovers from before they'd perfected the atmospheric shields. Torrential rains used to flood the streets and seep into the buildings, flooding the bottom floors Later they perfected the atmospheric shields, and the drains fell into disuse. But they might get us closer to any structure still standing beneath us."

Rowan passed into a neighboring room. "Here!" he called.

They joined him, standing over a large grate that led into darkness. "Give me a hand." They all knelt and lifted the heavy lattice away. Raven aimed his pyrometer into the hole. The reading came back at normal levels. "I'll go first," he said, and lowered himself down the drain. He held on to the lip of the floor before he let go, and landed a couple feet down. He turned on his headlamp, sending shadows scattering along the storm tunnel. "Looks good." His emitter's red flash bounced off the walls. She checked hers, making sure it still worked, remembering all too well that the night stalkers prowled storm drains during the day, keeping to the shadows.

One by one they dropped down. Raven consulted his PRD and headed toward the old facility.

They came to a place where the ancient rush of flood waters had caused part of the floor to weaken and collapse. Raven aimed his pyrometer beam into it, again receiving normal readings. He lay down and shone his light through the hole. "I think this is it. I see an old desk down here."

As Raven lowered himself through, H124 aimed her beam back the way they'd come. She could almost feel things staring at her, boring into her back, slowly closing in with clawed feet. Rowan jumped through, leaving her in the tunnel with Byron.

"You okay?" he asked.

She turned back. "Yeah. Just . . ."

"Creepy?"

"Exactly."

"You next."

She dropped through, landing beside Rowan, and Byron followed. As his beam passed through the hole, H124 thought she caught a glimpse of a slinking form in the tunnel above, but decided it may have just been Byron's shadow.

On the lower level, her beam revealed a series of offices much like the ones they'd seen in the other aeronautic facilities. They traversed corridors, passing offices with dusty tables and chairs and old computer equipment. Raven found a set of stairs, and they descended a floor. The next door had a lock like the ones Dirk had hacked back in Delta City, but this one had already been burned through with a pocket pyro sometime in antiquity. The door stood open a crack.

Her brow creased as Raven turned and met her gaze. This wasn't a good sign.

Together they shoved open the rusted door and entered a huge workspace like the ones they'd seen before. Work tables laden with tools, empty coffee cups, and blueprints lay scatted around the room.

In the center stood the glassed-in room, where more white suits hung on hooks.

H124's heart sank into her stomach. The glass room was empty.

Chapter 19

"Where is it?" Raven asked, his voice cracking. He rushed to the glass room and forced the door open. The spacecraft section, if it had ever been built, was not here. He turned, incredulous. "This can't be."

H124 hurried to a nearby table littered with papers. She shuffled through them—blueprints, calculations, statistics. She found a binder on a desk with "Current Project Status" written on the side. She thumbed through it. At the back, she read the last two entries: *Completed at 2040 hours. Awaiting status on other sections. Celebration tonight!*

The final entry read: *Funding cut off. Awaiting word from the other facilities to see what we can do.*

H124 turned to the others. "It was done. The last entry says they were just waiting on the other sections."

"And we have those," Raven added.

"So who took this piece?" Byron asked.

"Maybe it was the first one to be moved? To join with the others and be assembled?" Rowan asked.

H124's heart sank even more. If this piece had been transported, and wasn't at the other facilities, that meant it had been waylaid somewhere en route in antiquity. They'd never find it.

"I don't think it was moved by them," Raven said, examining the lock on the glass room. "This was forced open. The metal's bent, the lock destroyed. Same with the outer door."

H124 examined the lock with him. "But who would have done this? Who would be down here?"

"This city was falling apart," Raven speculated. "This is one of the few stable areas. It's possible the PPC was down here, assessing damage from the coal fire."

"And they took it?"

"The tech might have intrigued them," Raven said.

H124 had an idea. She moved away, bringing up her PRD comm window. Willoughby answered right away.

"H! Are you okay?"

She nodded. Willoughby sat in his extravagantly decorated office, his hair neatly styled, his usual tailored suit impeccable.

"How are you? Safe?"

"So far, so good," he said in a voice that didn't entirely convince her.

"You think they're on to you?"

"An exec paid me a visit, asking some strange and rather specific questions. I'm not sure if Olivia tipped them off with some lie, or if they really have something."

"I think you should get out of there. Transfer to another city."

"I might have to."

"Listen," she said. "We're at the aerospace facility beneath Basin City. But someone has taken the spacecraft section. Would the PPC keep any records of finding something like that?"

Willoughby leaned back in his chair. "It's possible. When Basin City failed, a lot of the PPC execs transferred to other cities, taking their records with them. If any of them came here, I might be able to dig something up."

"Can you see what you find and get back to me?"

He nodded. "Will do."

The comm window closed.

"And now?" Byron asked.

"We wait," she told him.

They milled around the room, absently picking up different tools. Byron drew patterns in the dust on one of the desks. Raven flipped through books and manuals. Rowan paced.

Finally her PRD beeped. She brought up the comm window. Willoughby looked nervous. "I think I found something." He glanced toward his office door.

"Are you okay?"

"I'm not sure. When I was digging around in the database, I got a strange 'Access Denied' message. I think they might be starting to shut me down."

"You need to get out of there," she told him again.

"I will. But first let me tell you what I learned before I got shut out."

The others gathered around her floating display.

"Before the city was abandoned, they were searching for pockets of natural gas that they could tap into with fracking. One of the energy techs found what they described as an 'ancient lab' and removed a device from it. It could be your craft."

"What happened to it?" Raven asked.

"The PPC took it to the main tower."

H124 remembered seeing it, its antenna toppled, the top of the building lying in ruins in the street below.

"Where in the tower?" she asked.

"There was an exec who collected antiquities on the 120th floor. I'm sending you a schematic of the old tower."

When she opened it, she saw that the floor lay below the broken section. A tiny gleam of hope sparked inside her.

"Were you able to learn anything about that thing inside Dirk?" Byron asked.

"I got locked out before I could finish the search. But I haven't given up." He got up and started stuffing things into a small satchel—his PRD, a multitool. "I have to get out of here. Call me if you need anything, and I'll let you know where I end up."

"Willoughby," H124 said. He stopped packing and faced her. "Be careful."

He smiled. "You, too, H." He signed off.

"The tower . . ." Rowan said. "I saw that thing on the way in. Isn't exactly in tiptop shape."

"But at least the floor is under the ruined part." H124 stuffed the project notes into her toolbag, and they filed out of the room. She checked her PRD. Dark would soon fall. They didn't have much time to reach the tower before this place would be crawling with night stalkers.

Chapter 20

Back on the city streets above, they headed toward the old PPC tower. They could see it looming above all the other buildings, even with its broken crown. They found a street with a clear line of sight leading directly to it. Raven led the way again, pointing his pyrometer at the ground and leading them around the unstable spots.

The western sky turned gold as the sun kissed the horizon. H124 and the others picked their way along the street, moving to alleys and neighboring blocks when they had to skirt around smoking cracks and unsound ground. As the sun dipped below the horizon, her heart started to beat faster. Every shadow seemed to come alive.

A sudden jarring sensation at her back sent her reeling. She didn't know what had hit her. Then she realized another earthquake had struck, sending a handful of bricks cascading down onto her back. She breathed out in relief.

They all bent low, waiting out the tremblor, moving on only when it passed. The clouds in the west went orange and pink, with a low-lying ripple of red beneath. It was beautiful, she thought, in spite of their circumstances. As the clouds went from red to violet to grey, shadows crept across the city. She moved in the gloaming, that short span when day and night existed at once, a time when she always felt that magic was close at hand and anything could happen. She tensed, staring into the deeper dark of alleys and the spots beneath collapsed structures.

Rowan's words came back to her. *Even Death Riders don't go there.*

As the dark lengthened, they all switched on their headlamps, and she kept checking their blinking emitters every few minutes. Something moved in the mouth of an alley as they passed, and a metal clattering followed.

She pivoted toward it, her headlamp piercing the void. A shape melted away into the shadows. She had the distinct feeling she was being watched.

"What was that?" Byron asked, stopping at her side.

"Don't know. Something big."

"So . . . not a roach then."

"Definitely not a roach."

He took her by the arm and urged her to join the others. Unslinging the energy rifle from her back, she kept an eye out for any areas they'd be vulnerable from as they progressed, aiming it in those directions.

Byron loaded his more lethal choice, the Henry repeating rifle.

They moved as a close-knit group, Byron taking up the rear, watching their six. She felt good with him at her back. She scouted the left side, and Rowan the right, while Raven concentrated on getting them through the dangerous terrain. Twice they had to navigate down cluttered alleyways, their progress slowed as they stumbled over piles of fallen bricks and metal beams. As they made their way down a third alley, movement above caught H124's eye. She pointed her lamp up, illuminating the corner of a decrepit building. Something darted just out of sight, moving along the roof.

"There's something up there," she whispered to Byron, who followed her beam. They saw the hint of a black shadow jerk out of sight.

At the end of the alley, Raven chose a route to get them back to the main thoroughfare that led to the tower.

Another clatter erupted from a side alley, and she lifted her rifle. Some way back, she heard the distinct sound of a manhole cover sliding open.

Byron moved to Raven. "Can we pick up our pace?"

"Only if you want to be burned alive," he retorted.

Furtive shapes loped at the edge of their beams, so she jerked left and right, ready to fire at the first sign of a night stalker. The tower was still a mile away. If they could just run along the main road, headed straight toward it, it wouldn't be so bad, but having to constantly divert their course was taking too long.

"I wonder how Onyx is faring back in Sanctuary City," she said, making conversation as her eyes darted wildly about.

"She's a great hacker," Raven said, eyes glued to his pyrometer readout. "I know she'll be able to do it."

Rowan checked his emitter, bringing up a small ultrasonic microphone to be sure they were still sending out signals. They were.

"You sure these things are going to work, Firehawk?" Byron asked him.

"I don't have any reason to think they won't. Except that they've never been tested."

"Great. Just the answer I was hoping for."

They had to stop completely when they came across a huge section of the city that had fallen into a chasm below. Sulfurous gasses spewed out, and in the dark, the fire burned brilliant red and gold in its depths. Raven led them to the left of it, and to her chagrin, they had to backtrack several blocks before he found a clear way onward. Moving along parallel streets, she watched as the tower grew no closer.

As she passed by an open window whose glass had shattered long ago, a wet hiss erupted, spraying her with warm spittle. The rank, moist breath washed over her, and she stifled a gag as the stench of rotten meat assailed her. She jerked away, aiming the rifle at the open window, beyond which a dark shape moved.

"They're everywhere," Byron whispered, moving alongside her. "More every minute. I don't think we're going to make it to the tower if we stay out in the open like this."

Raven maneuvered them along a wide, steaming crack, and once more they resumed their progress. Now true night had set in, and she could see the streets of the city glowing crimson around them.

Something leaped over them, jumping from one roof to the next. H124 grabbed Byron's arm. "Do you think they can see us?" She pointed her beam up, but the thing darted away. "I mean, see our lights, our movement, just like we see them?" Raven's idea that their eyesight had been compromised was just speculation.

Byron studied the rooftops, aiming his rifle as he did. "I don't know."

"The ones in the arena . . ." She thought of how they moved in on her and Dirk. Had they been looking at them, or echolocating?

She moved toward Raven. "Should we switch off our lights?"

"I wondered that," Rowan put in.

Raven glanced down at her. "I think if they could see us, like how we see, they would have attacked by now. They can sense our movement, but I think the emitters are working. They can't quite pinpoint us."

"I don't like this," Rowan said.

"I, on the other hand," Byron put in, "am having a swell time."

They moved back into formation. The tower was closer now, only a quarter mile away, and H124 allowed the smallest iota of hope to grip her. She'd appreciated the light quality of the new heat suit earlier, but now that she jumped at every hint of movement, and often had to lift her rifle, she felt encumbered by it. Her range of motion and vision weren't good enough, and it made her heart beat even faster.

She spun as she heard a shuffling noise to their rear, then the unmistakable sound of another manhole sliding open. Her light fell on the dark circle in the ground, and a smooth, black head ducked out of sight as her light gleamed across it.

The team moved closer together, rifles at the ready. She heard another furtive shuffle and spun again, heart crawling into her throat.

She'd expected to see something climbing from the storm drain, but instead what she saw made her hair stand. The street behind them was alive with crawling things, a horde of swarming, writhing black bodies, creeping forward on all fours, eyes green and reflective in her headlamp.

"Oh, shit . . ." she breathed.

The tower now lay only a few hundred feet away. She pointed her pyrometer at the ground between them and the main door, coming up with nominal readings. "I think we need to run," she told them.

Moving as one, covering all directions, they began to sprint. Behind them the swarming mass of night stalkers lunged forward, snouts lifted, smelling the air, wet mouths glistening with eager fangs.

She ran faster. A hundred feet. Fifty. Raven reached the door, and he and Rowan forced it open while Byron and H124 pointed their rifles at the seething mass of predators.

As the creatures crept closer, gaining proximity to the emitters, a few of them shook their heads and jerked backward. A few more did the same. Raven shouted, "Come on!" and she turned to see the door open, Rowan waving them through.

They darted into the PPC lobby, and Byron and Rowan slammed the door shut behind them.

H124 spun, searching the vast foyer for any hint of the creatures. She switched off her light as it flared on the front doors, their thick glass still intact. Beyond, green eyes glistened in the darkness, drawing closer.

"Are they in here?" Byron asked.

"Not in this room, anyway," she gasped.

As they caught their breath, H124 opened her faceplate to take a long drink of water. She wanted out of the heat suit. It was starting to close in on her. She needed to be able to fight, to see all angles of approach. She felt trapped in the thing.

The others followed her lead, taking long drinks. She checked her PRD, hoping Willoughby had left her a message telling her he was okay. But her inbox was empty.

After they'd all rehydrated and rested for a few minutes, H124 turned toward the stairwell. "It's going to be a long climb," she told them.

Chapter 21

The stairwell door came open with a little forcing, and they started up.
"Why are there so many night stalkers here?" H124 asked Raven.

"No one's sure, but this place seems to be ground zero for them. We've studied their population dispersal, and this place seems to be where they all radiate from. It's the night stalker epicenter."

By the twentieth floor, H124's legs were already starting to tire, and they still had one hundred flights to go.

When they got to the twenty-fourth floor, the ceiling above the stairwell there had collapsed, sealing off any farther advance on those stairs. They backtracked to a floor below and opened the door to the twenty-third floor.

They passed exec offices, production rooms, transmitter offices, and something called "Efficiency Monitors." Though covered in dust, most of the offices looked like the execs had simply stepped away. The cavernous silence of the place lent a chill to the air, and H124 could feel the hairs pricking on her neck. She started to feel like her oxygen wasn't working properly, so she opened her face plate again.

"Oh, god, me, too," Byron said, lifting his.

The others did the same. "Keep an eye on your gas sensors. We don't want to accidently walk into a cloud of sulfur dioxide."

They tried a stairwell at the other end of the hall, and started up that one, but it was blocked farther up, so they had to use the hallways of floor forty-four. This floor looked different. Instead of separate offices, the entire floor contained a single lab. It had once held several glass doors, but these lay shattered. Strange medical pods stood against each wall, tanks with viscous-looking fluid that had grown dark and stagnant.

She stepped through one of the shattered doors. Metal tables stood around the room, fitted with restraints. H124 felt a cold sweat erupt on her back. "What was this place?"

Something that looked like crusted blood was smeared all over one of the tables, and a thick, dried pool of it had drenched the floor beneath.

Rowan moved to some of the equipment, examining it more closely. In a cabinet at the far end of the room, he discovered an ancient PRD. The casing was cracked, but when he paired it to his own, the floating display flickered and came on. He waved through pages of notes, then paused on a video. He engaged it.

H124 drew up beside him to watch. A man in a grey medical suit and surgical mask faced the camera. "Experiment 254. We've successfully paired the DNA. These workers should be able to go deeper, access areas of complete black. We used a recombinant Q35 sample with the previous Experiment 54's DNA splice to achieve what has been our best result yet." H124 could see writhing bodies strapped to the tables behind the man. A shriek rang out as one of them struggled against its bonds. It shouted, but no comprehensible words came out. The voice sounded strange and garbled, as if talking through a malformed mouth. "We have every reason to believe that the next generation of workers should be ready within the week."

The video ended. Rowan flipped through more notes, and then a series of graphic images depicting the experiments, human workers with altered DNA, scenes of what looked like torture. H124 turned away to find Raven standing behind her.

He placed a hand on her shoulder. "So the night stalkers are . . ."

"People they altered to work in the deep fissures and find fuel extraction points," Rowan finished.

Byron still stood across the room, staring down at the dried pool of blood. He met H124's eyes.

She bolted out of the room, and to the next stairwell. The others followed. She was able to cover fourteen floors before that stairwell also proved to be blocked by debris from the collapsed ceiling. She backtracked down the hallway one floor below. The entire floor, like the one they'd just been on, was comprised of a lab with tables and restraints. She took a service stair up a floor, and peeked down the corridor. This floor was also a giant lab. She went up flight after flight, peeking down the different levels, finding twenty-two more genetics labs.

She decided to run up the narrow service stair. Suddenly her stomach tightened, and a sour taste filled her mouth. She swallowed the urge to retch.

A moment later, Rowan caught up with her. "It's okay, H," he told her.

"No, it's not. Those workers . . . like me . . ."

"It's a terrible place. But these people failed."

"Only some of them did," she countered. "Willoughby said a bunch of the Basin City execs transferred to other megacities when this one got too bad. There were no repercussions for any of this."

Rowan took her in his arms, and she pressed her face against his heat suit. "I'm sorry," he said.

She heard Raven and Byron closing the distance between them, and wiped the corner of her eye.

"You okay?" Raven asked as he reached them. "That was tough back there."

She pulled away from Rowan. "Your de-extinction lab was so beautiful. This is . . ." She readjusted the pack on her back. "Do you think they know they were once human?"

Raven shook his head. "Maybe." He waited. "Probably."

At the next floor, they encountered another collapse, and had to switch back to one of the other stairwells. She climbed up, hearing water dripping somewhere. She caught a whiff of something foul and rotting.

As they climbed higher, they heard the stairwell door bang open above them. Everyone froze. She heard someone breathing up there, then a voice. "Hello?" it called down. It was a man's voice, cracked from disuse, weak and barely audible. She leaned out over the railing and stared up, seeing a bearded face blinking back at her.

"Are you . . . real?" the man asked. His long hair, matted and grey, hung in tangles around his shoulders. His face was smeared with grime, and his clothes hung in tatters off his gaunt frame.

"Yes," Raven said beside her. "We're real."

The man erupted into a sob, and collapsed on his landing. Raven took the stairs two at a time to reach him, then bent over him. "Are you all right?"

The man grabbed Raven's arm, weeping as he clung to him. "I can't believe it . . . I've waited so long . . . didn't think I'd ever see another human being."

As H124 reached him, she caught the reek of urine, and the odor of his soiled clothes.

"Where did you come from?" Raven inquired.

"The Badlands. I came in here to strip down one of the transports. Then those things came. I've been hiding here ever since."

"How long ago was that?" H124 asked.

He stared up at her, blinking vacantly. "I don't know. Six months? I've tried to leave a number of times, but I haven't been able to."

Rowan helped him up, and he hobbled to the stairwell door to steady himself. "You'll take me with you, right? Take me out of here?"

Raven nodded. "Of course."

The man broke down again, his deep gasps making his body shudder. "Let me get my things," he told them.

They followed him through the door and to the hallway beyond. He limped along the corridor, stepping into an exec office. The place stank of rotten food cubes and fecal matter. He hobbled over to a couch he'd been using as a makeshift bed, and rummaged through the dirty sheets that looked as if they'd been red draperies at one point. He started gathering his meager possessions into a small satchel. Rowan watched him move a PRD into the bag. "Wow, that's an old model PX. You can't get those anymore."

The man looked up at him in confusion. "What do you mean? This thing's brand new."

Rowan wrinkled his brow. "They stopped producing them twelve years ago. They only made a few of them. Things were great for intercepting internal messages from the PPC. Made it easy to know the troop movements. The PPC figured out that little hack and stopped making them."

The man frowned. "You're crazy. I stole this thing the week before I broke in here. Stole it right out of the factory in Delta City."

Rowan knelt down next to the man as he crammed a pocket pyro and an old, rusted multitool into his satchel. "Are you saying that the week before you arrived here, that PX was on the production line?"

The man nodded, then, in terrible epiphany, widened his eyes. "Are you telling me I've been here for . . . twelve years?"

"I'm afraid that's what it sounds like."

The man stopped packing. He was frozen in time.

"How have you survived here?" Rowan asked him.

The man opened his mouth, but no sound emerged. He rocked back on his heels, then plumped down on the floor. "Kitchen's full of food cubes . . . been drinking rainwater . . ." He licked his lips, mind reeling. "*Twelve years?*"

"I'm sorry, friend. What's your name?"

At first the man didn't answer. He just stared around, dazed. Finally he whispered, "Malcolm."

Rowan extended his hand. "I'm Rowan." He introduced the rest of them, and Malcolm nodded at each in turn, mouth still hanging low.

Finally he stood up, slinging his satchel over his shoulder. "Let's get out of here."

Raven hurried to the office door. "We have to do something before we go," he told Malcolm. "You're welcome to wait here if you like. We'll pick you up on our way back."

"No way," Malcolm said, his voice returning. "You'll forget all about me."

"We won't," Raven assured him.

"I'm coming along," Malcolm said, his jaw set.

"All right then," Raven agreed.

As they filed back into the hallway, Malcolm asked Rowan, "What does your PRD look like?"

Rowan paused. "Excuse me?"

"Your PRD. Let me see it."

Rowan pulled it out, and Malcolm snatched it out of his hand, He examined it from all angles, and switched it on. Rowan's was code-protected, so he couldn't see any of the screens. "What's the code?" Malcolm demanded.

Rowan reached for his PRD. "We'll set you up with your very own once we get out of here."

"No!" Malcolm shouted, shoving Rowan's hand away. He stuffed the PRD into his satchel. Rowan stared back at him, but the man's dark eyes glittered wildly beneath his crop of grey hair.

"You can hold on to it for a while," Rowan said, "but I'm going to need it back to order our lift out of here."

Malcolm pushed past him, clutching his satchel to his side. "Where are we going?"

"Floor 120," Raven told him.

"You go first," Malcolm ordered, gripping the satchel as if they would rip it out of his hands at any moment.

Raven took the lead, followed by Rowan. Malcolm glowered at H124 and Byron and said, "Well?"

"Oh, no, mate. You first," Byron said, speaking for the first time since they met the man.

Malcolm turned with a grunt, starting up the stairs behind the others. Byron gently took H124's arm, holding her back. "I don't like this. My gut is singing like an angry drunk with a bottle of cheap whiskey."

"I don't feel so great about it either," H124 whispered back.

They resumed their laborious climb, ascending another twelve floors before they had to switch to a different stairwell.

"Why do you think there aren't any night stalkers in here?" she asked Byron, keeping her voice low.

He glanced up at the others. "Don't know. The PPC made their own towers to last. Maybe this building stayed strong enough to withstand their invasion."

"Or maybe," she said, still whispering, "they avoid this place because it's where they were made. Where they were tortured." She met his eyes. "It's like the House of Pain."

"The House of Pain?"

"It's from a book I read, *The Island of Doctor Moreau.* This crazy scientist created these animals, stitched them together using vivisection, twisting them into things they weren't, forcing them to speak, to walk on two legs . . . their pain was excruciating."

He stopped and blinked at her.

"After that, they never wanted to return to the House of Pain," she went on.

"That was in a book?" he asked, astounded. "Like something you'd read for fun?"

She gave a shy laugh.

"Sounds like a real heartwarming story."

The others had gotten a floor above them, so they started up again, but came to an abrupt halt when Malcolm bounded back down from the overhead landing. "What do *your* PRDs look like? I want to see them." He gestured at her. "And I want to see that energy rifle, too. I've never seen tech like that. Did you get it here? I want to see it."

"No way," Byron said. "Just keep moving."

"I said," Malcolm enunciated, spitting out each word, "I—want—to—see—that—rifle." He stared down the stairs.

"And *I* said," Byron snapped, "*No way!*"

Malcolm dashed down the stairs, clashing with Byron on the landing. The latter lifted his gun, hitting him in the head with the rifle stock. Malcolm crumpled like a rag.

Raven came from above, jogging down the steps. "What happened?" He saw Malcolm lying at Byron's feet.

"Crazy dude rushed me."

Malcolm slowly got to his feet, holding his head. H124 saw that he bore a fresh cut on his cheek. Silently he turned and climbed up toward Raven, then kept walking up. "I just wanted to see it," he moaned over one shoulder. "You didn't have to hit me."

"This is too weird," Byron whispered to H124.

They resumed their climb. When they passed Raven, the Rover said, "The guy's been here a long time alone. He's probably forgotten how to be around people."

"That's one way to put it," Byron said.

At last they reached the 120th floor. It consisted of a single luxurious office. At least it had been luxurious at one time. As H124 looked through the door, she saw dusty vases and sculptures, a grime-coated desk and couch, and furniture in disarray.

And there, on a pedestal in the center of the room, stood the spacecraft section.

"*Yes!*" H124 cried out, punching the air with her fist.

They tried the door, but found it locked with a secondary system; a backup was in place in case the power ever failed. Using Dirk's workaround, Rowan powered on the lock with his PRD, and cut and reattached wires. It took him a few tries before the heavy steel door finally slid open.

Raven rushed to the section, looking it over. He let out a huge sigh. "It doesn't appear to be damaged."

"What is that thing?" Malcolm asked, drawing closer.

"The last piece of a puzzle," Raven told him.

"What kind of puzzle?"

Raven slung off his pack and unfurled the maglev sled. "The puzzle that will save all of our lives."

As the copters aligned themselves, Malcolm got even closer, pointing. "What's that thing?"

"It's going to carry this section out for us."

Gently, Raven and H124 lifted up the glass enclosure, and set it aside. He draped a clean skin over the craft, and it adhered to the spacecraft section, sealing it off. Then the maglev snaked out its levers, inserting them under the craft until it was lifted onto the sled. Raven set up the maglev to follow him.

Other antiquities lined the shelves and bookcases on the walls, including some thin, framed books. One was called "Incredible Hulk #181," another "Detective Comics #27," and still another "Amazing Fantasy #15." She also found a strange collection of artifacts among them. One was a black and white clay bowl with geometric designs. It looked very old. A smooth wooden club lay next to a white sphere that had red stitching, both covered in dust. She picked up a gold, metal circle with a little button on top. When she pressed it, one face of the object opened, revealing a surface with numbers. Then she picked up a flat, square case next to it, and brushed off the dust. On the outside she could make out the word "a-ha" below a picture of three men, and when she opened the case, she found a disk similar to the ones she'd first located in Delta City. She placed it in her satchel. Beside it stood a cube with grooves, each side a different, vibrant color. She blew the dust off this as well, and found that she could turn each side to mix up the colors. She returned it to its original pattern, and placed it back on the shelf.

In a glass case, she found a cylindrical brass object tipped with more glass at either end, one side being narrower than the other. There was also an ancient-looking paper map, and a round, brass device with N-S-E-W written on it.

As they readied to leave the room, H124 moved to the expansive window overlooking Basin City. Hundreds of fires gleamed as far as she could see, twinkling red in the darkness.

They had begun to head out of the door when Malcolm suddenly picked up a chair and heaved it against Raven's back. As Raven staggered forward, Malcolm ripped the energy rifle off his back, and shot him with it. Then he turned it on Byron, who dove to the side before he could fire. H124 flung herself behind the large desk. She brought her rifle around to the front, but Rowan beat her to the shot. He fired off his weapon, and a brilliant, sizzling light engulfed Malcolm. The old man fell to the floor, knocked out and jittering.

H124 hurried to Raven's side as Byron wrenched his rifle from Malcolm's grip. He found Rowan's PRD in the man's satchel, and handed it back.

Rowan increased his rifle to a higher setting. As Malcolm stirred on the floor, Rowan kept it trained on him.

"What should we do?" asked H124.

"Leave his ass," said Byron.

Raven thought a moment. "He'd just follow us. Let's keep him with us so we know where he is."

Malcolm sat up.

"You have two choices," Rowan told him. "We shoot you and leave you for dead, or you walk in front at gunpoint. Either way, you do something like that again, and you're dead. You can rot here."

Malcolm sat up, running his hand over his face. "I'm sorry. I don't know what came over me." He wobbled to his feet, then grabbed the desk to steady himself.

Placing Malcolm in front, they started out of the room, the maglev hovering behind Raven. But before they reached the stairwell door, Malcolm turned and darted down the hallway, rounding the corner. They heard a door slam.

They all looked at each other, half-puzzled, half-worried.

"You should have just killed him," Byron confessed. "Someone like him wouldn't think twice about killing us."

They filed back into the stairwell and began their descent, the sled humming along. H124 was two floors down when the stairwell door next to her banged open. Malcolm collided with her, knocking her onto her back. She pushed at him, but his bony frame fell on top of her. He started ripping at the pack at her shoulders, trying to wrench it off. Then his hands closed around the energy rifle, and it went off, hitting the wall. She shoved him off just as Rowan snatched the back of the man's coat. He thrust Malcolm against the wall, and again he fell.

Malcolm lay there shaking. Then he struggled to his feet, once more refusing to stay down. "I need your tech more than you do," he said, straightening his tattered clothes. "This is the score I've been waiting for."

Raven helped H124 up. Rowan upped the setting on his rifle yet again.

Malcolm's eyes glittered at the sight of the spacecraft section. "That thing must be valuable if you risked your lives to come get it."

"Not in the way you're thinking," Raven told him.

Malcolm reached into his dirty satchel and whipped out a knife with a serrated edge. "I'm taking it. And something tells me you're not the kind to kill a man over a piece of tech." He started for the sled, brandishing the knife. "But I will. I'll kill any of you who come closer." He was halfway to the sled when Rowan shot him. Malcolm collapsed, his body convulsing on the floor.

"Did you kill him?" Byron asked.

Rowan checked the setting on the rifle. "No, but he'll be out for a long time. We'll be well out of here."

Byron marched back up to the landing and slung the Henry repeating rifle off his back, aiming it at the prone man. Raven grabbed the muzzle. "No!"

Byron's eyes were fixed on him. "Why not?"

"He's helpless right now. You can't shoot him in cold blood."

"The hell I can't. He's going to wake up and start hunting us again. We had to put him down three times in how long? We can't risk it."

Raven kept holding the muzzle. "He's just desperate. Confused. He's been here for so long he doesn't know how to react. Probably all he's thought about for twelve years is what brought him here—stolen tech."

Byron's rifle kept on the man's head, but Raven stepped in front of it. "No, Byron. He's not PPC or a Repurposer. He's one of us. One of you. A Badlander."

"Maybe he *used* to be one of us."

"He still is. Let's just leave him."

Reluctantly, Byron lowered the rifle. He nudged the man with the toe of his boot. He didn't stir.

They all started down again.

Before long they reached another blocked stairwell, but were able to pass through the door into a hallway. The entire floor was comprised of two huge exec offices. They each had their own cocktail bars and medpods, collections of antiques, and slide-away beds that folded into the walls. They passed through to another stair, and continued to descend. H124 stopped halfway down the next set of stairs, listening. "What is that?"

Everyone paused. "I don't hear anything," Raven said.

Rowan pressed his ear against the wall. "Wait . . . yes, I hear it, too. A scuttling sound."

She placed her hand against the flat surface. "Is this an exterior wall?"

Raven checked his PRD and the old PPC tower blueprints that Willoughby had provided. "Yes." H124 pressed her ear flat, hearing a scratching on the outside of the building. "I think it's—"

A deafening explosion wracked the stairwell. She grabbed on to the railing as a huge chunk of ceiling crashed down right next to her. Then another one hit her in the back, pinning her facedown on the stairs. She thrust her elbow up, shoving it off. Pushing to her feet, she tried to assess the damage. She coughed in the billowing dust, and brought the back of her arm to her mouth. Her ears were ringing. She looked up to see a small hole in the side of the building. The stars glimmered beyond. The hole was only a foot or so wide, but in no time a grey set of claws snaked through. Green eyes stared back at her, reflected in the beam of her headlamp.

As more dust settled, H124 took in her surroundings. The ceiling and a portion of the wall had collapsed, blocking her off from Rowan and Raven. On the stairs above, Byron coughed, waving away the dust, trying to peer through the billowing cloud. She stared down over the railing. The stair was completely blocked, and she saw no sign of the others. "Rowan!" she shouted. "Raven!"

She heard one of them cough below.

"Are you all right?"

"Yes!" came a muffled reply. "But we can't get through to you."

She moved down a few steps and started digging through the rubble, moving aside ceiling tiles and chunks of interior wall. Above her the things scratched and clawed, attempting to widen the hole.

Byron rushed down to help her, heaving debris out of the way.

The stairwell door slammed open above them. Malcolm appeared, holding a detonator. His smile faded to a scowl when he saw them below. "You were all supposed to die!" he shouted.

He scurried down the stairs, brandishing his knife, and Byron stood up, unslinging the rifle from his back. But Malcolm was too quick. As he flew down the stairwell, H124 rose, spinning to face him just as Byron grabbed Malcolm's hands. She was reaching for the rifle on her back when suddenly Malcolm's hand came free in the struggle. He went off balance, driving the knife forward. H124 tried to step back, but found herself too close to the wall. She felt the knife sink into her side, a burning sensation that pierced her insides.

"Noooo!" Byron shouted. He regained his hold on Malcolm's arm, and twisted his hand violently. H124 slumped to the ground.

All the while, the night stalkers clawed through the weakened wall with furious energy. One already had its head and shoulders through. H124 stood, unslung her energy rifle, and focused it on Malcolm. She was about to fire when something hit her back, sending her sprawling. She spun as claws dug into her shoulders, flinging the beast against the far wall.

Byron grabbed Malcolm's knife hand, wrenched his wrist, and seized the blade. He drove it right through Malcolm's throat, stabbing him over and over. Blood spattered his heat suit.

The night crawler zeroed in on her again, just as a second one squeezed through and leapt down. Her emitter wasn't making a damn bit of difference. Then she looked down. The device wasn't blinking. The explosion had broken it. She snatched it off her suit, shook it, pressed the power button. Nothing. A third night stalker crawled through the opening. They closed in on her with a snarl.

"We have to get upstairs!" she shouted. "Get past the door!" Byron threw Malcolm's body aside, sending it tumbling down the stairs. The night stalkers leapt on it, growling and tearing into his torso. Scarlet sprayed the walls as Byron and H124 backed up the stairs. But two more night stalkers pushed through the hole, instantly spotting them.

"I don't get it," Byron said. "How can they see us?" He looked down at her emitter. "Yours isn't blinking!"

"I know." Another slinking beast snaked its head through, then dropped down. The creatures lunged up the stairs. Byron fired off a few rounds, nailing a few, but more kept surging forward. They stared at her, ignoring Byron completely.

Taking her by surprise, Byron shoved her to the side. She flew against the far wall, and the night stalkers swarmed over him, ripping into him.

"Byron!" she shouted, then looked down at the flashing light on her chest. He'd slapped his own emitter on her.

She lifted her energy rifle and fired repeatedly, sending the night stalkers skittering on the landing. She couldn't crank it to the lethal setting as long as Byron was in physical contact with the creatures. It would kill him, too. She reached the stairwell door, and kicked it open. She blasted the night stalkers, one shot after another. Then she dialed it up to the lethal setting and hit the ones away from Byron in the stairwell, before focusing her fire on the ones pouring in through the hole. When the stunned creatures fell away from Byron, H124 sucked in a breath. His heat suit had been torn open, his torso eviscerated. She could see the exposed lining of his stomach, the wet glistening of a rib. Blood pooled beneath him in a thick stream. His face had been shredded. His head slumped forward, and she could hear blood bubbling in his lungs. But he was breathing. She quickly grabbed the collar of his heat suit and yanked him through the door, slamming it shut behind them.

The floor contained more luxury exec offices, so she prayed one of them had a medpod like the others. The slice in her side burned as warm blood trickled down, her left leg slick and wet inside the suit.

She dragged Byron down the hall, skirting around fallen cabinets and large decorative vases that had shattered long ago.

She left him for a moment to run into the first office, and was thrilled to see a medpod in the wall. It was fitted with a theta wave receiver and manual control, but neither had power, nor did the medpod. She had to use Dirk's workaround. Panic threatened to seize her, but she forced herself to breathe and still her thoughts as she took the power cell out of her PRD. She tore off the panel in front of the TWR, and inserted the cell. She held her breath, waiting for it to power on. A green indicator light flashed, and she sent the message for it to open the medpod. It beeped, and the medpod wall panel slid away, allowing the pod to lower itself down.

She tore the power cell out of the TWR and inserted it into the medpod. But it didn't power on. It wasn't strong enough. Dread filled her heart. She stood there, blinking, then ran back to Byron. She tore the PRD off his wrist and darted back. After pulling out its power cell, she daisy-chained it to her own. The medpod blinked, then whirred, and all the lights came on. She gave a gasp of joy and raced back to Byron. He lay on the floor, completely still, a lake of blood pooling around him. Grabbing his collar, she dragged him into the office, and started unlatching his heat suit. It was hell to get off, stiff and cumbersome, but she managed to pull his body free.

Then she propped him against the wall, threw one of his arms around her shoulder, and hefted him to his feet. She couldn't hear him breathing.

She staggered over to the pod and lifted him in, straightening his body as the glass closed.

It started scanning him, instantly sterilizing his wounds. The surgi-laser went to work, repairing his torn tissues and organs, mending his skin. His pulse, so weak, was barely a blip on the display. The pod sampled his blood, and created a synthetic to tide him over. It injected him with it, and slowly his heart rate grew stronger.

H124 stood with her hands against the glass, watching his face. The surgi-laser repaired his damaged cheek and forehead, mended the wound in his throat. He started to look like his old self, and his breathing normalized.

She returned to the stairwell door, making sure it was still closed. For an added precaution, she dragged over a heavy display case and jammed it against the door. The cut in her side screamed in pain, resisting her every move. She then made a circuit of the floor, checking the other stairwells and barricading them.

The door to the exec office had been jammed open sometime in the past, and she couldn't close it.

When she returned to the medpod, Byron was still undergoing surgery. Feeling the wet, warm blood, she shucked off her heat suit and lifted her shirt to examine the knife wound. It was deep. She tore off part of her sleeve, wadded it up, and applied pressure. Then she slumped down next to the medpod, keeping an eye on Byron's vitals. She couldn't call the others without her power cell, so she waited, gripping her side. The slash burned, but she tried to tune out the pain.

She didn't know how long she sat there, her mind going over the events, hoping against hope that the others were safe.

"It seems as if I owe you," a familiar voice sounded. "Again."

She looked up to see Byron sitting up in the medpod, staring down at her.

She got to her feet, wincing in pain. Red lines ran along his face where the surgi-laser had done its work, but he looked well.

She smiled. "And I owe you."

His eyes dropped to the blood-soaked sleeve she had pressed to her side. "We need to get you in here." He struggled to get out, his face twisting with discomfort. She knew that medpods worked wonders, but you still had a lot of healing to do on your own afterward.

As he got out, the glass door sealed shut, and the pod disinfected itself. When it was finished, Byron pressed the lid release again, and helped her inside. As the glass sealed over her, she removed the crusted rag from her side. It scanned her, the familiar green light sweeping over her body. Then it administered a numbing agent to her side, and went to work sealing and cleaning the wound.

As it worked, she watched Byron through the glass, who stood peering in at her. She gave him a sad smile. When all was done, the lid opened, and Byron helped her out.

The pod cleaned itself and retreated into the wall. They removed their power cells and put them back into their PRDs.

"I'll let Raven and Rowan know we're okay," she said, bringing up a comm window.

Rowan's face came into view, dusty and sweaty. "H! Are you still stuck on the other side? We've had no luck digging. There's just too much debris."

"Don't dig," she told them. "There's a horde of night stalkers on the other side of it. We barely got out of there. Byron was hurt bad . . ."

"Where are you?"

"On the floor above. I put him in a medpod up here, but we're fine now. How are you two?"

Raven came into the picture. "We're fine here. Little knocked around, but nothing serious."

"And the sled?"

Raven nodded. "It wasn't even hit."

She let out a sigh of relief.

"Are you hurt?" Rowan asked.

"Nothing too bad," she lied. "My emitter's broken."

Rowan's eyes went wide. "Damn."

"I'm not going to be able to get out of here while it's still dark."

"Then we hole up and wait," Raven said.

"What caused that collapse anyway?" Rowan asked.

"Malcolm," H124 told them. "He came after us again. Had a detonator." The image of Byron stabbing him repeatedly played through her head. "He's dead."

Rowan clenched his jaw. "I should have just killed him."

"We'll get to a safe place, wait out the night," Raven told her. "We'll let Gordon know the plan."

"Okay," she agreed, and they said their goodbyes and signed off.

She moved to the couch and sat, her side protesting, but the pain was much less sharp, so she could almost ignore it. Byron sat beside her, and together they surveyed the burning city below.

"What a strange place," he said quietly.

A particularly bright fissure glowed red and gold, illuminating the smoke above it.

"I'd say we could get some sleep, but there's no way I'm falling asleep with those things outside the door."

He gave her a rueful smile. "Yeah, me neither." His green eyes flashed. "I didn't think I was going to make it."

She met his gaze. "Why did you do that?"

She could feel his intense stare all the way to her core. "Why did I give you my emitter?"

She nodded.

"I couldn't stand there and watch those things hurt you." He paused. "You're unlike anyone I've ever met. You have this singular purpose, this altruistic bent that's almost alien to me. Since the first time we met, I've felt this connection to you. And now here I am, alive when I should be dead, fighting to see this vision of yours through to the end."

He brought up his hand, rifling his fingers through her hair at the back of her head. A flutter of pleasant chills washed over her, and she stood up, suddenly unsure. Byron matched her movements, shifting to stand in front of her.

His eyes locked on hers, and he drew close, bringing his arm around her back. The scent of his breath was inviting, evoking a visceral response. He pulled her into him, their bodes flush. The warmth of him spread over her, every part of her tingling. His green eyes locked on hers, his gaze penetrating, burning.

A conflict rose up inside her. His lips were mere inches away, but she held back. She remembered the night they met, lying together, the feeling of his body against hers. "I . . ." she began to say.

"Yes?" The scent of his warm skin made her feel strange, drunk. "I sort of have this thing with Rowan."

He pressed against her, hips touching hers. "I know. But you've fought by my side. My pulse races at the sight of you, ever since our first night together."

"When you tied me to you in your bed?" she breathed. She meant it to sound funny, take him off guard, but instead he drew closer.

"Yes. It took me by surprise. I could feel you next to me, not just your body, but your *spirit,* burning away in the darkness."

Her eyes wanted to close, to breathe him in, to bridge the distance, but she tried to resist. "But Rowan . . ."

"You don't owe him anything. Is there a reason you can't be with me?"

His lips brushed hers, and the feel of them made her eyes close against their will. "I don't know . . . I don't know anything about this kind of thing. It's all new for me."

"If you don't feel anything, just tell me," he breathed, his lips grazing hers again. Her head started to spin. She felt intoxicated, her lips on fire, every part of her surging with a strange desire.

His hands felt strong on her back, and his fingers moved up into her hair. She sighed with pleasure at his touch. Then his lips met hers, pressing sensuously, his kiss fiery and passionate, sweeping over her.

She felt herself starting to melt away, to sink into him. His arms pulled her into him. He kissed her deeply, his tongue enticing her with completely new sensations. His hips moved against hers, eliciting an unfamiliar longing, her heart pounding in new places. She felt dizzy, and ached for him to touch her.

She went off balance, but he held her close, kissing her now with so much fire that she felt a primal desire to sink her fangs into him. A growl came out of her throat, low and erotic, and his eyes flashed in response. They staggered against the wall, his hands roaming over her, making her moan.

She opened her eyes and met his gaze, unsure of what came next.

She heard something then, a scrabbling at the door. She turned to see another pair of green eyes—this one much less inviting—peering into the office.

A night stalker had breached a stairwell barricade. They froze.

Her heat suit was within reach, so she lifted it so the emitter faced out. The beast crept into the room, moving its head, mouth open in a snarl. Its gaze swept the room as it entered, lifting its snout and sniffing.

She and Byron remained still as it approached, eager tongue licking its lips. When it got within two feet, it shook its head and backed off, moving away. It continued to lope through the office, sniffing, and finally left.

Byron exhaled. "That was close."

"Byron," she whispered, pointing at the office door. More luminous green eyes appeared. The creatures slunk into the room, snouts lifted, hissing and snapping at one another.

They approached Byron and H124, but she clutched the heat suit closer, hoping one emitter was enough to protect both of them. Right now, pressed together, they might seem like a single object.

Two of the night stalkers approached, breathing them in, then shook their heads as the emitter grew too intense. They backed off a little, though they knew something edible stood directly before them. They looked to one another, making otherworldly whining noises.

Byron put his arm around her as dozens more entered the room, closing in on them, confused, but aware of their presence. The emitter was working for now, but if it failed, they were both dead.

In time the night stalkers sensed the futility, and filed out of the room. Byron turned to her. "We need a safer place to hole up. If this thing fails . . ."

H124 thought about the expanse of city, of ferrying the spacecraft section across the unstable ground, of the gases that might corrode the clean skin.

"How close would you say we are to the top of the building?" she asked.

"You mean where the antenna and upper stories fell off?"

"Yes."

"A dozen or so floors. Why?"

"Think we could make it up there? Get outside?"

"Out there? Those things are crawling all over the side of the building. It's exposed."

"I know, but if we could get up there instead of having to cross the city with the spacecraft piece . . ." She brought up her PRD comm window. Rowan answered somewhat groggily. He was clearly trying to rest.

"H? Everything okay?"

"Yes." She felt a little odd talking to him now, and her cheeks burned. "Are you still in contact with Marlowe, the helicopter pilot?"

He nodded. "She's at the new camp."

"This might sound crazy, but what if we climbed out to the top of the tower, and she picked us up there?"

He lifted a brow. "That doesn't sound crazy at all, actually."

Raven stirred, and moved into frame. "It would save us from endangering the spacecraft section."

"There's just one catch."

"What's that?" Rowan asked.

"We're not going to last the night up here. The night stalkers breached the barricade, and we only have one emitter. It hurts their ears to get close, but they can sure smell us, and if they get brave enough . . ."

Rowan ran a hand through his blond hair. "Can you get somewhere safe for now?"

"We're just about to do that."

"Let me contact Marlowe. See how far out she is, when she could get here."

"Thanks." She ended the call, and looked to Byron. "Let's find somewhere more secure. Something with a steel door." She thought back to New Atlantic, to the most sturdy areas of its PPC Tower. "Maybe an old server room, or an exec office with a door still intact."

They folded up their heat suits and stuffed them into their packs. They barely fit, but it was better than being encumbered by them.

Byron reached his hand down. She took it, his palm rough and warm. In the nearby stairwell, they could hear the hissing predators, searching for prey. This was going to be tough.

Chapter 22

They moved down the hall in silence, searching for an area with a sturdy door. Byron had insisted she wear the emitter, so she moved in front of him, shielding him, energy rifle at the ready. He walked with his back to her, also brandishing his weapon. The other exec office on this level had a door that wouldn't close, so they slunk into the service stairwell. It was clear for several floors up and down.

"Which way?" he asked.

"Let's head up. Maybe Rowan has reached Marlowe."

And so they ascended, reaching the next collapsed section. Here they entered the stairwell door, headlamps shining in the dark corridors beyond. They listened for any hint of movement, but heard nothing. This floor also held several labs, and they moved to the first one. Its door was still intact, and together they forced it open. Slipping inside, they checked the room, finding it thankfully empty. Returning to the door, they slid it shut, and blocked it with a thick metal cabinet.

H124 moved to a chair and sat. "And now we wait."

Byron took a seat across from her, watching her. She could feel the weight of his gaze. Her stomach was doing somersaults. She felt a strange, wild sensation, as if for the first time in her life she had no idea what she was doing.

She felt that if she looked at him, the room would erupt in fire. She breathed slowly, forcing her heart to slow, but the tingling didn't go away. Her mind turned over and over, thinking of the night stalkers, then Rowan, then . . . She turned her head, and found his eyes smoldering at her.

Her heart started thudding. She longed to feel him again, breathe in his scent, but her heart and mind were conflicted.

Her PRD beeped. Rowan's face flashed on the screen. "I've reached Marlowe. We're in luck. She can get here in about two hours."

H124 looked at her clock. "It's still going to be dark then."

"We'll have to be cautious. We can meet you up on the top of the tower."

"Be on the lookout for those things," she told him. "They could have spread through the whole building by now."

"Let's lie low, then make our way to the top just before her arrival."

"Sound good."

"How is Byron doing?" Raven asked, coming into view.

She looked over at him, but quickly averted her eyes. "He's better."

"Good."

"You two be careful," she said.

Rowan smiled. "Always."

They ended the transmission. Byron slid off the chair and stretched out on the floor. "My whole body aches." He placed his headlamp next to him, providing a soft glow over the room.

"I'm not surprised."

He took off his jacket and folded it up, creating a makeshift pillow. Then he held his hand out.

She lay down next to him in the dim light, placing her head on his chest. She listened to his heart beating. She thought of the first night they'd done this, and how much had transpired since then. He lay on his back, eyes closed, his inviting lips parted slightly. His breathing came deep and even, but she couldn't tell if he was falling asleep. She studied his profile, his long hair spilling down over his makeshift pillow, the rough of his whiskers. They lay like that for a long time.

Then, as if he could sense her gaze, he turned his head and opened his eyes. His breathing quickened. He rolled onto his side to face her, resting his hand on her waist. She felt a flutter there, an electrical surge.

"I'm burning for you," he whispered, leaning closer. True to his word, he pressed his lips against hers in a fiery kiss that made her whole body tremble. She wrapped her arms around him, feeling his muscular back. He rolled on top of her, his hair cascading around her face. The feel and taste of him made her heart race. His hips writhed against hers, eliciting waves of pleasure through her body.

Her PRD started to beep. She heard it as if it were a distant thing, at first not understanding what it was. Then she melted out of her reverie, slowly waking as if from a warm dream. Byron sat up. She brought a hand to her head, stilling her thoughts, her body, then lifted her PRD.

Raven appeared in the comm window. "Marlowe was able to leave faster than she thought. She estimates that she's thirty minutes out."

H124 nodded, her head swimming. "We'll meet you up there."

"Okay." He signed off.

She felt conflicted again. In a few minutes, she was going to see Rowan. What was she to him? She had no experience with this kind of thing, yet she felt her heart being pulled in two different directions.

"Are you okay?" Byron asked, placing a warm hand on her cheek.

"I'm not sure. I feel very . . . strange." There was something irresistible about Byron, but she didn't know if it was because of the dangers they'd faced together, if that had created some powerful bond, or if it was something about him in particular.

They stood up, grabbed their packs, and checked their weapons.

"Should we go now or wait a little longer?" she asked him. "As soon as we leave, we might not find another safe place to hole up."

He rechecked the chamber of his rifle, and made sure extra rounds were handy in his satchel. "I say we go now. The stairwell could be blocked up there. We might not even be able to reach the top, in which case she'd have to pick us up on the street."

She moved to the door, where Byron suddenly took her in his arms, holding her so tightly that for a moment she couldn't breathe. He bent his head down, kissing her deeply. Then he pulled away, meeting her eyes. "Let's go."

They pushed the cabinet off to the side, and slid the door open. The hallway was empty, soundless. H124 made sure the emitter was still functioning, and in back-to-back formation they headed for the nearest stairwell, and began the climb.

They had gone only a few floors up when they heard the stairwell door above creak open.

A familiar rasping filtered down, the sound of breathing through a ruined mouth. Then another hiss joined it, and a fervent ululation passed between the creatures. She was starting to recognize their sounds. This cry usually meant they were calling to others. Byron thumbed behind him, and they crept backward down the stairs. The beasts started down, claws clicking with every step. H124 reached the landing and stared down just as the door on that level opened. She hoped wildly it was Rowan or Raven, but instead a clawed grey hand came into view, curling around the door's edge.

Byron burst forward, kicking the door as hard as he could, slamming the fingers inside. The night stalker on the other side howled in agony.

Byron wrenched open the door, firing the rifle point blank into a cluster of creatures on the other side. The flash of the muzzle lit up the corridor beyond, where dozens of green eyes glittered back. Then he kicked the door shut and ran down the next flight of stairs, H124 right behind.

When she heard the door above open again, she spun, firing her rifle into the mass of night stalkers overhead. Byron reached the door at the next landing, and wrenched it open. He shone his light down the hallway, seeing nothing but an empty corridor. They ran inside, desperately searching for something to block the door.

She pointed to a large desk in an executive suite. They ran over to it, hefting it between them, and lumbered back to the entrance. They'd just tipped it on its side when the door started to open. Panicking, they slammed it against the door like a battering ram, driving the things back.

The handle turned, and the beasts tried to get in.

She and Byron took off down the hall, searching for another way up. She figured Rowan and Raven were well below, still heading up. They quickly scouted their way to another stairwell, and made the ascent.

They reached a section where a large slab of steel had crashed down on the stairs. She checked the building's schematics. "This is it," she said. "The top."

They braced their shoulders against the steel, lifting to no avail. Byron slung off his pack and set it down in the pool of light made by their lamps. He pulled out his pocket torch and donned a pair of dark goggles. As he lit the torch, shadows danced. He brought it up to the metal, cutting a hatch in it. Sparks flew to the ground, cascading hypnotically. "Stand back," he said, nearing the end of his rectangular cut. She moved against the wall as the piece of steel clattered to the ground. Night air blew in over them. Byron lifted his hands, gripping the rough edges of the cut, and started to pull himself through. She grabbed on to his hips, pulling him back down. "No way. I've got the emitter. I'm going first."

He met her gaze, his jaw set. Before he could protest, she jumped up through the hole, and hoisted herself up.

The broken rooftop didn't have much space for them to walk. There was only the remainder of the steel sheet that had fallen over the stairwell, and a few metal girders leading off toward the edge of the building. The wind howled around her, bringing the stench of rotten eggs. Much to her relief, there weren't any night stalkers prowling around.

Byron started to come up, but she held out her hand. "Wait a sec. It's pretty exposed up here. Let me call the others."

She put in a call to Rowan and Raven, telling them the sequence of stairwells they'd used to get up there. Raven thanked her and signed off.

She overlooked the city. The stairwell had deposited them near the west-facing wall of the tower, and she marveled at the sheer size of the forlorn metropolis.

Before long she heard the others in the stairwell below.

"Up here!" Byron called to them.

As she peered down through the makeshift hole, Raven came into view, sweating, black hair plastered to his face, gasping for breath. Making the climb all at once was taxing. Rowan followed soon after, his heat suit draped over one arm, his grey shirt drenched with sweat from his chest. She was struck with the memory of their first meeting in New Atlantic, hiding out in that small, dark room, hearing the Repurposers pass by the door, her heart thudding. He'd saved her life. Gotten her out of the city. She wished she knew if the conflict she felt was normal. Wished she knew what she was doing.

The sound of a helicopter's beating rotors drew her attention back outside. "I hear Marlowe!" she called, with an open-mouthed smile.

Then she saw the eyes. Green orbs, staring out at her from the far ledge. She swept her light around, spotting the crouching shapes pulling themselves up over the building's edge, slinking across the exposed girders, drawing closer.

"Night stalkers!" she shouted.

Byron grabbed the edge of the hole, and heaved himself up. He slung the rifle off his back and started firing, the booms cacophonous in the quiet night as dazzling flashes burst from the muzzle. H124 fired hers as well, hitting a few in a volley of beautiful light. The creatures fell inside the building, while others toppled off the tower.

Rowan climbed up and stood by her side, also firing away, felling as many as he could. Raven climbed through the hole just in time to see a fresh wave of night stalkers emerge from over the ledge. H124 stood close to Byron, trying to protect him with the emitter.

The others did the same, forming a tight circle, shooting in all directions. As the pounding of Marlowe's helicopter loudened, H124 scanned the western sky. She saw the blinking red and blue lights, and freed a hand to flash her headlamp at Marlowe. The helicopter turned on a spotlight, scanning the sides of the tower, sweeping up.

Marlowe drew closer, and the light hit the rooftop in a dazzling blaze. Night stalkers hissed and loped away, covering their eyes, wailing that eerie ululation that had given her nightmares ever since she'd first encountered them.

Marlowe played the spotlight around, skimming the roof, the light sending clusters of night stalkers skittering away like roaches. Then she was hovering above them, the rotor wash blowing H124's hair into her eyes. A ladder jutted down from the belly of the helicopter.

Raven looked to Byron. "You go first. We have your six."

The crack of Byron's next rifle shot was deafening. "No way. You're going up with that sled. It's why we came."

Raven hesitated. Finally he unclipped his emitter, slapped it on to Byron's chest, and started to climb the ladder. It whipped violently in the wind, but he held on, the maglev sled floating next to him. He reached the helicopter, and swung inside. The sled disappeared behind him.

"Okay!" Byron shouted above the rotor wash. "Now you!" He nodded at H124, who slung her rifle on her back. Gripping the cold metal rungs, she scaled quickly. A few times the wind gusted so powerfully that she had to stop climbing, and hang on tight. But soon she reached the helicopter, and Raven pulled her on board.

Byron insisted Rowan go next. The latter threw his rifle over his back, and obliged without any hesitation. Marlowe did her best to shine the light on the rooftop, but there were just too many creatures closing in on Byron. Finally he had to grab the ladder and climb before Rowan was all the way to the top. Marlowe lifted the chopper, carrying Byron away from the desperate night stalkers braving the painful sound of the emitter to slash toward his legs.

H124 lifted Rowan on board while Raven latched the sled and spacecraft section down, as Byron climbed the rest of the way. When he reached the top, they pulled him up. Wasting no time, Marlowe took off, the winch reeling the ladder back inside.

As she banked, H124's stomach took a dive into her shoes. The others held on, struggling into the seats and buckling themselves in.

When they were clear of the city, H124 clasped Marlowe's arm. "Thank you," she told her, with genuine affection.

Marlowe flashed a grin. "Glad I could help."

H124 leaned her head back in the seat. She closed her eyes, relaxing for the first time since they'd landed outside Basin City. They'd made it out.

"Listen," Marlowe shouted. "I've contacted Gordon. He had to refuel, but he sent me the rendezvous coordinates. Shouldn't be long before we're there."

H124 took the opportunity to call Willoughby. He answered right away, and she breathed a sigh of relief. "Where are you?"

"Outside Delta City."

"So you're safe?"

"Yeah, but it was close. Repurposers were on their way to my office. I barely got out."

"I'm so glad you're alive." She had to shout above the helicopter's rotors.

"I did get some intel on that device in your friend."

"What did you learn?"

His expression was grim, his mouth a pale slit. "You can't get it out without a special extractor tool. It's paired with the device when it's implanted, and only a code from the extractor tool can nullify the effects of the device. Then the tool enters the brain and pulls out the sphere."

"Do you have one of those extractor tools?"

He shook his head. "No. I'm sorry. It's still very experimental. You'd have to find the specific one tied to his implant. I learned that Olivia has the extractor. I tried to make it to her office before I left, but Repurposers were everywhere."

"I understand."

"I'm meeting a contact in a few minutes. I'll let you know if I learn more."

"Thanks, Willoughby." She signed off.

As Marlowe flew them safely away, H124 took one last glimpse at the ruined city. Beyond, she spotted Gordon's Vega waiting for them on a flat, brown plain.

Before she knew it, Marlowe set them down, and they filed out.

"Thanks again," she told the pilot.

Marlowe gave her thumbs up and took off without a word, banking away into the night.

They trudged wearily toward Gordon's plane, anxious to deliver the last piece of the craft back to Sanctuary City.

Chapter 23

When Gordon landed them in Sanctuary City, H124 headed straight for the medical lab. She stopped at the window. Inside, Felix worked at his desk while Astoria sat beside the medpod, watching her brother through the glass lid.

Felix saw her and stepped out. Astoria looked up, spotting H124 with weary eyes, but made no effort to get up.

"What's his status?" H124 asked the doctor as he emerged from the room.

"No change, but the countdown continues."

She told him what Willoughby had said about the special extractor tool.

"That might be his only chance then, if such a tool exists," Felix told her. "I've tried everything, but there are no precedents for this thing."

H124 nodded toward Astoria. "How's she holding up?"

"She's been very quiet."

"She's not berating you or telling you what to do?"

He shook his head. "Silent as stone."

As he went back to work, she watched Astoria through the glass. The warrior met her gaze. H124 felt as downcast as Astoria looked. All her fire was gone.

H124 had started down the hall when she heard Astoria leave the med bay. She glanced back to see her pacing in front of the lab's window. Byron emerged from the lift, joining his old friend at the med lab door. She watched their brief exchange, Astoria speaking with slumped shoulders, defeated. Byron gripped her shoulder, but she shrugged it off.

He stood there a few more minutes, trying to comfort her, but she just shook her head and retreated back into the med lab.

Left alone, Byron spotted H124, and started off down the hall. When he reached her, Astoria shot back into the hall. She bit her lip and stared after them, then glanced back to her brother.

"Byron. Wait."

"What is it?" he asked, as she caught up with them.

Tears glistened in her eyes, threatening to pour down her cheeks. She wiped at them roughly. "I need to tell you something." She gave a sigh. "This thing in Dirk." Her eyes met H124's. "That PPC exec . . . your grandmother? She told me they'd put something inside him, that he would die if I didn't cooperate. She wanted information, and said she'd kill him, that she could do it any time she wanted, no matter how far away we were." She crossed her arms and sniffed. "I didn't believe her. I thought after we got out of there that he'd be safe.

"But she kept contacting me. Wanted to know locations, information. Specifics about our plan to divert the piece that's going to hit BEC City. I blew her off. Then Dirk collapsed, and I realized she wasn't bluffing when the doctor found that sphere. I didn't know what to do. She was going to kill him . . ."

Byron touched her arm. "What did you do?"

Astoria looked up, helpless, the tears now spilling freely down her cheeks. "I contacted her. She wanted to know if we were going to be successful in saving BEC City. I told her I thought we were, about the craft with the nuclear payload. She forced me to grant her access to the craft, and to locally lock us out. She wanted to know where we were, where the Rover stronghold was."

H124 felt all the color drain from her face. "You didn't tell her about this location?"

Astoria shook her head. "No. I got her control of the craft, then told her she had to save Dirk. If she didn't, she wouldn't get any more information from me. But by then the sphere had already started its countdown. Until I give her this location, she's not going to save him. I don't know what to do."

"What else did you tell her?" H124 said, dreading the answer. Her stomach went sour.

"Where we keep the Silver Beast."

Byron's jaw fell open "No—Astoria, you didn't."

She hugged herself, rubbing her hands up and down her arms. "I did, Byron. While you all were in Basin City, an airship destroyed it."

His voice sounded weak. "And Chadwick?"

"He'd already left the area after storing it."

Byron let out an explosive sigh. "Well, at least there's that . . ."

"But she didn't deactivate that thing. She says I still have to give her the Rover stronghold location, or she won't save my brother."

Byron ran a hand through his hair. "I can't believe this."

"We can't trust her," H124 said, feeling sick. "We have no guarantee she'd save Dirk even if you did tell her. In fact," she added, thinking back to what Willoughby had told her about her mother, "I doubt she would."

Astoria's chin trembled. "I don't know what to do. He's dying."

H124 told her what Willoughby had learned about the extractor tool before he escaped Delta City, and Astoria's head lifted, her eyes catching the slightest glint. "You think she has it?"

"I think we need to get there and find out."

"But how will we get in? You say Willoughby's gone, and the Beast is destroyed."

H124 met her eyes. "You're sure you didn't reveal the location of Sanctuary City?"

Astoria shook her head. "I would never do that."

"Okay. Let's go talk to Raven."

* * * *

They found him and Rowan in Engineering, where Rivet and her team were beginning to assemble the three pieces. Tools lay scattered on every surface, and all of them wore special suits to keep everything sterile and static-free. H124 pulled Raven aside, apprising him of Astoria's confession.

Raven watched Astoria silently as she explained, then hurried her toward the astronomy lab. "Let's talk to Orion. See where we stand."

The astronomer looked up from his display as they entered. "We don't have much time. If we don't detonate it soon, we'll miss the window to change this thing's course."

Onyx closed down her floating display. "I can't get in," she said with disgust. "I've tried everything. We're going to have to go there in person and shut them down on their end. I've pinpointed where they're hacking from." She brought up a schematic of Delta City, zeroing in on a PPC tower there, and then straight on Olivia's floor.

H124 felt a crushing disappointment. "But how will we get in? Willoughby's gone, the Beast is destroyed . . . We'd be back to accessing the CO_2 vents, and those are too far away from that tower."

Astoria crossed her arms, pacing again. "We have to get in there. Get the extractor tool."

Raven lifted his head, and laughed absently. "I just had the craziest idea."

Byron narrowed his gaze. "Why do I get the distinct feeling this is going to get us all killed?"

Raven grinned. "Well, it might get two of us killed." He gestured excitedly. "We've got these prototype flying suits. You said Willoughby hacked a hole in the shield by replacing the streams of the citizens who maintain it, right?"

She nodded.

Raven continued. "If Onyx could use that same method to hack a hole in the top of the atmospheric shield, Gordon could fly over the dome, dropping two of us above the hole. Then we fly in, land on the tower itself. Look. Here." He brought up a schematic of the tower on his PRD. "There are balconies on the upper floors for the exec living suites. We could land on one of these."

H124 nodded. "We could land undetected on Willoughby's balcony. They might not have replaced him yet, so his suite would be empty."

Byron held up his hand. "Just to be clear, you're talking about falling thousands of feet to land on this tiny ledge?"

Raven nodded. "Exactly."

"I'll do it," Astoria said. "No offense to any of you, but I'm not trusting my brother's life to anyone but myself. I'm going. Besides," she added, looking down, "I want to make things right." She walked to the door. "Show me these suits."

Raven stared at her. "I don't think so. How can we trust you now?"

Astoria's eyes brimmed with tears, but more so with defiance.

Finally H124 stepped up beside her. "I trust her. She'd never risk Dirk's life. She told us what she did, didn't she? She could have given away our location, but she didn't."

Raven pursed his lips. "Okay, then." He led the way to the armory, where he lifted down two small sacks with straps. "We only have two of these suits," he told them. "They stow away in this small pack." He lifted one so they could see the case, no bigger than a couple of bricks. He held up a small, round disk. "This syncs with a PRD. You can then control your pitch and yaw, angle the chute to gain speed or slow down. They're not perfect."

"Can a suit carry two people?"

Raven shook his head. "No. We're still designing a tandem jumper. Only two of us will be able to go."

Rowan stepped up, looking at it. "I can go."

"No, it's got to be me," H124 said. "There are going to be TWRs between where we land and Olivia's office. I know how megacities work. I can get us in and out."

Rowan moved to the rack of energy rifles. "You're going to need weapons."

Astoria stepped forward. "No. We can't bring shock rifles. It's too risky. If we hit the extractor tool, it could fry it out." She selected an old 9mm handgun and checked it over, then grabbed a handful of magazines, stuffing them into a satchel.

Byron crossed his arms. "I'm with Astoria. No half-assed weapons anymore."

H124 knew the stakes. She grabbed a .45 pistol, some extra clips and magazines, then selected a sonic hand weapon from the rack. She adjusted the setting so it would be enough to render someone immobile, but not kill.

Astoria donned a tactical vest and draped a belt of grenades across her chest. She threw a second vest to H124.

Though her body burned from fatigue, H124 returned to the airstrip with the others. Gordon was sleeping in the back of the Vega. He snorted awake, struggling to sit up.

"Feel up to another flight?" she asked him.

He rubbed his eyes. "Rarin' to go. Where to?"

"Delta City. And you won't even have to find a place to land."

He cocked a brow, so she explained the plan. "Are you kidding me?" he asked, mouth agape.

"Nope," she told him.

He shook his head in disbelief, his eyes wide. "Well, alright, then."

She and Astoria stowed their gear while their pilot refueled.

Rowan hugged her goodbye at the runway. "You be safe, H."

She nodded meekly, hugging him back, her emotions conflicted.

Byron handed her a second pistol. "Take this. And here are some extra magazines and clips." She put them in her satchel. "Don't take any unnecessary risks. Kill if you have to." He embraced her, half in friendship, half in longing, then stepped out of the plane's way. Rowan gave him a cursory glance, but H124 tried not to think on it.

"Keep us posted!" Raven shouted as Gordon started up the engines. The propeller filled the night.

"We're going to watch over Dirk," Byron called out. "Don't worry!"

She and Astoria boarded the plane, stealing a last look at their friends. Then they buckled in, looking across at each other.

"You ready for this?" H124 asked.

Astoria checked her weapon, then holstered it. "Never been readier. I'm going to end every one of those PPC fuckers."

Chapter 24

For a moment H124 didn't think she'd be able to jump. She stared out at Delta City's atmospheric dome below her, the crowded buildings and streets, so tiny from this height, looking like a grey blight after the beauty of Sanctuary City. She thought of the desperate lives of the people pressed into a space not big enough to accommodate them all, and of the treacherous, vile ways of the PPC. A queasy feeling washed over her as she thought of her own confined life in New Atlantic, how ignorant she'd been then, a cog in the cold machine of a grasping and heartless regime.

And now she had to jump into the core of it. Cold sweat formed at her back and neck.

Astoria held on to the door frame next to her, staring down with an exhilarated grin. "You all set?" she shouted to H124 above the roar of wind.

"I . . ."

Lowering her goggles, Astoria stepped to the lip of the plane and leapt out. H124 gripped the door frame with a swallow, knowing she had only a narrow window on this pass. She pulled down her goggles with a trembling hand.

"You got this!" Gordon called from the cockpit.

As her stomach reared up in protest, she dove out. The air pushed against her as she opened her chute. It jerked her back up, her teeth clacking together. She sailed down, seeing Astoria below. The dome glowed beneath them, and to her right, she saw the hole in the amber light where Onyx had hacked an opening. She adjusted the chute's controls, aiming it toward the aperture. She made her body more aerodynamic.

Below her, the PPC tower's antennae came into view through the hole, the blinding lights on either side bringing tears to her eyes. Astoria zipped through the hole, followed moments later by H124. They sailed past the bristling antennae, circling the tower, and H124 spotted Willoughby's ledge on the eastern side. She aimed for it, angling her body to slow the descent, adjusting the flight suit's controls. Astoria landed deftly, tucking her body into a ball and rolling to a stop against the ledge railing.

H124 approached the ledge too fast, so she had to make an abrupt adjustment as the balcony loomed up beneath her. She landed hard on her feet, stumbling forward, but managed to remain upright.

Astoria had already pressed the button on the suit to reel in the chute, which folded itself neatly away into her small backpack.

H124 did the same, feeling at once both dizzy and terrified. She half expected troopers to storm out onto the balcony, but their entry had gone unnoticed.

Astoria unholstered her gun. "Let's go."

H124 moved to the balcony door. The room beyond lay in darkness. She hoped they hadn't installed anyone in Willoughby's quarters yet. She stood next to the glass, reaching her mind out to any TWRs. She found one, and sent a signal to it. The balcony door slid open, and a cool breeze washed over them.

"I'll never get used to that," Astoria told her.

They entered Willoughby's living pod, and H124 lifted her goggles, resting them on the top of her head. The familiar scent of Willoughby hit her. She still couldn't believe he was her father. It was all a strange dream. H124 checked the map of the tower on her PRD. "Olivia's office is three floors down."

H124 waved her hand over the door release, and they stepped out into the hall. Moving quietly, they filed past a number of other exec living quarters, eventually reaching the maintenance stairwell. They hurried down the steps, stopping three floors down. Astoria cracked open the door, peered into the hall, and pushed it open wider.

H124 remembered this corridor. She'd taken it during her escape from Olivia's office. She crept left, toward the rear door of Olivia's office.

They paused then, as light spilled into the dark hall from under the door.

"She's still up," Astoria whispered.

H124 brought up a comm window to Onyx. When the hacker's face appeared, Astoria moved into the frame and asked, "Is the signal still coming from the same place?"

Onyx waved through her display. "Yes."

"How's Dirk?" Astoria asked.

"Still unconscious, I'm afraid."

Astoria reached over and closed the window without saying goodbye. "We have to go in now," she whispered.

"Agreed."

Astoria chambered a round.

H124 withdrew her sonic weapon from its holster, and aimed it at the door. Astoria nodded to H124.

She tried the TWR, sending the unlock signal, but it wouldn't open. It was security locked from the inside. H124 used her old workaround method, sending a signal for the TWR to both lock and unlock simultaneously. The panel started to smoke and then caught fire. The door unlocked, opening.

Astoria shoved it to one side, extending her gun with her free hand.

Olivia sat at her desk and snapped her head up. She flung her palm against her chest. "What the—" As her eyes fell on H124, she closed her mouth.

"Where's the device?" Astoria demanded.

"What device?" Olivia stood up, backing toward a panel in the wall behind her.

"Don't move!" Astoria shouted, training the gun on her. "The device that you're using to kill my brother. He's dying!"

Olivia's gaze fell to her desk, where a slender metal rod lay. H124 didn't recognize what it was. It could be the extractor tool, or a weapon for all she knew.

Olivia started backing away again. "I said," Astoria snarled, *"don't move."*

But the exec continued to back up, so Astoria took a knee and fired right through the desk at Olivia's legs. The older woman screamed in agony, and keeled over on her side, clutching her knee. Astoria stormed around the desk, throttling the woman by the throat. She dragged her out into the center of the room.

"Be sure no one gets in that door," Astoria told H124, nodding to the main entrance.

H124 went to it, adjusting the lock readout to the maximum setting. No one was getting in without Olivia's permission now, and she was in no state to give it.

"Tell me where the extraction tool is. Now!" Astoria shouted, leveling the gun to Olivia's head.

"Astoria—" H124 began to say.

When Olivia didn't answer, Astoria jerked the gun down and fired it again, blowing away the woman's other kneecap. Olivia screamed as the blood jetted out, spattering her immaculate white suit. "Please!" Olivia pleaded. "It's in a d-drawer—in my d-desk. S-second one down . . ."

Astoria gestured for H124 to retrieve it. She hurried to the desk, checking for any kind of trap, then tentatively slid it open. Inside lay a surgical tube with a small claw on one end. H124 held it up. "Is this what controls the sphere?"

Olivia nodded, gritting her teeth, sweat beading on her forehead.

H124 came back around the desk. "Where are you jamming the spacecraft from?" she demanded. Olivia pursed her lips and closed her eyes.

Astoria kicked her in the side. "Where?" she shouted.

When she still didn't receive a response, Astoria stomped down on her arm, pinning her wrist against the ground. Then she fired point blank into the woman's hand. Olivia shrieked, and H124 felt a little sick.

H124 knelt down beside her. "Don't you understand? It's not just going to destroy BEC City. A terrestrial hit that big will cause firestorms, earthquakes. We'd all suffer."

Olivia opened her eyes, and tortured tears joined a river of sweat to meander down her face.

Astoria stomped down hard on her forearm. "Your other hand's next. Then your head. Don't think a medpod will help much with that."

"Okay," Olivia whispered, shaking. "Okay. Go to the main display. Enter this code."

H124 hurried to the woman's desk, and brought up her main display. At the terminal window, she paused.

"ENT145OVERRIDE," Olivia told her.

H124 entered it. A stream of data came in. She opened a comm window to Onyx. "I'm in," she told the hacker, then turned her PRD's camera so Onyx could see the display.

The hacker nodded approvingly. "This is good. Okay. Enter the following just as I'm typing it here."

She typed in a series of complex commands, and H124 entered them into the terminal verbatim. The terminal window shut down, then rebooted.

"Now enter this," Onyx added, providing additional coding. "This will lock them out."

H124 typed it in, then turned to see Astoria staring down with utter contempt, her pistol trained on Olivia's head.

"Stay on the line," Onyx told her. For a few tense minutes they waited. Blood pooled beneath Olivia, as sweat dripped from the tip of Astoria's nose.

"All right!" Onyx yelled.

H124 heard Orion cheering in the background. "We're back in. Going to launch the craft now, maneuver it the right distance, and detonate. It's going to be close."

Onyx looked at her. "You did good."

Raven bent down into the frame. "Get the hell out of there, H."

H124 closed down the display, then vaulted over the desk. She looked down at the bleeding wreck that was her grandmother. "You lied about Willoughby."

Olivia's gaze fluttered as she focused on H124. "Is that what he told you?"

"You arranged the death of your own daughter."

"That's what he wants you to believe."

"She was going to reveal to the world what you really are. A monster."

"He's playing on your emotions. Can't you see that?" Olivia whispered. "He can't be trusted."

Astoria aimed at Olivia's head. "Let's finish her off."

H124 reached out, staying Astoria's arm. "No. Let's just leave."

Astoria glared at H124. "She'll just crawl into a medpod." She looked back at Olivia, dark eyes dripping with hatred. "She tried to kill my brother. He still might die."

"Let's just go. We have to get back to save him. We have to move fast."

"I could put a bullet in her head by the time I finish this sentence."

"She's my grandmother," H124 said. "Let's just go."

Reluctantly, Astoria lowered her gun, and spat on the crippled woman's face. Eyes cast downward, H124 hurried back to the maintenance door, and slipped through. She and Astoria hurried down the hall, back to Willoughby's old quarters.

They still had to get out of the city. She patched through to Onyx again. "We're ready," she told the hacker, and sent her coordinates. They climbed out onto the balcony, where the wind whipped violently around them. This high up, the streets below looked distorted, the sheer height playing tricks on H124's sense of perspective. Far below the roofs of smaller buildings bristled upward, too many to count. They watched the atmospheric shield, glowing not too far from their location.

Astoria started to pace. "We should have killed her," she snarled, snugging her pistol back into its holster. Then the shield flickered, and a hole opened. It was considerably lower than where they stood now. If they angled their suits just right, they could sail through.

"Okay. Let's go!" Astoria latched the extractor tool safely inside her tactical vest. She then leapt off the balcony, her chute opening behind her. She adjusted the flight controls, sweeping perfectly toward the shield opening.

H124 stood on the edge of the balcony, trying not to look down. She lowered her goggles, took a deep breath and leapt. She brought up her PRD as she soared, making a few slight adjustments, gliding closely behind Astoria. They sailed downward, wind streaming through their hair.

As they soared over the top of one of the buildings, its roof door slammed open. PPC troopers stormed out, their flash bursters setting the night afire. H124 veered wildly, narrowly missing an electrical blast, its radiance burning her retina. But Astoria wasn't so lucky. A flash hit her, and her flight suit malfunctioned. H124 saw her bank out of control, the chute fluttering erratically behind her. She sailed past the roof with the troopers, but H124 could tell she was no longer in control. She veered toward her friend just as the roof of a second building loomed up below. Astoria tried to pull up, but she came in too fast. She jabbed at the display of her PRD, but already she was plummeting. H124 watched as she collided with the roof of a third building. There she tumbled to a stop, tangled up in the chute.

H124 aimed toward her, coming in a little slower than she had before, and managed to land a few feet away from Astoria. The chute retracted into the pack, and H124 ran to her friend. A fist punched out from the bundle of the chute, and H124 helped Astoria unwrap herself.

The warrior got to her feet, throwing off the lines from the chute. "Fuck!" she shouted. "The damn thing's fried." She punched at the display, and the chute started to retract, then stopped. "It's not responding."

H124 looked off in the distance, where the hole in the shield still held, a dark polygon in a wall of glowing amber.

Astoria manually bundled up the chute and ripped the pack off her back, then crammed it inside. Strapping it back on, she looked to H124. "I'm not getting out of here with this."

"Can't mine carry both of us?"

"You remember what Raven said. They were only starting to develop a tandem jumper. We're too heavy."

H124 looked to the roof door. "Then we climb down. This looks like a residential building. There won't be anyone out and about. It'll be a clear path all the way down to the street. Then we make a break for the shield."

Astoria looked over her shoulder at the hole's placement. "Onyx'll have to hack a hole at the top of the retaining wall. No way we'd make it up that high," she said, gesturing at the current hole.

H124 brought up her comm window. "Onyx. We need you to open a different hole, one just at the top of the wall."

"Is everything okay?" she asked.

"Astoria's flight suit has been fried."

"Okay. I'm on it." She switched off.

"All right. Let's start down." H124 ran toward the roof door, but it slammed open before she got there. Garbed in black, face shields down, PPC troopers streamed out by the dozens. She couldn't believe how many there were. They just kept pouring out, like a plague of beetles.

There was no way they were going to make it down the stairwell, now choked with soldiers. H124 ran to the ledge, staring down the side of the building, trying to spot an old fire escape or drain pipe, anything they could climb, but the walls were smooth. No ledges, nothing to hold on to.

The troopers closed in, training their flash bursters on them. Down below, more soldiers flooded the street, energy rifles pointed up at them.

Even if they got down to the street, there was no way they'd get through all those troopers.

"Astoria! What do we do?" H124 called. Astoria ran to her side, gazing off the side of the building.

Astoria turned and faced the advancing soldiers. H124 whipped around, standing side by side with her, heart hammering in her chest. Then Astoria grabbed her by the shoulder, and yanked her close. "Take this!" she said, sliding the extractor tool into H124's vest.

Astoria shoved her off the roof.

H124 tumbled down, grappling against the violent air to reach her PRD and turn on the flight suit's control. The chute whipped out, jerking her upward and knocking the wind out of her chest. She gasped, struggling to look back over her shoulder. She saw Astoria grab her grenade belt and run from the edge, bellowing a war cry. Moments later a great explosion claimed the entire roof. Fire bloomed upward, followed by a billowing cloud of smoke and debris.

"Astoria!" cried H124, helpless. Below her, hundreds of jolts flashed out as the troopers fired on her. She angled the suit away from them, tears pooling in her goggles. "Astoria!" she shouted again. She glanced behind to see the upper stories of the building aflame, fire licking up into the darkness.

Ahead, a new hole opened in the shield, down by the top of the wall. She looked back to see the troopers in the street pushing out a massive sonic gun, training it on her. She'd seen the destruction it could wield when they'd attacked Black Canyon Camp. She whipped to the side, flying erratically, zigzagging, doing all she could to survive.

The hole loomed closer, and just as she heard the dull *whump* of the sonic weapon fire, she sailed through the shield, into the darkness beyond, gliding over the rivers of excrement seeping out from the city.

She kept sailing, staying aloft as long as she could, clearing the vile, reeking streams and fast approaching a barren hill. She tried to get more lift, hoping for a thermal, but came down hard in the dirt, tumbling on her side. She lay there, immobile, the flash of the explosion imprinted on her retinas, playing itself over again on the dark vault of the sky.

Finally she pulled off her goggles, and wiped her eyes on her sleeve. Through the amber glow of the shield, she could see the fire atop the building. She lay there, watching burning debris cascade down the side of the edifice and drop out of sight behind the retaining wall.

"Astoria . . ." she whispered into the night.

For a long time she remained there, feeling the cold dirt against her face, watching the fire burn. Then the hole in the shield flickered and sealed.

Her PRD beeped, and Raven's face appeared. "Are you out?" he asked.

She couldn't answer. Her voice had left her.

Then another call came in. Gordon's face flashed on her display. "You get out okay, kiddo? I'm waiting to come get you."

She swallowed, finally reaching a hand up. She sent him her coordinates, then lay back in the dirt.

In the city, the fire raged on.

Chapter 25

In Sanctuary City, H124 sprinted to Felix's office. She handed him the extractor tool, hoping that it hadn't gotten fried when Astoria had been hit with the flash burster. Immediately getting to work, he shut off the device's transmission. Delicately, while she watched, he placed the extractor tool against Dirk's skull. A thin, snaking arm came out, latching onto the sphere and pulling it out.

The doctor dropped the sphere into a metal dish and sighed, shoulders slumped. She looked to the display with Dirk's vitals. They were stable. The medpod repaired the hole left by the extractor.

"Will he be okay?" she asked.

Felix turned to face her through the window. "He'll need a few days of rest. But yes."

Running footsteps drew her attention down the hall. Byron rounded the corner, boots thumping as he ran. "H! Tried to meet you out on the airstrip, but they said you'd taken off running. How is he?" He stopped in front of the window. She couldn't look at him. "He's going to be okay," she said, with a sore throat.

Byron glanced around. "Where's Astoria? Can't believe she'd miss this."

H124 turned her back to him.

She felt his warm hand on her shoulder. "What is it?"

The lump in her throat was so painful she could barely speak. "She didn't make it."

"What?" He sounded incredulous. "But she . . . she can't be gone."

"I'm sorry." H124 pulled away, and hastened down the hall. She took the lift to the surface, and walked out into the night. The moon was almost full, lighting the forest in silver.

She sat down at the base of a tree, drew her knees up to her chest, and let herself cry. Insects filled the night air with their song. Bats darted by, their translucent wings silhouetted against the moonlit sky.

When the lift door opened, Raven appeared, the wind catching his long hair. He tucked it behind his ears, spotting her by the tree.

He sat beside her, letting silent companionship drown out the tension. "Byron told me about Astoria."

She met his eyes in the dark. He lifted his arm, and she leaned her head on his shoulder. He wrapped his arm around her. "Good people have lost their lives in this fight," he told her. "But she saved her brother, and now you've saved countless more." She looked up at him. "Orion detonated the nuclear weapon. He thinks it'll be enough to nudge the fragment off course, but he says it's going to be close. Now we just have to wait."

"And the big one?" she asked.

"Rivet's making good progress on assembling the craft. Now all we need is a bomb, and a way to launch it."

H124 beheld the stars, a mesmerizing panorama untainted by light pollution. She could see the entire expanse of the Milky Way out here in this amazing place.

"See that collection of stars there?" Raven pointed out a pattern with a very bright white star in it, the brightest star in the sky. "We call that constellation Tłish Tsoh, or Big Snake. It's a constellation used in healing ceremonies." He pulled his knees up and brought his free arm around them. The night air pressed in, cold and invigorating. His breath frosted as he said quietly, "Dirk will heal now. Astoria made sure of that. She died for a purpose. Not everyone can say that."

Raven's PRD beeped. He brought up the comm window. Orion came into view. "This is it," he told them. "This is going to be a very close call."

"Want to go in?" Raven asked her.

She wiped her eyes, and nodded.

He helped her up. They returned to the lift, then headed over to Orion's office. He had set up a simulation window and was using radar to track the fragment. "I've got some bad news," he told them as they entered the small room. "It's not going to miss. Not entirely."

Byron, Gordon, and Rowan stood near Onyx and a host of other Rovers beside, Nimbus among them.

They watched the fragment in the simulation hit the top of the earth's atmosphere. H124 held her breath as it dove down into the stratosphere. It skimmed along, staying high, and everyone in the room held their breath.

The fragment was streaking through the stratosphere.

Orion inhaled. "This is going to be one hell of an airblast."

Onyx's hands flew over her virtual keyboard. "BEC City just went down. No transmissions are coming through. It's totally dark."

H124 gritted her teeth as the fragment hurtled onward. Then it exited the atmosphere, shooting back out into space without making landfall.

The room was quiet for several heartbeats.

"Wait a minute," Onyx said. "BEC City's back up! I'm getting a weak media stream from them. They're okay!"

A cheer went up. H124 blinked in disbelief. They'd done it. Gordon whistled, while Raven and Rowan thrust their fists into the air. Raven let out a laugh. Orion clapped, and Onyx flopped back into her seat, exhausted.

"We did it!" Raven told H124.

H124 felt numb. Slowly the reality of what had just happened dawned on her. They *had* done it. They'd diverted the massive fragment. And if they could avert that one, they could reroute the main asteroid.

She thought of the forest outside, of the wildlife roaming along the grassy plain above.

It could be saved. It could all be saved.

Shattered Skies

If you enjoyed *Shattered Lands,* be sure not to miss the third book in Alice Henderson's Skyfire Saga.

A Rebel Base e-book on sale October 2019.

Acknowledgments

Many thanks to my amazing editor, James Abbate, for his excellent work and enthusiasm for the series, and to Martin Biro for making the *Skyfire Saga* part of the Rebel Base imprint.

Patrick Bartlein, Professor of Geography at the University of Oregon, was incredibly helpful when it came to my climatological research that went into this novel.

Thanks to the Launchpad Astronomy Workshop at the University of Wyoming, dedicated to bringing accurate science to science fiction. The week I spent there was one of the most enjoyable of my life.

And thank you to Jason, who has solidly had my back and offered endless encouragement over the years, and to Becky, whose years-long friendship I absolutely cherish.

Meet the Author

Alice Henderson is a writer of fiction, comics, and video game material. She was selected to attend Launchpad, a NASA-funded writing workshop aimed at bringing accurate science to fiction. Her love of wild places inspired her novel *Voracious,* which pits a lone hiker against a shapeshifting creature in the wilderness of Glacier National Park. Her novel *Fresh Meat* is set in the world of the hit TV series *Supernatural.* She also wrote the *Buffy the Vampire Slayer* novels *Night Terrors* and *Portal Through Time.* She has written short stories for numerous anthologies including *Body Horror, Werewolves & Shapeshifters,* and *Mystery Date.* While working at LucasArts, she wrote material for several Star Wars video games, including *Star Wars: Galactic Battlegrounds* and *Star Wars: Battle for Naboo.* She holds an interdisciplinary master's degree in folklore and geography, and is a wildlife researcher and rehabilitator. Her novel *Portal Through Time* won the Scribe Award for Best Novel.

Visit her online at www.AliceHenderson.com.

Shattered Roads

In a future laid waste by environmental catastrophe, one woman in a shielded megacity discovers a secret hidden within—and the nightmare of what lies beyond.

The Skyfire Saga

Her designation is H124—a menial worker in a city safeguarded against the devastating storms of the outer world. In a community where consumerism has dulled the senses, where apathy is the norm and education is a thing of the past, H124 has one job: remove the bodies of citizens when they pass away in their living pods.

Then one night, H124's routine leads her into the underground ruins of an ancient university. Buried within it is a prescient alarm set up generations ago: an extinction-level asteroid is hurtling toward Earth.

When her warning is seen as an attempt to topple the government with her knowledge of science, H124 is hunted—and sent fleeing for her life beyond the shield of her walled metropolis. In a weather-ravaged unknown, her only hope lies with the Rovers, the most dangerous faction on Earth. For they have continued to learn. And they have survived to help avert a terrifying threat: the end of the world is near.

Printed in the United States
by Baker & Taylor Publisher Services